Sexy Stories To Keep You Up All Night

Vibrations of love . . . Dial "S" for phone sex . . . The video revolution meets tion . . . The jo The new bisex Professor of De otic climates . . . The sexual voyages of a sailor . . . *and so much more!*

EROTICA FROM PENTHOUSE

Today, more people enjoy a sex life than ever before in history. And erotica both reflects and contributes to this newfound freedom. In EROTICA FROM <u>PENTHOUSE</u>, ordinary people describe their most intimate moments in their own uncompromising terms. It's liberated. Literary. And wonderfully sexy.

EROTICA
FROM PENTHOUSE

THE EDITORS OF *PENTHOUSE*

WARNER BOOKS

A Time Warner Company

WARNER BOOKS EDITION

Cover design by Don Puckey

Warner Books, Inc.
1271 Avenue of the Americas
New York, N.Y. 10020

Visit our Web site at
http://warnerbooks.com

 A Time Warner Company

Printed in the United States of America

First Printing: January, 1990

10

CONTENTS

INTRODUCTION

It is a little sobering to realize that the dark ages of erotica extended to within only a quarter-century or so of our considerably more enlightened times. In 1960, D. H. Lawrence's 1928 masterpiece, *Lady Chatterley's Lover*, was finally declared to be not obscene by the British courts. That was the opening shot of what later came to be called the Sex Revolution. In another five years' time, other landmark works like Henry Miller's *Tropic of Cancer* and *My Secret Life* by the anonymous Victorian businessman who called himself "Walter" were being enjoyed by an appreciative American and British public. Today the erotica of the average man and woman is commonplace.

This phenomenon—ordinary people describing their most intimate moments in whatever terms they choose—is peculiar to the twentieth century. Lawrence, no doubt, would have denounced this democratization of bawdy literature—his own rather pedantic version being primarily a vehicle for high-minded moralism. But Miller, Anais Nin, and other pioneers of American erotica would likely have found this trend something to cheer about. After all, they used to write about the pleasures of the flesh mainly for money and for the fun of it.

As such, they were much more in the tradition of Francois Rabelais, whose own works were the high-water mark of the last great sex revolution in Western civilization. That all too brief undraping of the European libido occurred in the early 1500s and came to an abrupt end when an outbreak of syphilis swept across the continent, helping to usher in the Counter Reformation and Inquisition.

In our AIDS-plagued time there is no guarantee that the tradition of unrestricted erotica will continue. But, science has caught up with the Rabelaisian temperament. Discoveries like the Pill and penicillin, as well as the work of theorists and researchers like Freud, Kinsey, and Masters and Johnson, have made it possible for more people to enjoy a better sex life than ever before in history. Erotica reflects and contributes to this freedom, and is also a bulwark against anal-retentive reactionaries who continue to confuse a deadly virus with the wrath of God.

The tradition of erotica in *Penthouse* is a long one, dating back to its founding by Bob Guccione in 1965. Like the reader letters, the erotic stories published in *Penthouse* and its sister publications are all guaranteed true and they offer a peek into the bedrooms of people from all works of life. Most of the stories collected in this volume were not written by professional writers (though writers have interesting sex lives, too), but by secretaries, policemen, lawyers, cartoonists, teachers and even a stonemason.

As editor of *Penthouse Forum*, I buy and assign such stories every month, and I am always amazed at the extraordinary variety of erotic life that exists beneath the conventional facade of so many people. It is as if I were a collector of orchids who continues to find new species after species, each one as rare as the last.

The only restriction I impose on contributors, other than the assurance of authenticity, is that an erotic story tell a tale between consenting adults. Erotica has outgrown its morbid Victorian preoccupation with cruelty, the exploitation of children, or for that matter with the mere cataloguing of copulation after copulation. It has even outgrown moralism—which is not to say that many of these stories do not contain a moral. Today's erotica is staking new ground—trying to be judged not on high-minded "redeeming literary, artistic, or social values". Whatever those are, they are the invention of blue-nosed courts; and literature—erotic literature included—has an obligation to tear them down.

Rather the erotica of today and tomorrow should be judged for its erotic value. If it's bad erotica, ignore it. But if it celebrates the joys of the flesh in a way that entertains, then we should celebrate it, pass it along to friends, and maybe even try to write some ourselves.

For obvious reasons, the names of the writers of these stories have been changed to protect their privacy and that of others described in their tales. But that is the sole concession made.

The groupings are only loosely thematic. But I have tried to represent the male and female points of view as equally as possible. After finishing the book the reader may find that modern erotica has another trait differentiating it from the pornography of the past—feminism. Good sex is mutual sex, and by extension good erotica is mutual erotica. Perhaps in some future court, sexually explicit literature will be judged by that salubrious criterion alone.

—John Heidenry

Prologue

✶

But let me get back to the woman on the bed who asked me if I
nted to sleep with her. Well, sure I did, but I had noticed lately
t the less time I spent with someone before we slept together,
less time I wanted to sleep with her afterwards. In fact, with
he women I couldn't bear to spend the night afterwards. I didn't
d fucking a stranger. But *sleeping* with one was different.
Somehow, deprived of the *longueurs* of a prolonged seduction,
ever built up the romantic illusions that are so often the sublime
ducts of sublimated sexual frustration. I never got to endow a
man with the magic—or to savor the magic already there within.
ked about this matter with a friend who was really popular with
men—so popular that he had a hard time finding any who would
up serious resistance, or allow him to enjoy a teased-out se-
ion. He told me how he'd given this problem a piquant erotic
t.
e started playing hard to get. "What I'd do," he told me, "is
to the point with a woman where we were close enough or
nate enough that we both knew we'd end up sleeping together
e of us made the first move. We'd both want to, you see, but
uldn't make the expected move. I'd make her seduce me. And
uldn't be an easy lay. I'd make it hard for her. I'd make it
ating. We'd end up at the end of an evening sipping an after-
r cordial in a bar and she'd be leaning up against me, rubbing
g against my thigh, whispering "Let's go back to my place"
ear, and kind of punctuating that with her tongue, if you
what I mean.
d sometimes I'd go back to her place and sometimes I
n't. But if I did I wouldn't always do what she wanted. I'd
playfully, until she ended up moaning, getting really frustrated
chy just the way men used to get. Then when we'd finally
t would be so hot, so intense, we would almost be like lust-
teenagers tearing into each other."
y for that delay. I was just about to tell you what happened
at sweet, sexy securities analyst asked me flat out to sleep
r. The thought did cross my mind to do with her what my
id with women—play hard to get. But that was a little too
d and even mean-spirited for my taste. And besides, she
o winsome and sultry there, sprawled out on her covers,
kimbo, giving me head with her eyes that, even though I
ally wanted to resist, I thought it might be misinterpreted
ant.

ARE WOMEN TOO EASY?

By Bruce Travis

Women go to bed with me much too easily. In fact, women
generally give in too easily. I know this assessment is provocative.
Women, if they read no further, will think this is some kind of
arrogant boast. Men will probably misinterpret my conclusion—a
call on women to put up more resistance to seduction. And both
sexes will assume that I'm advocating a return to repression and
Moral Majority rule.

No. All wrong. What I'm talking about here is a *tactical shift* in
the ground rules of the seduction game to make the play more
exciting. For example, some of the most intense erotic pleasures
occur before the decision is made to go to bed. And those sus-
penseful, anticipatory, teasing, toying, breathtaking, heartstopping
moments of escalating arousal and resistance are too often lost in
the accelerated art of modern romance.

Look at it this way. If exquisitely prolonged foreplay before actual
penetration is desirable, if exquisitely prolonged intercourse before
orgasm is desirable, it stands to reason that exquisitely prolonged
seduction is likewise desirable.

Yet the 70s systematically destroyed seduction. It wasn't just the
instant lovelock of LSD-eye contact or the instant intimacy of encounter ecstasies or even sexual sophistication that destroyed it. Or
maybe it was. Sophistication, that is. I have the feeling that after
casual sex became common, not to say commonplace, most intelligent men and women grew adept at sizing up the opposite sex.

3

From the first mutual glance, from the very quality of initial eye contact, they knew just whether they'd eventually sleep together. This development removed a lot of suspense, or a lot of romance and, I suppose, a lot of frustration in some cases. But there are those who believe romance is more than sublimated sexual frustration.

It may be a problem of communication. Women don't realize that many, many men appreciate the subtle gradations of a slow but intense and *smoky* seduction. They believe that men still want what they used to want—the selfish ego satisfaction of instant seduction success.

But now that men tend to sense, or scent, success from the beginning, the symbolic value of an instant consummation is diminished. And if men don't display eagerness for instant sex, that is, going from first kiss to first fuck without an intervening candlelit dinner, women feel they are being rejected. However, as I learned recently, women don't always have to be sweet-talked out of a first-night fuck.

I was at the party of a friend when I spotted Delilah (not her real name) leaning against the refrigerator and smiling at me as I looked for an opener.

"I'm looking for an opener," I said, as I rifled my friend's kitchen drawers.

"Men always are," she said, winking at me.

That was Delilah, full of teasing, sexual insinuation in her eyes and her smile. She had glossy auburn hair and a fresh-scrubbed Irish face sprinkled with freckles. I was completely charmed. But I couldn't tell whether the come-hither wit was a put-on or a come-on. There was the same mystery about her clothes—a starched white-lace, high-collar blouse and Brooks Brothers ladies-floor cardigan. She was prim and ladylike, befitting her position as a securities analyst of a Wall Street investment banking house.

She said her job was to analyze computer-generated performance charts in search of erotic stocks.

"Erotic stocks?" I asked. "What are they like?"

"The ones that have been building a base for some time and are already rising in volume and velocity. I have to get a feel for what I call their 'hot plateaus.' "

I liked the way she touched me for emphasis. I liked her so much I was nervous asking for her number.

"Uh, would I be remiss asking for your phone number?" I said as we parted.

"Remiss?" she said. "You'd be a fool not to." On the ‍ I felt that I was falling in love.

A week later we had dinner out together for the first ‍ knees touched under the table. It provided a genuine erot‍ of innuendo to even the driest discussion of commoditie‍ and leveraged options. We skipped dessert and went b‍ place.

We sat on her bed drinking wine and listening to N‍ records. I savored each moment of anticipation. And th‍ I could suppress it no longer, she said, "Would you li‍ with me?"

Let me interrupt this story for a moment to cite so‍ wisdom on the central question of contemporary seducti‍ lilah's question raised. I found this gem in a book called‍ the autobiography of Rona Barrett. It's not a piece of ‍ wisdom, but rather a proverb from one of the ancie‍ Hollywood, Louis B. Mayer of MGM, on the relations‍ the frustration of desire and the theory of narrative form‍ to the mystical mogul Mayer, "There's only one g‍ that's a delayed fuck."

Yes. The delayed fuck. In my opinion this is a ne‍ of erotic *intensity*. It doesn't have to be the prudish‍ minded slow-down that gave delay a bad name v‍ teenagers. So much of recent erotic literature has be‍ or simple-minded reaction against *this* kind of delay‍ Erica Jong's "zipless fuck" in *Fear of Flying* and t‍ stranger-fuck of *Last Tango in Paris*.

Do you remember that scene in *Last Tango in Pa‍ and Maria Schneider are lying naked together a‍ their introductory fuck-at-first-sight? Schneide‍ Brando to see if they can "come without touch‍ Brando waits a few seconds, then jokingly asks he‍ yet?" But it seems to me that with an artfully‍ people *can* get so horny for each other that they ‍ come just by looking into each other's eyes. I k‍

The full sexual potential, the often thrilling sex‍ gazes, is almost never realized. Erotic eye co‍ (to use the term from *Stranger in a Strange ‍ psychedelic era) used to lead to instant psych‍ an artfully delayed fuck, eye contact can almos‍ head with the eyes," as one woman I know ‍

But three days later, as we were lying in bed together talking about that moment, we came up with another solution.

"Did you like it when *I* asked *you*?" she asked me.

Well, I told her, I loved it. But I tried to explain how I sometimes missed the Age of Delay, the long slow seduction, the thrill of surmounting every sensual gradation on the way to all-the-way.

At first I thought she had taken offense.

"Oh, I see," she said. "I know what you want. You want me to be a cock-teasing bitch—the kind that leaves you high and dry, gasping for more, until she gives in and makes you feel like a real stud. Is that it?"

Well, I said, that wasn't exactly how I'd put it. But I did concede that I liked cock-teasing girls. The ones who curl their tongue around the tip of your cock. The ones who can make licking their lips seem as if they're licking your cock.

I thought she might be offended by my analysis, but she just laughed. She was *into* it. "I like to tease cocks," she admitted. "I don't like to hop right into bed, but I guess with the ratio of men to women I do feel this pressure to be a sex bomb on the first night. I like the slow build-up. In fact," she continued, "tell you what. From now on this lady is going to be *very* hard to fuck. At least for you," she added, with expert cock-teasing bitchiness.

Well, I'm here to say a kind word for cock-teasing. And the reverse—cunt-teasing, or whatever you want to call male resistance to seduction.

The whole of the next week she refused to see me. Wouldn't even take my calls at her office. Then Saturday afternoon she called me up and asked me if I wanted to help her shop for a sexy camisole. Choked with lust, I could barely manage to mumble agreement to meet her at a New York store specializing in classy silk undergarments like camisoles, teddies, tap pants and the like. When I got there she dragged me into a dressing room, whipped off her jeans and proceeded to try on one after another heart-stoppingly seductive undergarment of the camisole sort. All the while, she was giving me delicious come-hither glances, rubbing against me in the close confines of the dressing room, giving me head with her eyes.

Half an hour later we were in a cab speeding up to her apartment, necking madly, urgently. But when we pulled up to her place she drew herself away, hopped out and said she was having dinner with her older brother that night and would see me next weekend.

The following Saturday night we met at a movie theater and spent about 119 of the 120-minute movie with our tongues in each other's mouth and our hands in each other's pants, trying to suppress gasps of lust. This time she hopped into a cab right outside the movie theater and didn't even let me get in with her—though she practically had to slam the door on my, uh, hand to keep me out.

The next weekend she invited me over to her place and answered the door wearing just her camisole. Pulling me over to her couch, she opened my fly and we had probably the most furious spasm of sex I'd ever experienced. Since then I've held out on *her*, with equally intense results.

It's my opinion that the artfully delayed seduction is the way to have the best of both worlds, the hot, feverish lust that's bred of repression and resistance, and the playful intimacy of post-Victorian sex. Now there are some who might say this is artificial, that it's not spontaneous. And that's true. I am talking about *artfully* delayed seduction. Perhaps it might be better if people put up more resistance to seduction "naturally"—if their resistance was sincere.

And perhaps with the return of repression in the 80s, with the shadow of herpes hanging over everyone, women will make it more difficult for men to get into their pants, and vice versa. And then I'll probably be lamenting the loss of the Golden Age of Easy Sex.

But I don't think so. I think both men and women should put up more resistance to seduction, not out of fear, but because of the pleasure principle. The longer people take, by the time they finally get around to actually doing it, the more they will have eroticized every sensory nerve, every look, every glance, every touch, every signature of the other's being.

And so when they finally do it, the sex will be not only less impersonal, but more exciting. Impersonal sex has gotten a kind of down-and-dirty reputation for being more exciting than genuinely intimate sex. If people would only learn to take longer to seduce each other, that first fuck—so often anticlimactic—would be infinitely hotter and more personal.

Not Just Your
Average Relationship

*

OUR FIRST VIBRATOR

By Michael Fletcher

When I asked Liz what she wanted for her birthday, I expected her to say perfume or jewelry. But she had something else in mind.

"A vibrator? Are you serious?" I said. She giggled nervously, but I knew that she meant it.

Liz was easily embarrassed and almost virginal in style. But her lascivious streak never failed to surprise me. She could charm dinner guests while playing with my cock under the table. I looked forward to shopping.

A few days later I visited a store called the Pleasure Chest, a 7-Eleven of sex toys and paraphernalia. Men in three-piece suits with blond, manicured girlfriends perused cock rings and crotchless panties. A gay couple in black leather and studded chokers examined a giant two-headed dildo with "lifelike veins."

The vibrators on display ranged in size and color from monstrous flesh-colored models to butt plugs that resembled night lights. Some were expensive semi-orthopedic devices with sponge-covered balls affixed. Others were strap-on affairs that promised stunning orgasms for the woman daring enough to wear one. Options included variable speeds and intensities, hand crank, AC-DC adaptors, kits with lubricants and spikey rubber sleeves.

I eventually decided on two sleek, white missile-shaped models like the ones that turn up occasionally in drugstores. Each package portrayed a woman smiling beatifically as she held the little bullet to her cheek. "Eases muscle tension," the copy proclaimed. The big one, about 10 inches long, was an inch-and-a-half in diameter near the ridged bottom and tapered to a point. The other was no longer than four inches and nearly the same thickness.

When I handed the boxes to a clerk in black leather and crew cut, he looked up in mock horror. "Two?" he intoned. "Aren't we being a little piggy?" I mumbled something out of embarrassment, but he paid no attention. With the nonchalance of someone who had tested vibrators a thousand times, he threw batteries into each one, twisted them with a flick of the wrist, then flipped them back into the box. Like a waiter reciting the specials of the day, he then advised: "Remove the batteries after each use. Keep them clean. Don't use them in the tub. Have a nice day."

Liz tore the wrapping paper away like a kid. "You really did it?" she cried. Then she started giggling "Two! Oh, my God."

I slipped the big one out of the box and turned it on. Liz gasped. "Jesus, it's loud, isn't it?"

"Don't worry," I said. "The neighbors will just think it's an electric toothbrush."

With the thing still buzzing in my hand I put my arms around her and lifted her skirt from behind. I slid it down her ass and between her legs. The sound was muffled as it disappeared beneath her skirt and touched her pantyhose. I drove it between her thighs and poked it through to the front. Liz's mouth dropped open with pleasure. I kissed her deeply while lifting her gently to her toes with the vibrator pressing against her cunt. She was moaning now as her weight brought the buzzing bullet into direct contact with her clitoris.

I put it between us and we held it with our crotches while embracing. Liz began to grind against me. I pulled down her pantyhose and took off my shirt and tie. We kissed deeply. My hand played with her cunt. It was open and wet as her outer lips gave way to my fingers.

I moved down to kiss her breasts and suddenly jumped. The vibrator was between my legs. Liz was rubbing it over my ass and against my balls. I felt a boiling sensation against my peritoneum, a buzzing throughout my testicles and inside me. "That feels weird," I shuddered, "but wonderful."

Liz smiled lewdly as she roamed with it all over my thighs and crotch. "A cock of my own," she giggled. "How do you like that?"

I was fully erect. I knew I would come in seconds if I entered her. So I took the vibrator and used it to caress her breasts and stomach. She closed her eyes and slowly parted her legs, pushing a pillow beneath her. "I'm the birthday girl," she whispered. "And I want my present now."

I felt like spurting my come all over her stomach. But I wanted to climax with her. So instead I knelt beside her on my haunches. I stroked her face with one hand and nuzzled the buzzing vibrator into her opening. Its quivering tip just barely nudged her cunt open. Liz moaned and whimpered and finally pleaded, "Oh, please, don't tease me."

Our lovemaking always had an element of taunting. When she was excited, I made her admit that she was a hungry little whore. That admission caused her last inhibition to snap and she would grow even wilder, bucking her hips and in a low guttural voice begging to be fucked.

So I teased her with the dildo, pushing it in slightly and withdrawing it. "We have a hungry little cunt tonight," I murmured.

"Please don't do this," she sighed. "Stick it in me. Please."

Bringing her knees up she swallowed three fourths of the vibrator. I pulled it out and slowly slid it back and forth again and again. It made wet smacking noises as it parted her pussy. She moaned softly, lost in the pleasure coming from between her legs. Then I began pumping her with a steady rhythm. I watched her buck to meet every thrust. The buzzing went from loud to soft as the shiny white cylinder slithered deeply in and out of her.

My voyeurism became rampant now. Wanting to see her pleasure herself, I placed her hand over my own on the vibrator. She grabbed it without hesitation and then she began plunging it into herself even faster than before.

While Liz was fucking herself furiously with the 10-inch dildo, I leaned over to retrieve the little one from the bedside table. My cock brushed her face. With her eyes still closed, Liz parted her lips and stuck out her tongue to find me. In a moment I was inside her warm mouth and her cheeks were contracting feverishly while she kept the big dildo tight in her fist.

She sucked me with groans of pleasure, arching her head and neck from the pillow. I snapped the little vibrator on and moved it down her stomach, toward her clit. When I penetrated her with it her jaw went slack and her body stiffened. My cock fell still shiny with saliva from her mouth.

"Oh, honey, keep it there. Please don't stop," she begged. I held the little vibrator lightly against her exposed clitoris and knelt back to watch.

It was a view I had never been privy to before. Liz's body was stiffening as if taking an electric charge. Her hands fell limply to her sides, but the big vibrator still jutted from her thick pubic thatch, held only by her muscles. From the look on her face, I knew we were in the countdown stage.

Suddenly her torso arched upward and a low, breathy "*Ohhhh*" came from her lips. She shook and quivered and gasped for nearly a full minute. I was voyeur and participant, feeling something close to wonder to see her in that state. She was so out of control, so abandoned to the pleasure coursing through her cunt, that I felt a small pang of jealousy. When her breathing returned to normal, I fought back my own greed and whispered in her ear, "Happy birthday."

I knew Liz would soon get horny again, but I was anxious. I reached over for a bottle of baby oil on the bedstand and dripped some onto my cock till it glistened. With one hand I lubricated myself until the oil made a popping sound. With the other I parted her cunt.

Kneeling between her legs, I pumped my erection, waiting for her eyes to open. I knew she loved to watch me do this. It reminded her of porno movies we had seen. When she finally looked at me a smile spread across her face and she raised her legs in the air. I slid into her with ease. She squeezed her cunt muscles in welcome.

"You feel so warm and big," she said. "Just let me lie here and get fucked by that big thick cock." She bit my lips, sucked my tongue and begged me to fuck her. "I'm so open, I'm so wet," she groaned as I slid in and out of her.

After about 10 thrusts I was ready to come. I wanted to hold back, but Liz was milking me with her cunt. I slowed down, and began to lick her breasts when I heard one of the vibrators snap on. Liz was pressing the small one—still wet with her juices—against my ass. The buzzing tip suddenly slipped all the way in. I started thrusting furiously, feeling nothing but that churning inside me and my come coursing up through my cock.

"Shoot it," she cried. "Shoot it into me, make me take it." I pushed my cock deep inside her. Liz was moaning—for me, for my pleasure—while holding the vibrator against my ass. With my last spasm I fell on top of her and we shared a deep, wet, tired kiss.

The two vibrators became a part of our sex lives. We named them Ho and Joe and even took them with us on weekends to the country. It was on one of those weekends that I raised the subject of her Christmas gift. She mused for a moment, then looked up at me with an innocent smile and said, "Batteries."

THE INDELIBLE AFFAIR

By Natasha Sarnoff

Max Perry owned a Greenwich Village jazz club and had made a lot of money. But the time we spent together wasn't in the city. He loved to fish. That's what he was doing the first time I saw him on Fire Island on a hot July day while I was still married. With my 14-month-old son slung on my hip I walked to the shoreline.

"What do you catch doing that?" I inquired.

"Usually not much," he answered.

His mouth was full and sensual, and behind his aviator sunglasses I knew his eyes were traveling my body. The baby pulled at the bra strap on my bikini, exposing the white flesh below the tan line and the outer ring of my nipple. Max examined the breast coolly. His detachment excited me, and I waited until he had finished looking before slowly pulling up the strap. I am tall with long legs, a flat belly, narrow hips and straight dark hair.

Max flung the rod over his shoulder and the line whistled past me beyond the low-breaking waves.

"I don't fish because of what I can catch," he continued. "I fish because I like standing here."

He reeled in the line and smiled at me.

"Can I try?" I asked.

His arm grazed mine as he put my index finger through the line and showed me how to release it. I handed the baby to him and cast the line in a perfect arc above the water. Max raised his eyebrows in approval.

"Not bad," he admitted.

"I have an older brother," I told him. "He taught me to throw a ball. It's the same motion."

I returned the rod to him and grasped the baby under his chubby arms. His mouth sucked at my shoulder.

"I have to go now," I murmured. "It's time for lunch."

"I'll walk you back," he said. We walked across the dunes to the house my husband and I had rented for the summer. I put the baby in his crib and, knowing what was going to happen next, returned to the shaded deck in back. Wordlessly Max positioned my shoulders against the siding and untied my bikini top so that my breasts fell free.

After examining them for a moment with the same detachment I had noticed on the beach he grasped the nipples and rolled them between his thumbs and index fingers. They hardened instantly and a rush of wetness dampened the crotch of my bathing suit. Then he ran his hands over my belly and pulled the bottom of my bikini down around my thighs. He passed his hand between my legs and then withdrew it. "Open your mouth," he commanded. I did and he inserted his wet index finger inside.

"Suck," he ordered.

I was weak with excitement, but knew what I had to do.

With leaden arms I reached up and removed his finger. "I'm sorry," I whispered. "Not now. I can't."

A flicker of contempt crossed his face, but then he shugged. "Are you sure?" he persisted.

"Yes," I replied.

He picked up the rod and walked off the deck and I went inside. I threw myself face down on the bed, put my fingers between my legs and masturbated.

I was on the beach with my husband the next time I saw Max Perry. I introduced them and we became friends. Max and my husband even began fishing together. Neither Max nor I ever mentioned what had happened between us on the back deck. Not until five years later, after I had ended my marriage and spent a summer in Europe, did Max and I become lovers. But by that time I was ready for him.

I arranged that trip to Europe very carefully, having sent my son to stay with my mother. I wanted to feel free to do as I pleased for the entire two months. I was 31 years old and had been married 10 years. But I was a virgin when I got married, I had remained monogamous during the years my husband and I were together and

I knew very little about sex. I intended to educate myself that summer, and I wasn't about to let anything get in my way.

My TWA flight was scheduled to leave for London at 10:30 on a June evening. I arrived at Kennedy Airport early, wearing a pair of blue jeans, sandals, a scoop-necked t-shirt and a slender gold chain around my neck. I carried only one bag. A friend in London had invited me to stay with her, but I hoped that would not be necessary. Before long, I saw what I wanted. He was in his late 30's, about 5 feet 10 inches tall with thinning, reddish hair, pale, freckled skin and a sturdy, muscular body. I got behind him in the check-in line and tapped him on the shoulder. "Listen," I said. "Would you mind if I sat next to you? I'm very anxious about flying, but I'll be okay if I just have someone to talk to."

He was an ex-trumpet player turned songwriter on his way to London to write the musical score for a film. That morning, when the flight landed, I checked into the Hilton with him. While he made his telephone calls I took a scented pine bath and then sat naked in his lap in an armchair with a view of Park Lane and Hyde Park. He kissed me, fondled my breasts and stroked my thighs. Then, after I had stretched out on cool sheets, he unbuckled his thick leather belt and dropped his jeans to reveal a healthy erection. Lying down beside me he gathered me to him.

I whispered, "Please, let me do this my way."

"Sure, baby," he murmured. "Anything you want."

I flung my leg over him and pounded my clitoris against his muscled thigh, moving slowly at first and then gaining momentum. It took a long while. Sweat ran from between my breasts and under my armpits before the tiny organ exploded and a feeling of relaxation flooded my thighs. Although I had virtually masturbated myself to orgasm, this was the first time I had ever come with a man. I felt exhilarated. "I did it," I cried as I fell back panting.

"Good for you," he laughed as he turned me on my back. Opening my legs, he put his cock inside me and galloped until he came.

The musician was the first of many men I knew that summer. My experience with him freed me. I became regularly orgasmic and my appetite for experiment sharpened as I wandered through Europe. In Rome, in the elevator of a hotel, I got off on the same floor with an American doctor and returned to his room with him. Straddled above me with his cock deep in my throat, he gently peeled back my labia and licked me to orgasm.

In Milan I showered with a Italian financier who had me bend over the sink while he inserted a soaped index finger into my anus and massaged my clitoris until I came. I learned to come in every position with a French poet (who could stay erect for long periods) simply by rubbing my clitoris against the base of his cock. By the time I left Europe I was a different person—no longer the unskilled housewife I had been when I arrived. But even though I liked all the men I knew that summer, I didn't want to continue seeing any of them. I had done what I needed to do and wanted to take a break from sex for a while. But that September, a week after I returned from Europe, Max Perry began calling me.

In the beginning I told him I wasn't interested. Over the years I'd seen him with dozens of women, never with any one for very long. The detachment that made him so sexually exciting carried over into the rest of his life and made him an unreliable lover. In an affair with Max Perry two things would be certain: it would be good, and it would be short.

"Max," I repeated in November, "I'm really not interested." I said the same thing in January and then, on an evening in February, he answered me back.

"Oh, for God's sake," he exclaimed, "I'm not interested in you either. But we're old friends. I've known you for years. Why can't we have dinner?"

I hesitated for a moment and then decided he was right.

"Okay," I shrugged. "Why not?"

I met him at a small French restaurant not far from his club in the Village. We sat side by side in a banquette. The sleeve of his velour shirt brushed my arm, and beneath my silk skirt I could feel his thigh pressed against mine. He had just returned from a week of fishing in the Caribbean and his face was deeply tanned. Involuntarily I began to wonder who he had taken with him. After dinner, outside in the cold air of Bleecker Street, I did not want to leave him. With a wet snow falling I leaned toward him with my fur coat unbuttoned and my mouth open, but he hailed a cab and kissed me chastely on the forehead. "Just friends," he gloated as he paid the driver and gave him my uptown address.

I waited a week before I gave in and called him. "I don't want to be your friend anymore," I confessed.

He lived in a penthouse apartment in the West Village. After he let me in he stretched out on the velvet sofa with his hands clasped behind his head. I sat opposite him in an armchair.

"So you don't want to be friends," he grinned.

"No," I said, "I really don't."

"Then why don't you come over here?" he urged. I kicked off my shoes and lay down beside him on the sofa. His hands remained clasped behind his head with that same detached attitude that had first excited me on the beach. I kissed him and he turned to me and with perfect control slowly explored my mouth with his tongue. He reached down and unbuckled his pants and opened the zipper. Then he stood up. "Show me what you can do," he demanded.

I thought about all the times I had refused him, and I knew he was going to make me pay for those rejections. But I had learned a lot in Europe, and I was going to enjoy making good the debt.

Kneeling before him I took down his pants. I kissed the insides of his thighs and licked his balls. Then, after sucking gently on the tip of his cock, I took him deep into my throat. "That's a good girl," he groaned, cupping my head in his hands and thrusting deeper and deeper. I ran my hands up and down his legs, moaning, twisting and whimpering with excitement. I was still dressed and I began to unbutton my blouse. "Wait," he commanded. I writhed until he finished with my mouth and withdrew.

"All right," he said. "Get up."

In the bedroom, although I wanted to rip my clothes off, he forced me to undress slowly. When I was fully nude he ordered me to lie down and spread my legs. I did. "Wider," he insisted. I did so and he sat down beside me and parted my lips with his fingers. He rubbed me deftly, stopping each time I was on the verge of orgasm.

"Oh please," I moaned.

"Not yet," he replied sternly.

He turned me over, positioned me on a pillow and came into me from behind, manipulating my clitoris with his hand and stopping each time just as I was about to come. Finally I screamed, thrashed onto my back and guided his hips into mine. He laughed and began to move rhythmically in tandem with me. His control was perfect. When I came, he began to groan and pound at me until he too came with a violent shudder. We lay drenched together and then fell asleep.

Max Perry and I began seeing each other several times a week. All of my sexual experimentation in Europe culminated in our affair. The depersonalized attitude he brought to our lovemaking turned me on in ways I never would have believed possible before my European trip.

When summer came we went to Fire Island, where we had first

met. With my son in camp we spent long weeks at the beach. It was there that our most powerful and erotic sex took place. I wore few clothes (never more than a bikini bottom in the house) which Max felt free to pull off whenever he pleased—sometimes when I was cooking or doing the laundry.

Once he bent me over a corner of the dining room table and entered me from the rear and then, just as I found the pressure unbearable, he pulled out, sat up on the table, pushed me to my knees and, holding my face in his hands, guided his cock into my mouth, where he came. Seeing my dismayed expression he ordered me to stand up and play with myself in front of him. I did so, my head bent with shame at my excitement. Just as I was about to come he removed my fingers, pulled me up on the table and gently licked me to orgasm with his tongue.

In the mornings we rose before dawn and went out to the beach. In a depression surrounded by dunes Max would take off his bathing trunks, sit down on a blanket and lean back. I would lie on my stomach, my head between his legs, my tongue busy.

Occasionally he would guide my head with his hands, pulling at my ears to direct his motions. I found this way of directing me unbearably exciting, and before we even began I was usually moist and groaning with anticipation. Although I was primed to come at a touch, Max never let me. When he was ready he would turn me toward him and tease me, sometimes with his fingers, more usually with his tongue or his cock. When he finally allowed me to come it was always explosive. One of my most vivid memories is of watching the sun rise out of the ocean with Max's body pounding on top of me.

That winter, with no local beaches available, Max and I went to Grenada, a Caribbean paradise with a number of deserted beaches, where we made love for hours. One night, in the bar of our hotel, Max met a beautiful, dusky-skinned local woman named Elita and invited her to join us at the beach the following day.

"I want you to see me with another woman," he explained. Just the tone of his voice excited me. Elita sat between us in the car the next day as we drove to the beach. While driving, Max parted her legs and ran his hand along the inside of her thighs. I grew wet watching him, half mad with jealousy.

At the beach Max spread a blanket and lay Elita down on it. She pulled off her skirt and wriggled out of her bikini. Max motioned that I was to take my clothes off as well while I watched them. "Sit there," he ordered, settling me alongside them. Then, after fondling Elita's firm breasts and spreading her legs with the same efficient and impersonal attitude he used with me, he played with her clitoris until she began to squirm with desire. "Isn't she pretty?" he asked me. I nodded dumbly, my body burning with excitement.

"Keep watching," Max commanded as he thrust into her over and over again in the hot sun. Finally, when I thought I could bear it no longer, he gestured for me to lie down alongside Elita, dismounted and shoved her toward me. We embraced, pressing our bodies together. Then she hovered over me, her clitoris pressed to my mouth, her tongue between my legs.

"That's nice! Good girls!" Max cooed. After a while he separated us, penetrated me and, with his thumb and forefinger caressing Elita's nipple, rode me until I came. Climbing on top of her he soon reached orgasm with a groan.

We took Elita to the beach every day for the rest of our stay in Grenada. I had a wonderful time and never saw Max happier. Even our sex together improved. It was as though the presence of a third person had brought us even closer.

Max and I continued seeing each other through the following summer and into the next fall. There seemed to be no end to the desire we felt for each other, but I knew our affair couldn't last. We stayed together for two years—longer, Max said, than he had ever been with anyone.

Oddly enough, the end came not after a quarrel or because of another woman. One typical night, after I had sucked his cock and licked his balls for a long time while a jazz recording played softly on the stereo, Max lifted my face to his and said, "I love you." He had never uttered those words before. I told him that I loved him, too. But I understood that love was not something Max could live with for very long.

Several months later he began seeing other women. Although he told me they meant nothing to him, I knew it was time for our friendship to end. I stopped answering his calls, walked around in a daze and didn't feel normal again for over a year.

I have remarried and gone on to live a happy life. I love my husband. We are close in ways I never could have been with Max, and the sex we have is fine, varied and often thrilling. I try not to think about Max. Sometimes I succeed.

SWAN SONG SEX

By Sandy Broca

It was early on a Sunday morning. More asleep than awake, I instinctively reached for Alan beside me. My hand grazed the hairs on his chest, then traveled down, lingering over his flat stomach and coming to rest on his penis. Soft, fat, shrivelled, vulnerable, it elicited the tenderest of feelings—and a challenge to make it harden.

With my fingertips, I began to perform a familiar erotic dance—teasing, gentle pulling, a squeeze, the rhythmic knead. The expected reaction occurred. With pride and pleasure, I twisted in bed so that I could take his erection in my mouth.

He groaned, cleared his throat. And then, in a voice still clotted with sleep, asked, "Should we be doing this?"

Stunned, suddenly made ashamed of my own innocent and natural sexual impulses, I stopped and let his shrinking cock tumble from my mouth. In the four years Alan and I lived together, we had made love more than a thousand times. Never before had he questioned the propriety of priapic pleasure. Then again, never before had we decided to break up—as we had yesterday—with only the logistics of who got to keep what and when to schedule the moving men's arrival to be worked out.

I touched his shoulder to answer him, then withdrew my hand. Overnight, the rules had changed—but we hadn't clarified just what the new rules were. He had told me it would be a month before friends moving to Denver would vacate their apartment so Alan could move in. It made no financial sense for him to leave my apartment to stay at a hotel or with other friends in the interim. Besides, I didn't want him to go, and he was still my best friend.

Last night we had cried together, mourning our relationship that lacked the mutual mandate to continue. In four years there had been countless good times, some admittedly terrible times, much laughter and the kind of warm feelings that couldn't dissipate overnight.

The problems that caused us to break up were not sexual in nature.

In fact, we had been compatible and easy-going lovers. Until this morning, sex had been an unquestioned source of pleasure, somewhat routine, but always satisfying. Our forays into erotic variations had delivered less satisfaction. What can you say about a man you seduce in the bath and who, upon leaving the tub, steps on and breaks his glasses? Only that he's sweet and clumsy and your heart goes out to him in a sentimental way that he doesn't always appreciate.

And that, I suppose, was the crux of our problem. After years of bending over thick textbooks, stifled by the poverty of graduate student life, Alan now held a well-paying job where people looked up to him. He wore expensive suits. He didn't want to be a sweet and clumsy puppy anymore. Lean and mean, the Lothario of the Eastern seaboard was more the fantasy image he gravitated toward. No more Mr. Monogamy (yet the ethos was there to the end—an open relationship would not suffice, a break-up was the license required for philandering to ensue). Suddenly Alan had become a freedom fighter in his private war against commitment, hurling his first Molotov cocktail last night. And the smoke had not yet cleared.

Looking at him in the early morning light, I felt a reprise of last evening's tears coming on, but I fought the impulse. My woman's tears had nearly drowned him, he'd shouted at me yesterday. So be it—no tears. Compassion and understanding weren't welcome guests at this moment, either. Toughness, decisiveness—those were the operative emotions in this new lexicon of leaving.

I sneaked a glance at his penis. It was semi-erect, making me think that even though he had one foot out the door emotionally, desire still lived at this address. Action was called for.

With a courage that was enacted rather than genuinely felt, I assumed a familiar position, my head resting on Alan's shoulder, a thigh sidled between his legs, my hand cupping that twin-sacced, hormone-pumping station that was the probable cause of our problems. I gave his cock an affectionate squeeze. It hardened perceptibly; he shot me an uncertain look.

"Yes, we *should* be doing this," I informed him.

He wavered. In his mind, I imagined, were all the logical reasons why we should institute a hands-off policy for the coming month. As of last night, we'd "officially" broken up; we needed this time to get accustomed to the idea of no longer being a couple; after making love for more than four years, there was something seedy about simply fucking for physical release; he wanted out—and the biological imperative of the act would send him off in the opposite direction.

A moment's more indecision, and *I* would be ready to hurl my belongings out into the street. "Aw, c'mon," I coaxed, my thigh hugging his, "I won't tell, if you won't." A smile curled his lips and his arms moved and encircled me. "All right. You talked me into it. Just make sure you don't get me pregnant," he warned, imitating the uncertain tone of a teenage girl in the back seat of a car.

The love we made that morning started out tender and familiar. Always the gentleman, Alan made sure I had an orgasm first by placing his hand between my legs and assigning each finger a specific task. His thick thumb located my clitoris and began pressing and circling it. His next three fingers made their way inside my vagina, and his pinky grazed my anus. It was a pleasant routine with no surprises, yet it always yielded the most delicious erotic sensations I had ever experienced.

After I climaxed, I started to reciprocate by giving Alan an all-over massage, starting at his chest and working my way down. When he was good and hard, I straddled his hips and lowered myself onto his waiting cock.

He captured a breast in each hand and began squeezing and pluck-ing at my nipples. However, they were oversensitive from my recent orgasm and I wanted him to stop. Flattening my body over his, I then got him to roll over so that we were in ye olde missionary position. It felt good and right and comfortable and sane; and the thought passed that if one had to be frozen in time, this wouldn't be a bad everlasting position to be in.

I cupped Alan's buttocks in my hands as he thrust and strained. Although I rarely climaxed when he was atop me, I still adored the special contact it afforded. I reveled in the firmness of his thrusts, the sounds and feel and smell of his warm skin on mine.

Suddenly his movements changed from rhythmic to more frenzied and intense. Thinking he was about to come, I insinuated a finger between his cheeks to stimulate him anally. It was the cherry atop the sundae, the action that invariably took him over the edge.

"No!" he practically barked. "Don't do that."

I retracted my finger and tried to concentrate on moving with him. But he was fucking at a pace I couldn't follow. Frantic, erratic, so deep it hurt. Pounding away at my body I could feel my insides becoming sore, and my enjoyment dissipated.

"Will you come soon?" I asked politely.

If he heard me, he didn't show it. Rather, his thrusts got deeper, harder. I felt like screaming. I wondered if this was what it felt like to be raped. "Alan, please."

The hell with you, I thought. I brought my finger back to his anal opening and practically stabbed him with it. He moaned, pushed into me cruelly a few more times, shuddered and came to a halt.

When he opened his eyes, he found me glaring at him angrily. "What was that all about?" I demanded.

He seemed not to understand. Then, abashedly, "I guess I just really got into it. Why do we have to do it the same way every single time, anyway?"

Hurt, I looked away from him. I'd never insisted we had to make love the same way every time, but I didn't relish being bruised either. He hadn't just made love to me; he'd acted out some sort of revenge fantasy. "Fuck you," I said and turned over. It seemed redundant.

As a freelance writer, one of the few professional perks I have is collecting free advice under the guise of doing research. So I phoned Dr. C. A. Tripp after Alan left for work on Monday. Dr. Tripp is the author of *The Homosexual Matrix*, which presents a theory of sexual "resistance" based on the idea that the obstacles to intimacy (such as anger or fear of losing one's partner) heighten our excitement in bed and make sex so piquant.

"Sex has an awful lot of stuff close to fighting in it, naturally," Dr. Tripp said. "Sex also carries a charge of affection." And it's the combination, the volatility that makes sex at the end of a relationship so different from all that went before.

"When you're together, you struggle for closeness," Dr. Tripp went on. "Succeeding violates all kinds of desires. So a couple back off, and the more they do that, the more they're attracted again. What very often happens is that once a couple agree to separate, they keep up sex."

The good doctor had something there. On Monday night, when I was deliberately cool to Alan during dinner and TV, he couldn't keep his hands away from me. While I was washing the dishes he came from behind, gently taking my breasts in his hands and hugging me until I felt his hardness against my back.

When we got to bed we made the sweetest love ever. Soft, tender, patient, and so filled with emotion that I thought my heart would break because he'd soon be gone.

In two days' time I'd had it rough and I'd had it tender. In the month that followed I came to realize there was no one definition of how a couple make their final sexual peace together, but some patterns did emerge before Alan shook my hand (yes, shook my hand!) and left with his suitcase.

As commitment lessens, so do efforts to please. In retrospect, I can now honestly admit that Alan was not the best lover I'd ever had. Before the break-up, we'd had numerous middle-of-the-night heart-to-hearts when I tried to explain my quite normal sexual desires to him. Cunnilingus, for example. I craved it; he avoided it. So I'd try to talk to him about why he didn't enjoy performing the act. He would deny disliking it, and for about a week we'd have oral sex every time we made love. And then he'd stop, seemingly having forgotten the discussion.

After we broke up, but were still living together, we didn't have cunnilingus again. I can't be sure whether it was spite, aversion or plain denseness that prevented it, but it became apparent that he wasn't terribly interested in pleasing me that way.

Good sex won't keep a partner from leaving. I'll admit it, I tried playing Scheherezade. We were more sexually active in our last month together than previously. Usually, it was at my instigation. I wanted Alan to know he was foregoing a good thing, and I wanted to leave him with plenty of memories. And, even more foolishly, I wanted to "store up" sex for the drought I anticipated.

So instead of doing my work when Alan left in the morning, I busied myself writing involved sexual adventures with a hero and heroine who carried our names. At night we'd hurry to bed and take turns reading the tales aloud and enacting the fantasies that appealed to us most, whenever possible.

It was fun and diverting. Yet, ultimately, it made life sadder. When I asked him after one multi-orgasmic, exhausting session, "Are you sure you really want to move out?" he said yes, and went to sleep on the couch. I spent the rest of the night feeling humiliated and impotent. Moral: If there is an optimal time to enjoy sex for sex's sake, it is at the end. Second moral: If someone is going to change his mind about breaking up, he will doubtless let you know, so don't ask.

Bittersweet sex is better than no sex at all. It's painful and difficult to end an intimate relationship, and sex *can* ease the transition. At least it did in my case. Granted, Alan and I would soon no longer be a couple, but it was reassuring to know I was still desirable to him on a sexual level. And when someone's leaving you, you question your desirability on every level. By remaining sexually active with your partner-not-to-be, you think: He wants me—but he doesn't want me. Confusion and ambivalence are fine buffers against flat-out rejection.

So it seems that end-of-the-road sex can be many things: It's terrible and terrific, sometimes both in the same evening. It's a way to communicate when other channels are closed. And, finally, it's a message that reads "I love you"—but not necessarily happily ever after.

SEX DURING DIVORCE

By Nick Edmunds

I felt skittish and scared and very much like a virgin as my wife led me by the hand to the bedroom of her new apartment. This was our first time together since our marriage had fallen apart seven months ago. And it had been years since either of us had enjoyed any of our lovemaking sessions.

Earlier in the evening, my new girlfriend, Roxanne, had kissed me goodbye and said, "It's okay if you go to bed with your wife. I know you want to." Her intuition proved correct. Up until now I was not sure whether I wanted to risk making love to my wife—to take the chance of being rejected as a lover as she had rejected the eleven years of our marriage. I was even more afraid to discover what new ways of lovemaking she had learned from new men.

But my dinner date with Corinne and the dancing afterward had been a ritual of reconciliation. Both of us were at that point in a separation where we wanted the other's approval. We made sweet talk, remembering only the good times, and slow-danced like high-schoolers. When we drove back to her apartment, which she shared with a graduate student, I did not have the nerve to hint at sex. We were kissing goodnight at the door when Corinne—honest and forthright as always—pressed her long body against me in a slow, sweet grind. Mentally I thanked Roxanne for giving her blessing to whatever would happen in the upstairs bedroom.

Corinne's bed consisted of a mattress on the floor piled with pillows and our old Sears set of Noah's Ark animals. The Japanese seascape etchings she had had since college were propped against the walls. Copies of *My Mother, My Self* and *How to Be Your Own Best Friend* lay nearby. Kneeling, she turned on the light.

Then she approached me, looking seductive in her Chinese print silk dress. She was wearing more makeup these days, and the dim lamplight made her face shadowy and mysterious. We played at kissing as my hands slid down on her full behind and she slanted her newly flat belly hard against my stomach. Mired in an unhappy marriage, I had seen her only as the source of all my troubles. Now making love to her on an unfamiliar bed was like coming in from the cold; it was like coming home to an exciting stranger.

When our marriage was going to hell, we talked a lot about "fixing" our sex life. But we never did anything about it. Our lethargy regarding careers and finances and plans for travel and children extended to lovemaking as well. Corinne had suggested long ago that I oil her body, then massage and eat her a long time with no thought of my orgasm. But we never did it. In turn, I wanted the contrasting excitement of her voluptuous dark-haired beauty and that of her petite blonde photographer's assistant. But we never set that up either.

We talked about keeping sex alive, but as time passed our lovemaking became an empty ritual—a way of scratching our libidinal itch. Then Corinne began asking for tenderness more than sex itself. When she did not get it, her desire waned and she took to eating cheesecake by the refrigerator at midnight. I started fantasizing about new lovers and kinky scenes from the bottom of a gin bottle. She got plumper and I got drunker. And even though she remained quite attractive—I think some men were turned on by her very abundance—and I never reached the pink-elephant stage of boozing, sex slowly deteriorated into a rare, awkward and lonesome thing for us.

"You know," Corinne said, unsnapping my pants to let my penis spring out, "it's so nice to be together like this. It's like the best of both worlds—to be like new lovers and at the same time to know each other better than anyone else."

"My God, you're stunning," I confessed, with just a tinge of resentment that she had gotten back into such sexy shape only after leaving me. She was wearing nothing but black panties now and I was amazed that, at 29, she still was the same incredible Amazon I had fallen in love with so many years ago. With her thin waist, ample breasts and long legs, she looked almost too good to be true. I just stared and stared.

"You look great, too," she said. "Trim, athletic. Well, we're both back on the meat rack now."

"How true," I admitted. For I, too, had immediately started shaping up for my own reentry into the competitive singles world, of course.

I straddled her waist and let my balls and cock rest snugly against her breasts, while leaning over to take her face in my hands and give her a deep kiss. This was going to be a fuck of high desire with a wife who was no longer mine. That dangerous excitement I felt was the same as if I were making love to another man's woman.

"What do you want me to do now?" I asked.

"Guess."

Fortunately, I had always had a good sense of what Corinne wanted, though the stress of our mundane life together usually short-circuited my willingness to give it. But now I had energy and will to spare.

Just before I went down on her, however, I did something for myself. I hunched my body down between her thighs and slipped my cock into her while her panties were still on. Dreamy memories of teenage car fucking came as I enjoyed the contrast of the black fabric pushed aside by my white cock. I pushed all the way into her, lifting her legs onto my shoulders. Then I rolled her panties down; she opened her legs for me and let her head fall back. Closing her eyes and clasping her hands behind her, she received me.

As I was kissing her cunt and moving my tongue slowly up and down her outer lips, my fingers squeezed and pinched her nipples, which I could feel swelling. She made a wordless, throaty sound as my tongue thrust deeply into her vagina. The taste and smell and feel of her were so familiar. I remembered that she did not like direct pressure on her clit, so I gently whipsawed two fingers alongside the hood instead.

Corinne's face was taut with pleasure—a look I had seldom seen in the last months of our marriage. She groaned happily as I put two fingers into her vagina and pushed deep, while my tongue continued its friendly circling of her clit. Steadily and slowly, forcefully but not too roughly, I finger-fucked her. She put one hand against her forehead and with the other hand swiftly brought herself to climax.

A moment later, as we lay side by side with her fingers wrapped around my erect cock, she said, "One thing I do thank you for is teaching me to want a man who really likes sex. Someone horny. Like you with your 18-year-old's erection."

"Is Jeff horny? What's it like when you're in bed with him, Corinne?"

"He thinks I'm the best kisser he's ever known. And he likes to eat me a lot."

I added a finger; now she was stuffed with four. I said, "Do you fuck a lot?"

They spent long evenings making love, she said. Jeff could stay hard indefinitely, even after he came. Once while driving around downtown, they pulled into the parking lot of the town library and made love on the front seat of his Mercedes.

I asked if he were well-hung and she said, "Actually, it's phenomenal how fat and long he is." I shoved my own cock as deep as I could into my wife's cunt and she sighed, "Oh, honey, that's just so-o-o-o good. Give me more." I quickly did so.

Later, I told Corinne about Roxanne. Our sex life was wonderful, I said, though no better than it had once been with Corinne, only different. I liked to pick her up, because she was short and curvy, and screw her against the wall with my hands supporting her bottom. Unlike Corinne, Roxanne was self-conscious about my going down on her. On the other hand, she loved me to enter her from behind.

"Will you put a finger—just one, and be careful—up me?" Corinne said at one point. I probed gently and slid my middle finger up her tight passage. Somehow, as we talked about Jeff and Roxanne, my wife and I had lapsed back into calm, almost meditative lovemaking. I tried to see Jeff in her eyes. Was she thinking of him as she pulled my hips deeper and harder into her? The thought that I would be back in bed that night with my new lover, and that my wife would soon lie with Jeff, gave me a sharp rush of desire, and I thrust into her with long, fast strokes. It was so good to bury myself in that place where so much of the joy and sorrow of our marriage had resided. And each pinch of her fingers on my nipples and the familiar rippling contractions of her cunt were tightening my balls and bringing the moment of release closer and closer.

She was bracing herself on her heels and arching her cunt, going for her orgasm. I felt my own start to generate from the base of my spine—and from my mind, where the hottest thought of all was that of coming together with my wife. It was exciting and also sad, because this endless fuck was entirely dependent on the fact that my wife and I were no longer a couple. Freed from the constraints of marriage, we could talk honestly about our other loves and ask for sex without hurting the other. Now it had come down to this moment of mutual orgasm, and we went for it.

After the sensations receded we lay together, letting our cock and cunt remain joined. We did not speak. We were at peace.

Sex Rites

*

MORNING BECOMES ERECTION

By Jimmy Crenshaw

During my sophomore year at a small liberal arts college in upstate New York, I found myself sharing a bed with a very cute blonde from my English Lit. seminar. We had made violent love following our *Chaucer* mid-term, and fell into deep slumber on a frigid winter evening. As the morning sunlight crept into her tiny apartment hours later, I awoke and watched admiringly for a few moments as her small, perfectly formed breasts rose and fell softly with each breath.

I felt the old familiar wellings and knew I had to have sex immediately. We had dated sporadically for two years, and I knew her tastes were not against A.M. couplings. So I didn't think it untoward at all to pull the covers back from her beautiful torso and place my face at the entrance of her pleasure center.

I began to lick her vaginal lips slowly, and then more intensely, almost hearing the yet unuttered moans of pleasure that always signaled my arrival at her erotic gates. Instead, this unpredictable co-ed opened her eyes wide, clamped her legs together and began to kick violently about my upper body. She shrieked hysterically: "You fucking pig. What the hell do you think you're doing? You fucking animal."

Never surprised at the capacity of the female to confound, I stayed calm while explaining: "I was engaged in the act of cunnilingus—something you urged me to perform for what seemed like hours last night."

"This is different. . . . It's like necrophilia," she screamed, grabbing the blankets and retreating to the living room.

Such are the pitfalls of the delicate art of morning sex—an erotic variant that I've been especially drawn to since coming of age.

Unlike most people I know, my introduction to sex came in the daylight. Whereas high school classmates boasted of losing their innocence in the back seats of cars bathed in moonbeams or in incense-filled bedrooms illuminated only by the flickering image of Johnny Carson, my manhood began as the sun rose over a lake in New England woods.

Kate and I met at a Boston rock concert less than 24 hours earlier. Fondling and French-kissing consumed us for the late night hours. Consciously or unconsciously, I can no longer remember, we saved the lovemaking for sunrise. In a sleeping bag dripping with early morning dew, we embraced—each naked from the waist down. Between kisses, we could see the vapors of our short breaths reflected in the dim light. When I climbed on top of the nubile 18-year-old and entered her, the sun broke through the trees. As I climaxed— all too quickly—I arched my head back and stared up at the blue sky and the clouds.

My first love laughed out loud when we finally exhausted all our youthful passions an hour or so later: "What a way to start the day," she giggled.

I couldn't agree more. There's nothing quite like licking breasts before breakfast or having coitus before coffee. Fortunately my lovers, by and large, have shared my taste in this regard. Yes, one does make concessions to the hour. For example, I never force tongue kissing in the A.M.

In fact, if a woman grabs my head, presses her lips to mine and sticks her tongue inside before we brush our teeth, well, that's exciting. The woman who ignores bacteria because she must have me then and there is a she-devil in my book.

My current wife is unpredictable on this score. And this can sometimes cause confusion. Some mornings I awake earlier than she and begin stroking her naked body. She sleeps on her stomach, so I begin with a light massage on the shoulders, move my fingers down her lower back, stroke her buttocks and move my fingers into the even more sensitive nether regions. If the Missus is in deep slumber, she usually remains oblivious to all this. But often my amorous maneuvers will prompt her to roll upon her back, open her eyes a crack and laugh wickedly. "Aren't you supposed to be out jogging now?" she will ask.

Thereupon I dive down upon her mouth and start caressing the nipples of her breasts. She'll raise her head to meet my kisses and fold her arms tightly around my neck. Off we go.

Yet other times, she'll move her head violently to the side as my lips near hers, and she'll bury half her face into a pillow, mumbling something about the clam sauce on last night's linguine. I usually ignore the rebuff, adroitly turning it into a rape fantasy scenario—grabbing her arms, pinning her wrists to the pillow, and fucking her while blowing in her face as she squirms. Such kissless passion has its own unique rewards.

My fondness for early morning eroticism stems in part no doubt from the fact that I almost always get up with an erection—a male physiological quirk that is unparalleled in the female erogenous zones. The boner is coupled with the need to relieve myself and the desire to have sex. This combination leads to intense internal deliberations. Dare I run to the commode, maybe wake the baby in the next room and lose the moment? Or do I grit my teeth, surrender to passion and get the ball rolling? To be honest, I usually go for broke.

But what about bed mates? Women with full bladders rarely enjoy horizontal folk dancing. Some have told me this after the fact: "Jeez, I'm glad that's over with. Excuse me for a moment, will you?" It's the rare woman, I've found, who will dive in despite urinary imperatives. I don't mind if they excuse themselves. I just wait patiently and pray that passions aren't doused by cold bathroom tiles.

Morning sex is risky business. I've had trysts ruined by Con Ed representatives wanting to read my meter; phone calls from friends who want to catch me before I've left for the office; and the incredibly antiaphrodisiac drone of giant concrete mixers working on the luxury condominiums next door.

I usually enjoy being the aggressor in sex—morning or night. But I've come to realize that perhaps no joy is greater than the startling realization that a lover is licking your penis while urging it and you to "wake up." I always follow that command.

Yet I've found some women who are quite inattentive to early passion. I went down on one lover as the bedside alarm clock radio switched on the all-news station at 6:45. After the headlines, weather, sports, an editorial on toxic waste removal, tips on how to beat the flu and the stock market report, my snoring beauty had yet to stir. Upset by her corpse-like responsiveness, I stormed into the shower. As I was towelling myself dry, she entered the bathroom. "Shit, it's after 7:30. Why didn't you wake me? I'll be late for work."

One has to be especially vigilant on the birth control watch in the morning. And it can be a pain. Women on the pill, for obvious reasons, pose the least hassle. Females with diaphragms—unless they are very much into it—don't relish all the rigamorole involved in preparing for another spermicidal assault. I don't mind sheathing my erection with a condom in the morning. It's better than the messy withdrawal method. But my experience has shown where there's a will, there's a way. No matter what the obstacles.

On one camping trip, for instance, the lovesongs of sparrows awoke me. I stared over at my lover huddled against my body in the sleeping bag in our tiny two-person tent. I began to rub my groin against hers, and she stirred appropriately, moaning with more than a little desire. "Let's make love," I said, putting my cards on the table.

"Okay, but I've got to get some spermicide. Hand me the tube over by my socks near the inside flap, will you, baby?" she purred gently.

As one who believes contraception is a shared responsibility, I gladly reached to the backside of the tent, grabbed a half-empty tube and laid it lovingly in her hands. She removed the cap with one hand, massaging my manhood with the other. While squeezing both tubes simultaneously, she began to laugh loudly: I had handed her the Crest. The sperm-killer was in our parked car on the other side of the extinguished campfire. Should she get out of the tent and retrieve it (the morning air in our Canadian campsite was so cold, a sheet of ice had formed on the tent)? Thank God, she said "No," preferring to impale her throat cavity upon my penis. As other campers fetched wood and water for coffee, they heard me yelling from the tent, "It feels so good, soo goood, sooo goodd. Sooo damn good." We received a lot of leers a half hour later when, passion spent, we arose, pumped up the Coleman propane stove and cooked flapjacks.

Sex in the morning shower is next to Godliness. My wife and I regularly enjoy standing intercourse while lathering each other. We don't plan such trysts. But I always hope they take place. It will begin innocently enough. "I'm gonna shower, honey. Wanna join me?'' I'll ask, climbing out of bed. "Okay, be there in a minute," she'll answer.

I get the water running lukewarm to warm and the bathroom steams up good and cloudy. My love climbs in after me, pulls the curtains closed and asks for her half of the bar of soap. We begin by rubbing the Dial on each other's backs. We then turn and massage the lather with slow deliberate strokes onto our bodies. I circle her breasts with my fingers and cup her nipples with my palms. She strokes my penis. I put a finger between her lips and squeeze her clit. And she strokes my penis. I begin to kiss her neck. She strokes my penis. I begin to suck her breasts, kiss her stomach and push her back against the wall. She strokes my penis.

As the shower spray shoots into my face and shoulders, I enter her while pushing her buttocks against the wet tile walls. Her legs circle my waist, her hands grab my neck and then the shower curtains. I pump and pump and she places her tongue in my mouth and bites my ear. The soap halves are now on the floor, shrinking in the drain.

Sometimes the action will cause the shower curtains to be torn away from the hooks that keep them in place. As we furiously fuck, the room fills with water. Finally, after a few moments, I come, and she pulls herself closer to me. Sometimes she will even come. Then we unhook ourselves and stand under the spray.

"I wonder who's talking with Jane Pauley today," my lover will say as she turns off the water.

"I don't know. Let's check it out," I answer as my penis shrivels up.

The days that I start with a sex act or two are my favorites. For no matter how bad things get, I know that I've already gotten laid. That always cheers me up.

DIAL S FOR SEX

By Marianne Scott

We called it our dinner-and-"Dynasty" date. Every Wednesday Patrick and I prepared a meal together at his Brooklyn apartment.

Then we would curl up on the couch to eat, drink and watch the latest episode of our favorite TV program. On this particular evening, I deposited the lasagna fixings next to the chianti, greeted Patrick with a kiss and headed for the stove. The phone rang and he answered it. Clamping his hand over the receiver, he exclaimed, "It's Shelly! Should I talk to her or tell her to call back?"

For a second I drew a blank. Patrick made an obscene gesture with the phone between his legs. Then I remembered. Patrick has never met Shelly. She discovered him by dialing numbers at random one day, looking for a phone sex partner. Since then she had called him a half-dozen times. Then he learned that she was a 17-year-old high-school student and discouraged her calls.

For a year he didn't hear from her. Now she had phoned him again. "Talk to her," I urged.

Patrick smiled. "Hold on a minute, Shelly," he murmured into the phone. "I'm going to take this call in the bedroom." He handed me the receiver and I listened, holding my breath. The next moment he picked up the bedroom extension. "Hi," he said.

"How've you been?" she replied. I recognized her voice from a tape Patrick had made of one of their telephone trysts. It was low and husky, just short of breathless, with a homely Bronx accent.

"I haven't heard from you in a long time."

"I know," she stated flatly. "I'm in my mother's bedroom. I was looking through some of her magazines and I started thinking about you."

"What kind of magazines?"

"*Playgirl*. What are you wearing?"

Quietly I filled two glasses with wine and made myself comfortable. Shelly was not wasting any time.

"I'm wearing jeans and no shirt." There was a pause. "Are you still seeing your boyfriend?"

"Sometimes. But he's off at college, so mostly I spend time with my girlfriend."

"Does she ever sleep over?" Patrick asked, lowering his voice suggestively.

"We hold each other in the dark, or lie on top of one another."

"How did that feel?"

"It felt good."

"Hold on a second," said Patrick. "I left a cigarette burning in the other room."

He appeared in the kitchen doorway. I held the receiver against my stomach to muffle our voices. "Is this grossing you out?" he asked. "Should I hang up?" I shook my head no. "Do you want me to talk her into an orgasm?" I nodded. Patrick smiled, then gave me a long, wet kiss—my reward for so eagerly agreeing to be his accomplice in this game of sexual subterfuge. I gave him the other glass of wine and we toasted before he disappeared once again into the bedroom.

He told Shelly that he had taken advantage of the break to remove his jeans.

"Are you wearing *anything*?" she demanded.

"Just my underwear."

"What kind of underwear? Bikini underwear?"

"That's right," he lied.

"The see-through kind?"

"How did you know?"

I almost laughed out loud. Patrick only wears ordinary white briefs.

"Why don't you take them off?" Shelly suggested. "I'm all naked. My pubic hair has gotten really thick. Do you want to hear me run my fingers through it?"

Patrick answered yes. Then I heard a rasping noise.

"Did you take off your underwear?" she inquired. "Let me hear yours."

"Okay," Patrick agreed. I had been mid-sip and tried not to choke. There was a silence. "Can you hear that?"

"No, do it again."

This time I heard a faint scratching. "Can you hear that?"

"Yes."

"So you like to touch your girlfriend," Patrick observed. "What would you do if she was there now?"

"Tell me what to do."

"Imagine she's lying on the bed beside you. She's completely naked, too. You bend over and take one of her nipples in your mouth. It's hard against your tongue and her breast is soft against your lips. Do you like that?"

"Oh yes. What do I do next? Where are you?"

"I'm on the bed behind you. You can feel my big hard dick against your ass, just pushing against your crack. How does it feel?"

"I'm pressing back against it. It feels so big. It would fill me up. Do you want me to suck it? Or lick your balls and ass? Tell me what to do."

I unbuttoned the fly of my jeans and slipped my hand between my legs. The scene the two had described was tantalizingly vivid.

"Lie on your back. I'm kneeling over your face. I want to feel your tongue around my cock. Now I'm pushing it in and out of your mouth." I could almost imagine the familiar taste and texture of Patrick's rigid cock on my lips.

"Your girlfriend's hands are on your ankles," Patrick went on. "She's spreading your legs apart. She's sucking you, flicking her tongue over your clit, and then pushing into your hot, wet cunt. She's fucking you with her tongue. You like that, don't you?"

"Yes," she breathed, just barely audible. I began to finger myself through my panties, trying to keep quiet. I was afraid she might hear me and hang up.

"I want you to slow down," Patrick continued. "So I take my dick out of your mouth and push your girlfriend away from you." I knew Patrick was also talking to me, orchestrating both of our rhythms.

"Oh no!" she protested.

"Yes. I want you to get on your hands and knees. I'm lying underneath you and my dick is pointing straight up at you. I want you to lower yourself onto it until you feel the head just beginning to enter you. I have my hands on your hips. Now tell me what you want."

"I want you to fuck me." Her voice was wavering. I increased the pressure on my clitoris and felt a heavy warmth spreading down the inside of my thighs.

"Say it again," Patrick insisted.

"I want you to fuck me. Hard."

"Now I'm letting you drop your cunt onto my cock. You can feel it go deep inside you inch by inch until you're all pried apart. But I'm not ready to fuck you just yet. Hold very still."

I stopped massaging my clitoris, anticipating her orgasm. I wanted to come with her. Shelly and I both groaned. "Don't be a selfish bitch," Patrick chided. "You forgot your girlfriend."

"Just tell me what to do," she gasped.

"She's kneeling behind us," he directed, "taking my balls into her mouth very gently and licking them. You can feel her breath on your thighs and ass."

I pleaded silently for Patrick to hurry. The sound of Shelly's moans made it difficult to hold back.

"Now you can feel the tip of her tongue against your cunt. She's licking around where my cock goes into you, trying to reach your clit."

"Fuck me. Please," she begged breathlessly.

"She's running the tip of her tongue up the crack between your ass cheeks. You can feel her tongue in your ass. She's fucking it just like it was another pussy."

"I'm coming now . . ." Her voice faded out as my own orgasm washed over me. When it subsided I reached over and quietly replaced the receiver in its cradle. Then I buttoned up my jeans and headed for the bedroom to get some firsthand attention myself.

Patrick was sitting fully clothed on the bed, smoking a cigarette. He too had hung up.

"She always hangs up as soon as she comes," he said, shrugging.

"That was great," I exclaimed, stubbing out his cigarette. Straddling him, I pushed him down on the bed. He put his arms very gently around me.

"You really didn't think that was weird?" he asked.

"I enjoyed it. Let me hear what your pubic hair sounds like," I teased.

"I was rubbing the hair on my head," he confessed, smiling somewhat sheepishly.

"No wonder we couldn't hear anything," I laughed. He smiled and flipped me over on my back. Slipping his hand under my jeans, he parted the still sensitive lips of my cunt.

"You did like that, didn't you?" he murmured, dropping his voice. "You're already wet."

"I thought you'd go on with her forever," I complained.

He plunged a finger inside me and I bore down against it. "I think you need something bigger in there," he observed. "Let's get these clothes off you."

"Why are yours still on?" I asked, pulling my sweatshirt over my head.

"I was saving myself for you. I would feel funny about jerking off while you were listening."

"Let me see your see-through bikini underwear," I joked, unbuttoning and pulling off my jeans.

Grinning, he stepped out of his jeans and then his white briefs.

"Come here," he ordered, pulling me down so that I was kneeling naked in front of him.

"Tell me what to do," I said, mimicking Shelly's Bronx accent.

He ran his fingers softly through my hair, then tightened his grip, pushing my face into his groin. "Suck me," he commanded in the same low, menacing voice he had used with Shelly. I gripped his cock at the base and took as much of it as I could into my mouth. Then he placed me on my back and tormented me with the tip of his cock. "Do you want to feel it deep inside of you?"

"Yes, please," I begged, still attempting a Bronx accent.

"Not yet." He lowered his mouth to my breast and flicked his tongue across a nipple.

"Imagine that one of my girlfriends were here now," I suggested, picking up the thread of fantasy. "The one you like best." I thought a minute. "But don't tell me who."

"Mmmm, okay. She'd suck your breast like this. And then she'd pull your legs apart." I felt his breath on the inside of my thighs. "She'd fuck you with her tongue like this." He pushed his tongue inside me and I pressed down against it. He pulled away.

"Where are you going?" I grabbed for his hair.

"Not yet. Don't be so selfish. Get on your hands and knees."

"Just tell me what to do," I replied meekly. Patrick had never been so domineering before and I loved it. I loved it a lot.

He positioned himself underneath me, holding me slightly aloft. I knew what he wanted to hear. "Let me go. I want to feel you in me."

"Say it right."

"Fuck me, Patrick. Please."

He allowed me to lower myself onto him. As he entered me I couldn't resist mocking him in Shelly's accent. "Ohhhh, I can feel you prying me apart . . ."

The punishment I had been asking for was a swift upward thrust from Patrick's penis. As he fucked me he reached around and slipped his finger into my ass.

"Don't forget your girlfriend," he growled in my ear. "She's fucking your ass with her tongue, just like it was another cunt, and you love it—right?"

"Right," I managed.

Later, as Patrick enjoyed his ritual post-coital cigarette, he noticed the time glowing on the digital clock. "Honey," he said, sounding not at all sorry, "I'm afraid we've missed 'Dynasty.' "

"Not to mention dinner," I replied, sighing. "Do you think she'll call again?"

SEX IN THE DARK

By Marco Vassi

When the jaded poet in the film *Reuben, Reuben* falls in love with a college girl of 19, she asks him what he sees in her. Wistfully he replies, "Innocence is the ultimate aphrodisiac." When I saw that scene I found myself nodding in agreement, remembering the delicious rush that comes when a trembling young thing exclaims in your arms, "I've *never* done *that* before."

Shortly after seeing the film, though, I had the tables turned on me by a woman of 22 who would not make love with the lights on, not even the illumination from a TV screen. Her excuse was shyness, an acute embarrassment at having a man see her naked. But once we were plunged into total darkness, all her inhibitions dissolved and she became hot, wild and wanton. The affair lasted four months and not once during that time did I ever see what she looked like while we were having sex. The experience affected me powerfully and at the end of it *I* was the one left trembling and exclaiming, "I've never done that before."

I don't have any principles or prejudice about whether sex takes place with the lights on or in the dark; each mode creates its own mood. But for the 15 years prior to this affair, I'd been moving in the direction of greater and greater exposure, not only through describing my individual adventures in print, but also by getting involved in swinging, party scenes, and erotic performance art, reaching a state where I felt completely comfortable having sex in a crowd or for an audience.

It was a heady period in my life, and in the history of the country, a period that came to be known as the Sexual Revolution. Like many others, I was swept up in the excitement and promise of a social movement and I lost sight of the price I was paying for pursuing idealistic visions, exotic sensations and a certain notoriety. As I became a cultic and even a public figure, my personal and private sexuality was sucked out of me and into the demands of the various scenes I was into, as well as into the lenses of many cameras. This left me without any organic sexual impulses, but rather with a highly stylized choreography that I could activate the way an actress can turn on tears. In short, I stopped enjoying sexual energy as a feeling and activity in itself and began using it only as a stage for mounting some erotic dance.

This wasn't so troubling when I was, say, at an orgy, but it worried me that I was no longer able to relax even when I was in bed with a lover. When a woman was giving me head, for example, I couldn't lie back and enjoy it but spent the time adjusting my angle of penetration to produce the most appealing curves on her lips as they stretched around my shaft. I was aware of all of this as a process, but only abstractly. It wasn't until I spent those four months making love in the dark that I realized how far I'd traveled from the ability to take a simple and uncomplicated pleasure in sex. One night, after we'd been together for almost two weeks, Becky went down on me for the first time, and I spent perhaps half an hour staring at my crotch in the perfect blackness of the room before I snapped out of my trance and registered the fact that I wouldn't see anything no matter how hard I looked.

I caught myself at a number of such posturings. I often assumed positions that established a certain angle between our bodies which, had there been lights and a camera, would have provided the most interesting shots. I carried over the tensions of erotic flirtation into the physical and emotional exchanges of intercourse, maintaining the psychological distance essential to the theatre of sex even while bringing my body closer to someone who had already surrendered all her roles. Instead of being a man expressing his desire, I'd become a performer endlessly polishing his act. And it was only in the dark that I became fully aware of how thorough the transformation had been.

I'm not at this point "denouncing" group sex or erotic performance art. These were extremely liberating activities for me and in a wider context they served the purpose of counterbalancing the repressive Puritan heritage of pushing everything into the closet. Taking part in an orgy frees one from the prejudice that two is some kind of sacred sexual number. Sex on stage makes one aware of the power of sex in commanding attention and even devotion.

And making love in the light under any circumstances fosters both an acceptance of the body and its functions, and an absence of shame or guilt. It also allows people to look into one another's eyes in which the transports of pleasure and joy shine through.

However, everything must find its proper balance. Prior to the 1960s we, as a nation, tried to keep everything sexual a secret. Since then we have indulged in a mammoth show-and-tell. What is intelligent, as always, is the ability to be flexible, which means neither suppressing erotic expression nor exploiting it. In our culture, both extremes have been tied to the visual. My spell of sex in the dark, by removing that dimension altogether, restored balance and flexibility in two ways. The first was simple deconditioning. All my "pornographic" gestures and attitudes became ridiculous with no one to see them, and so just faded away. The second was a restitution of the other senses, as well as elements of sexuality that are more basic than sight.

Take breathing for instance. A karate instructor I know is fond of saying, "It doesn't count if you're not breathing." In the dark, as I let go of my attachment to form, I found that my breath became fuller, deeper. The more visual an experience is, the more cerebral it is. During such self-conscious behavior there is a strong tendency to hold the breath and crank up the excitement level through oxygen starvation and carbon dioxide intoxication. When the focus of attention drops from the eyes to the breath, sex becomes a far more sensual experience. When the breathing is restricted, the muscles are kept tense, and sex turns into a charged skirmish that may be highly stimulating but not deeply satisfying. Theatrical sex always left me flushed and exhausted. But when I began to return to a more organic sexuality I found that an hour or more of hot licks made me feel refreshed and rejuvenated.

The next rediscovery in the dark was the sense of touch. Instead of using my eyes, I let my fingers do the walking. I found it deliciously sexy to explore my lover's body without first sizing it up visually, to approach it like a child with an unknown object, without associations, sliding from smooth skin to eruption of hair to viscous center between the thighs. The most intriguing thing was to put my hand on her body and not recognize what part I was touching.

The second sense to come alive was hearing. Just as a blind man can make a map of the world from sound, so having sex in the dark made me far more sensitive to the noises my lover was making. I learned to follow the cycles and shadings of her excitement not from facial expressions and body postures, but from the sighs, moans, whispers, cries and groans she produced as we moved from the first light kisses of foreplay to the explosion of orgasm.

The third sense to assume new prominence was smell. Perhaps the greatest overall conspiracy against sexuality in our culture is the war on the sense of smell. Yet this is the most basic of the senses. We are bombarded with advertisements to scrub ourselves daily and rub deodorants into the body's natural hollows, and even to mask the aroma of the vagina itself. In the dark, when visual cues are removed, the body's smells are a voluptuous invitation to the most intimate exploration. The odor of sweat, secretions, and the crevices of armpits and buttocks make a compelling aphrodisiac.

In addition to breath, relaxation and the senses, sex in the dark awakens the feeling of mystery. In darkness it is easy to forget your identity, the identity of the person you're with, or even which planet you're on. With the two basic orientations of daily life removed— visual cues and vertical posture—it's possible to sail off into a mood of unknowingness. After a month or so of sightless lovemaking, I didn't feel that I was having sex so much as that sex was having me. All my egotistic concerns dissolved as two blind creatures pressed against and penetrated one another, and were hurled from the cliff of self-awareness into the abyss of rapturous oblivion.

At the psychological level, this melting into mystery emerges as freedom of fantasy and emotional expression. In the dark you can imagine anything and you can have any look or attitude you want. While visual sex does have its values and virtues, it also tends to inhibit us in the way we express ourselves. When the light is on we don't ordinarily let our faces show anger, stupidity, bestiality, boredom or other "negative" emotions. We become as polite in bed as at the dinner table. And the degree to which I'd become mannered hit home one night when, in the midst of one of my best ravishment routines, my entire body erupted with the sense-memory of the joyous wildness I used to feel before my sexuality was choreographed, at which point I began to ravish the lady in earnest.

Those four months in the dark served as a purification ritual for me. When that process was finished, I wanted to move into a regular, balanced cycle of darkness and light in our lovemaking. But she was afraid that if we put the light on, that would "break the spell." Maybe it would have. The relationship was a failure in too many other areas anyway and we never found out what might have happened next. We parted and went our separate ways.

Although the affair ended, its effect continued. I subsequently spent six months in celibacy and then began living with someone on the condition that I would say or write nothing about our sex life together, thus completing my return to a totally personal, private and even secret sexuality.

It feels good, although still a bit odd, to have arrived at such a conventional solution. One night last month I was talking about all of this with a few old friends and comrades from the early days of the Sexual Revolution and one of them remarked that I was sounding very conservative these days, and that some of my views could even be endorsed by fundamentalists. I saw that he was right and had to smile at the way the wheel of revolution keeps meeting itself coming and going.

When the wheel was turning in the direction of liberation, it was good to open all the closet doors and sweep away the stultifying hypocrisy that was our official national policy on sex. But now that the movement is back in the other direction, it's time to admit that the previous period of letting a thousand orgasms bloom did leave pockets of corruption—the wastes produced by commercial exploitation of liberated sexual energy and the diseases spawned by unbridled debauchery. Then perhaps we wouldn't have to swing all the way back to the "right," but find instead a middle way between massive suppression and total license.

As individuals we have little control over the larger movements of history. But each of us can strike a balance in her or his own sex life and thereby be a stable element in the greater process instead of adding to the confusion. Those who are still keeping themselves in the dark because of fear or prejudice need to let some light into their bedrooms and their minds. Those who are overly dependent on visual stimulation, on sexual theatre and erotic imagery need to shut the door, pull the curtain over the window, turn off the light and, in what Dylan Thomas called "the close and holy darkness," remember how to *get down*.

When we are no longer afraid of or addicted to the light or the darkness, then our sexuality will be free.

FANTASY GAME

By Eric Perry

I knew Kevin for less than a month, and never met his wife. But when he invited Kathy and me to join them for an evening of erotic games, I could hardly contain my excitement. At first my wife was skeptical about a sex game for two couples with no swapping. "He said you didn't have to switch partners," I told her.

"And she's pretty?"

"She looked beautiful in the photo . . . great legs."

"And you're a leg man." Kathy leaned over and kissed me. I fondled her breast and kissed her back. "Yes, but no one has better legs than you, darling."

"And he's good looking?" she asked coyly.

"About 6-foot-2, slim, with sandy hair and a nice moustache—just your type."

"M-m-m-m . . ." Her tongue found mine and she began unzipping my pants. "Okay," she whispered. "Let's meet them."

Kevin and Sheila lived in a lovely old section of Long Island. As we drove up the driveway, I had butterflies in my stomach. Kathy was attired in a skimpy black dress and red ankle-strap high heels that previously she only wore in our bed.

Kevin welcomed us warmly and introduced Sheila. Slim and strikingly pretty, she stood in four-inch black heels. Her tight skirt showed off the curves of her legs and ass when she moved, while under her filmy blouse was the hint of a lacy bra. I was utterly enchanted.

Soon the small talk turned intimate. Kevin and Sheila steered the conversation to sexual fantasies.

"Most of ours involve everyday situations that become sexual encounters," Sheila informed us. "That's how we devised our little game."

"Ah, yes, the game," I mused. I was very aroused by now.

Kevin picked up a white leather binder from the coffee table and

50

handed it to us. We started leafing through the pages with photos of two couples cavorting in various stages of undress.

"Each page contains a different fantasy to be acted out," Kevin said. "There's a three-minute time limit for each one and we put our clothes back on between each fantasy. Then things don't get out of hand and everyone becomes more and more turned on."

The fantasies were divided into categories. "Ones" were cute and flirty—like a man opening his partner's blouse and squeezing her breasts while the other couple watched. Another had him raising her skirt. The "twos" were more daring: a girl with her skirt pulled up around her hips, with one man pressing a vibrator into her cunt while she sucked another's cock. Kathy was beginning to breathe heavily.

Before we got to the "threes," I suggested we just start playing. Sheila led Kathy out of the room. When they returned, my wife was blushing. Adorned in pale blue stockings and little white anklets with red high heels, she sat down and darted her tongue playfully into my ear.

Sheila announced that the fashion show was about to begin. Kevin pushed the table out of the way. Then he positioned his wife in front of us, gently ran his hand over her blouse, and caressed her breasts. Boldly, Kathy put her hand on my cock. Then Kevin unbuttoned Sheila's blouse and exposed a lacy bra that barely covered her nipples. Sheila's eyes closed in ecstasy as he pinched through the bra. Kathy and I began kissing each other as we watched.

Kevin then knelt to stroke his wife's legs. Slowly, he pushed up the hem of her skirt, stopping at mid-thigh. Her hose were sheer and dark, defining the provocative curves of her legs.

"Higher," said Kathy. "Let's see more."

Kevin raised the skirt up above Sheila's stockings, which were held by a black garter belt.

"Do you like my panties?" asked Sheila, pointing to her black bikini panties.

"They're beautiful," Kathy murmured as she kneaded my cock through my pants.

Kevin now held Sheila's skirt up to her waist. We could smell her wetness as she pressed against him. Sheila opened her legs slightly to allow Kevin to insert his hand. After he withdrew, the silky crotch remained tightly nestled in the crease of her cunt.

"Now it's your turn," I told Kathy. Sheila buttoned her blouse and took Kathy's hand. Kathy slowly rose and stood before us.

Kevin kissed my wife on the cheek as Sheila sat beside me to watch the second part of the fantasy unfold.

Kevin slowly cupped Kathy's full breasts. The sight of another man fondling my wife was incredibly arousing.

"Open her dress," Sheila ordered. Kevin unzipped Kathy's dress and lowered it down her back. She wriggled and the dress slipped down her arms.

I was startled by the snugly fitting corselet pushing her breasts up over the lacy cups. Kevin playfully traced his fingers over the edge of the bra.

"How does that feel, Kathy?" Sheila asked.

"It feels wonderful, orgasmic. He's squeezing so hard."

Meanwhile Sheila stroked my cock through my pants. I worried briefly about what Kathy would think, but she was too preoccupied to notice.

"Show us more," Sheila insisted.

Kevin grazed Kathy's thighs and toyed with her garters. Then he tugged on the white satin panties, causing them to press against her cunt. Turning her around, he bent her over to show us how vulnerable and available she was. Pulling the panties to one side, he revealed one of my wife's delectable cheeks. Then he poked the satin into her ass as Kathy began writhing her hips against his touch. His other hand played with her cunt.

It took us all a few moments to regain our composure. As Kathy dressed, we took deep breaths and long sips of our drinks.

"This beats Trivial Pursuit," I joked and everyone laughed. "But how can you keep up this excitement without coming?"

Sheila confided that there was no penalty for orgasm. But the longer we delayed climax, the better it was when it finally occurred. Kevin announced that the game got more interesting when we reached the "twos." I couldn't wait.

"How about doing Hot Flashes?" Sheila asked. "We all write a short fantasy, a hot flash, on a slip of paper, then we read them in turn and act them out."

Sheila handed out pencils and paper. "Now remember," she cautioned, "we only have a minute to act each one. Be sure to specify who does what to whom."

Each of us finished quickly, folded the slips of paper, and placed them on the coffee table. "Eric, why don't you read the first one," Sheila suggested.

Closing my eyes, I picked up Kathy's note. She wanted to suck both men simultaneously. Sheila expressed her delight. Kevin and I obediently stood in front of Kathy, who promptly unzipped us. Wrapping her fingers around our cocks she stroked us gently. Pulling down Kevin's briefs, she exposed the head of his cock. It bobbed, then stood straight out, long, thick and rigid. Next she lowered my shorts below my balls. My cock, too, stood out slightly uptilted.

Kathy proudly displayed us and gently pulled both shafts, then licked the tip of my cock, fondling my testicles. She repeated the process with Kevin. I loved watching her play with his penis.

"Go ahead," I urged her, "put it in your mouth."

She took the head in her mouth. I could almost feel the swabbing tongue that Kevin was now thrilling to.

Kathy next sucked on me. Grasping both cocks firmly, she pressed the two heads together. I had never felt another man's cock next to mine, and the sensation was strange and exciting, like one's first French kiss.

Opening her mouth wide, she took in as much of both tips as she could, licking each shaft in turn. Finally, she accommodated both cocks in her mouth at once.

Sheila now read the next flash. She wanted to suck my cock while Kevin spanked her. I sat next to Kevin on the couch. Sheila lay across his lap. She took my cock and probed the tip with her tongue as Kevin spanked her through her skirt. She moaned as he brought his hand down hard. Her mouth held my cock tightly.

Kevin roughly yanked her skirt up. Sheila wriggled to allow him to work it up over her ass. As she writhed her hips, her long stockinged legs and spike heels kicked defiantly in the air while her black-laced cheeks jiggled at his touch. Meanwhile her head bobbed up and down, playing with my loose foreskin.

Kevin's hand came down hard again on Sheila's ass. As he bared his wife's cheeks I began to feel an undeniable rush. "I'm going to come," I warned.

Kathy began kissing me as the first burst hit. Sheila sucked voraciously. I was filling her mouth with come while Kevin pried her legs apart and spanked her again. "I love you," Kathy whispered as Sheila swallowed my come and licked my cock clean.

Now it was Kevin's turn. Having spent myself, I was to be an observer. But my hair-trigger cock sprang to life as Kathy read Kevin's flash: "I would like to pleasure Kathy and Sheila simultaneously with two vibrators."

I could not resist stroking myself as he positioned the women side by side on their hands and knees. Then, slowly pulling down their panties, he took two shiny gold vibrators and switched them on. "Spread your cunts," Kevin ordered.

Carefully he inserted the humming tips into each gaping vagina. The buzzing grew alternately softer, then louder, as he worked them in and out. Both wives squirmed as he dildo-fucked them faster and faster.

Then it was time for my hot flash. I wanted Kathy and Sheila's mouths to meet around my cock. The thrill of two tongues licking me was surpassed only by the sight of two women tongue-kissing as their mouths met at the tip. Afterward we advanced to the "threes."

"This one is our favorite," said Kevin, opening to a page depicting two couples sucking and fucking.

The instructions called for one pair to assist the other in sliding cock into cunt. The second couple then took their turn at fucking while the first lovers helped them. Play was to proceed to a natural conclusion with no time limit. Kevin and Sheila were the first pair.

Kathy lowered Kevin's shorts and began to suck him. I removed Sheila's bra, admiring the pink spice-drop nipples. They jiggled pertly as I sat her on the coffee table. The sound of Kathy slurping Kevin's cock was wonderfully exciting. Taking hold of Sheila's high heels, I spread her legs apart. Then I began running my tongue lightly from the instep of her shoe slowly up the inside of her dark silky leg.

Pausing at the top of her stocking, I licked along the edge, feeling the delicate texture of the nylon and the cool softness of her inner thigh.

"Eat me, Eric. Please eat me," she begged.

I pushed my tongue deep into the moist cleft. Gently prying apart the lips with my fingers, I alternately sucked and blew. Sheila groaned loudly.

"Let's make them fuck," Kathy said to me.

I instructed Sheila to lie on the floor on her stomach. Placing a pillow under her head, I raised her ass so that her cunt was presented for Kevin.

Kathy positioned Kevin behind Sheila and continued to suck his penis. I parted Sheila's cunt as Kathy slowly introduced the head of Kevin's penis. The two slowly began to fuck. I sat on the edge of the coffee table so that Sheila could take me into her mouth.

Kathy stroked Kevin's cock as it plunged in and out of Sheila. "Can you get your finger in, too?" Sheila asked Kathy. As my wife complied, Sheila began to come. I pressed my cock deep into her throat.

Kevin had not come yet when I suggested we switch roles. He did not object. Kathy sat astride me, facing away so that Sheila could kneel and lick us both as we fucked. Kevin climbed on the couch beside us so he could offer his penis to Kathy's mouth. She accepted his offer and sucked him as my cock buried itself deeper into her cunt.

Kathy and I fucked furiously. Sheila withdrew my cock from Kathy's cunt and plunged it into her mouth. Then she carefully reinserted it into Kathy. She repeated the process over and over until I thought I would burst. Suddenly I felt the torrent mustering, as though I had never come before in my life. I looked down to see Sheila take the first burst into her mouth. Seconds later she pushed my shaft into Kathy's cunt.

Thrusting even deeper into Kathy's mouth, Kevin shouted, "I'm coming!" The first drops spurted against Kathy's cheek and she quickly swallowed the head. With Kevin's come dripping down her cheek, Kathy began to tremble. All three of us had climaxed at once. Sheila rose to lick the semen off Kathy's cheek. We all fell into a sweet kissing embrace.

The effects of our night with Kevin and Sheila were enduring and delightful—like an extended afterglow. When we arrived home that night, exhausted as we were, we could not take our hands off each other. We fucked ourselves to sleep. The next morning my cock was still rigid. Over and over again we recalled the details of the incredible adventure which now took on the aspect of a vivid wet dream. As we made love we fueled our passion with questions about how his cock tasted in her mouth or how wet Sheila's cunt had been.

We decided definitely to see Kevin and Sheila again, but not too soon or too often.

The attractive couple and their game were like rich delicacies, to be savored in measured portions.

Desperately Seeking Adventure

*

STEAM HEAT

By Eva Girard

As an artist, I am used to unusual situations. But nothing had ever prepared me for my bizarre encounter with Jonathan. Paula, a mutual friend and fellow photographer, hired us to help her photograph a fund-raising party for the new aviary at the city zoo. We were assigned to take Polaroids and present them to the guests as mementos. Paula decided that the job definitely called for us to dress up as birds.

Paula's boyfriend Daniel joined us. A makeup artist and designer, he had fashioned outfits with wing-like sleeves and a peacock tail. He was decorating my face with feathers and sequins when Jonathan arrived. Only a pair of fishnet stockings kept me from being naked.

"Your costume is in the corner, Jonathan," Paula ordered. "Put it on and Daniel will do your makeup next."

I watched Jonathan undress. He was long, lean and nicely muscled, like a swimmer. As he dropped each garment to the floor, he continued to stare at my breasts and hips. I found his blatantness arousing and stared back.

At the zoo pavilion we paired off. Jonathan and I wandered around taking Polaroids and giving them to the guests. Many asked to be photographed with one of us. Jonathan enjoyed posing me. While positioning me he would whisper in my ear, "Eva, you have very shapely legs," and surreptitiously run his hand over my ass. Or he would straighten the straps of my bodice and smooth the pleats over my hips. I found his caresses exciting. Once he cornered me as I was reloading my camera. He slid his hand through the open back of my dress and fondled my breasts.

"I have to see your face," he murmured, squeezing my nipples. "I like what I've seen so far." I searched through the folds of his costume, found his cock and fondled back. For the remainder of the job, I thought only about how it had hardened in my hands.

Afterward we went back to Daniel's studio. Paula and Daniel disappeared into the bedroom. As I leaned over to take off my shoes, I felt Jonathan embrace me from behind.

"Let me help you with your dress," he said.

Peeling off the bodice, he ran his hands over my breasts. We began to kiss passionately. Nearby was a table covered with soft fabrics. Jonathan lifted me onto it. Placing his cock at the opening of my vagina, he gently pushed in half an inch and paused, then advanced the entire tip of his cock and stopped again. He entered me a half-inch at a time, occasionally pulling out and starting over again. This sweet torture made me desperate. I tugged at his hips, but he resisted penetrating me all the way.

So I knelt down before him and with my tongue circled the tip of his cock. I took him into my mouth slowly, a little at a time, sucked and stopped. He grew excited and wanted to thrust deeply into my mouth, but I resisted.

"Come inside me again," I urged. He thrust into me again and again until the deep waves of pleasure rippled through us.

Later we dressed each other in street clothes and left the studio. The streets were surreally lit by the star-filled March sky. We walked, holding hands, in the direction of my house.

"This is one of my favorite streets," Jonathan told me. "A city heat pipe runs under it, so almost every block has a sidewalk steam vent. Look." He pointed to one ahead of us that was spewing large white clouds. "Would you let me photograph you in that one night?" I laughed, amused at the idea. Many artists had asked me to pose before, and I always declined. But imagining myself in one of Jonathan's strange photographs was appealing.

"Yes," I replied, turning to him. "I might be able to help you."

Jonathan phoned a few nights later. "Wear something you can easily slip in and out of," he instructed me, "and I'll pick you up at midnight."

I put on my kimono and a long blue cape. Half an hour later I found myself naked, along with Paula and Daniel, in an alley in a deserted part of the city. In the middle of the block, a street vent emitted a steady mass of steam. We huddled around it, trying to find warmth in the near freezing night. Jonathan mounted his strobe on the camera. Then he wordlessly slid his hands down my neck and shoulders, peeling back my cape and kimono.

"Stay near the vent and you'll be warm," he advised. He moved several feet away and began to view the scene through the camera.

For a crazy instant I thought of the hundreds of times my mother asked if I dressed warmly enough. Then, leaving my clothes where they fell, I stepped to the edge of the vent. To my surprise, I had entered a warm, wet world not unlike a steambath. And as I glided around in the hissing vapor, I began to enjoy the alternating gusts of cold and hot air.

"That's it," said Jonathan, "keep on moving in and out of the steam."

"This must be New York's version of Old Faithful," laughed Paula. She and Daniel soon joined me. The three of us danced in slow motion around the vent.

"Eva, keep dancing," Jonathan cried. "I want Paula and Daniel to kiss." I moved around them as they embraced, thinking of Jonathan and me.

"Now the three of you together," Jonathan directed. Paula drew me into their embrace so that I was sandwiched between them. Her hands stroked my thighs, then glided up my waist and cupped my breasts. Daniel lifted my face to his and gave me a long kiss, his tongue probing deeply. When he rubbed his erection on my thigh, I gasped with pleasure.

"Eva, put on your cape and come here," Jonathan said. "I want you to watch them." He photographed Paula and Daniel's lovemaking while I looked on with frustration and envy. Then he put down his camera, opened my cape, knelt before me and began to suck and lick my clitoris. His tongue, then his fingers, pushed me to the edge of orgasm. I began to unzip his pants, but he drew away and began packing up his camera equipment.

I assumed he was shy about making love in front of Paula and Daniel. This thought mitigated my sense of rejection. When he dropped me off at my house, I began to caress his cock through his pants. But again he stopped me. I felt acutely disappointed, but said nothing.

"Stay with me," he whispered cryptically before driving away.

A few days later Jonathan called to say the photographs were fantastic. He asked if I would pose again, this time with André, a French sculptor and friend of his. I agreed.

"Nice secluded spot," mocked André when we arrived at the location Jonathan had chosen. The only thing that obscured us from the traffic that whizzed by was a row of shabby forsythia.

"It's an excellent vent," Jonathan exclaimed, admiring the clouds that escaped from the street grille.

André and I shed our clothes and stepped close to the vent. He was blond, uncircumcised and well built. As he moved around me, striking various poses, he looked like a statue.

"The Rape of the Sabine Woman," he called out, lifting me up.

"That's good," Jonathan said. "Now let's see the Rape of the Sabine Man." André and I laughed, amused at the idea that I could overpower him. "And Eva," Jonathan added, "can you make the pose less metaphorical and more specific?"

Then I understood. Certainly André did, because he became instantly erect. Before I could decide if I wanted to pursue this latest development, André embraced me. I submitted, closing my eyes and pretending that it was Jonathan's cock I was sucking. When André groaned with pleasure I looked up. Jonathan had stopped photographing and was watching us. But we did not make love that night either.

Over the next several weeks I posed with painters, writers, an Ethiopian who sold Arabian horses, an editor at the city newspaper and other photographers. Sometimes there were as many as seven or eight of us gathered around a vent.

Several times the police came. Only one officer was outraged enough to threaten us with arrest. Two showed us steam vents where we could photograph with more privacy. Almost all of them wanted to watch us work, but none accepted our invitation to be part of the group.

The mood of the evenings varied. Everyone involved took the project seriously, but there was also much hilarity among us. What many of the sessions had in common was sex. All the nakedness and touching was hard to control, and sometimes people would begin to make love.

Jonathan liked to direct people toward or away from me, manipulating events so that by the end of every session I was always aroused but never satisfied. When he dropped me off at home we would often begin to have sex. He slowly unbuttoned my blouse and sucked my breasts until the sweet tension between my legs turned to a sharp ache. But he would not allow us to make love.

I increasingly resisted Jonathan's scenario. At first I assumed each time we went out that we would spend the night together. But as the "next times" began to accumulate, discomfiture and confusion overwhelmed me. Paula's appraisal of Jonathan as a neurotic ceased to be an amusing comment. I began to see him as a brilliant sadist. But when he kissed me good night I sensed his fervor. We were playing the game of continence to its farthest limit.

When spring arrived, Jonathan decided to have an end-of-the-season venting session. He invited Paula, two German filmmakers and me. Afterwards Jonathan brought out two bottles of champagne. We stood around the vent toasting one another.

"I don't really have any steamy photographs of myself," Jonathan announced. As he undressed he looked at me.

"Eva, you should be part of this," he asked. Weeks of repression had inured me. I pretended not to have heard him. He began to move in and out of the steam.

"Eva, I want you in these photographs," he murmured, staring at me.

I took off my clothes slowly to hide my eagerness. But as I approached him my heart was pounding furiously. His cock was already large and hard. A current of intense joy ran through me when his slender, naked body embraced mine.

"Finally," I whispered, and we began to kiss passionately. He slipped his hand between my legs and the sensation was so acute that I started to come.

He spread his legs. My hands glided down his waist and massaged his groin. When I crouched before him and slipped him into my mouth, he groaned with pleasure. I was oblivious to the clicks of the camera and thought only of his hard cock.

Steam swirled around us. Jonathan pulled me up, grabbed my leg and put it around his waist. I lifted myself up, locking my legs behind him. The head of his cock found my vagina. When he penetrated me I thought I would faint. He moved in and out, pushing and thrusting, bending his knees for better leverage. A gust of steam swept us like a warm hand caressing our bodies. I reached down and fondled his balls. He began to thrust more quickly and I felt myself exploding.

"Come with me," I pleaded. I was contracting deeply, furiously. "Eva," he cried with a violent shudder.

Jonathan and I have made love many times since that night. I realize now that the period of celibacy he put us through was his peculiar way of bonding us together. Neither of us has ever forgotten the trauma of intensely wanting but not having the other.

The steam vent series created a controversy when the photographs were exhibited. Several critics denounced them as indecent, others hailed them as highly original. I find the photographs, like their author, beautifully eccentric. A favorite is one the art world will never see. It shows the ashen, shocked faces of the two Germans watching as I mounted Jonathan.

I WAS A COKE WHORE

By Jodi Jettson

Until recently I was a coke whore, trading sex for cocaine. A man named Carl introduced me to the drug. He asked for nothing in return. Yet it was inconceivable to snort with him all evening and then not sleep with him. Later I met Ted, an acne-faced fellow from St. Louis, who told me outright that he expected to fuck me at the end of a long, hot, coke-snorting night on the banks of the Mississippi.

Many more men and a lot more cocaine followed. The pattern never varied: I snorted their lines of white powder, drank their booze and then went home with them. The coke made me feel uninhibited and giddy. I usually wanted to have sex after being high. When I closed my eyes and lay down, I could surrender completely to the sensations of my body. And it made no difference whether I was attracted to the man or not, since it was his cocaine that I lusted after. Then I met Frank.

I had moved to northern California from Chicago to attend college. During the first few weeks I found small-town life lonesome. One Saturday, hoping to find companionship, I went to a local hangout popular with the students. A reggae band was playing. I ignored stares from the fellows at the bar and took an empty seat at the end. A tall man stood next to me, watching the musicians. I paid no attention to him until he asked me to watch his drink for a moment.

"Sure," I said. "What's it going to do?"

I stared at the glass as though waiting for it to perform a trick. The man laughed and walked away.

A few minutes later he returned, sniffing and wiping his nose and wearing the telltale grin of someone who has just snorted a line. I was envious. I had not done any cocaine since leaving Illinois and I shivered at the thought of those sensuous crystals crawling up my nose.

"Your glass hasn't done anything yet," I told him, motioning toward his drink on the bar. He looked surprised, then bent over his drink and yelled, "Goddamn it, I'm tired of this dead-beat act of yours. Now stand up and dance!" Then he looked at me, shrugged and asked me to dance. Afterward he invited me out to his car for a line, just as I had hoped.

We sat in the front seat for hours, talking and snorting. Finally I went to retrieve our coats at the bar. Without saying a word, both of us knew I would be going home with him. That is how things are between a man and a woman who share cocaine all night. The attraction is not mutual desire but a need to keep the party going.

But Frank was different. As I soon discovered, he liked sex even more than coke. Both were my chief preferences in life, too, but in reverse order. Since he wanted to fuck and I wanted to snort, we made a tacit, subtle agreement, the way you automatically move closer to the fire when you're cold.

Frank was a voracious, insatiable lover. A tongue flick or touch of the hand on his crotch gave him a stubborn erection. He could literally make love all night, though I made sure we stopped frequently for cocaine. Those were the moments I liked best. Even though Frank was a thoughtful lover, he did not excite me. I achieved orgasm with him no more than once or twice. He seemed more like a drinking or snorting buddy than a sex partner.

After a month, I could not even look at Frank without tasting that acrid powder in my nostrils. If he visited me during the day and did not give me a few lines, I felt angry and resentful. So I decided to ensure a regular supply. The next time he came over, he sprawled out on my couch and started chatting. I walked over, unzipped his pants, and began giving him a blowjob. His cock immediately grew hard. He had an enormous penis and it gagged the back of my throat. Finally he moaned and his semen spurted out. I swallowed every drop.

"Whew," he sighed, "what did you have for breakfast today?"

That night he returned with two grams of cocaine and a bottle of champagne.

We cruised the bars regularly, drinking and snorting coke in the restroom or outside in his car. Often, people who were strangers to me approached him. Then Frank would disappear for a few minutes to make another drug deal. Or we went to parties where people gave him money and he cut out the lines of cocaine on top of a coffee table.

Some nights we snorted so much cocaine that I felt too wired to make love to him. My body twitched and my mouth was dry. But Frank was never too stoned to screw. So I would force my jumpy body down onto the bed with him, letting my nervous tongue roll over his chest. Then I lay trembling and agitated while he penetrated and thrust into me. After he came, I always got up and snorted again. My desire for cocaine was becoming as unquenchable as his for sex.

Yet snorting did affect me sexually in different ways. Sometimes when I was high, my body yearned for physical sensations. Each touch was isolated and intense. Frank's fingers on my skin felt like static electricity. But at other times I was indifferent to his caresses. My body seemed to freeze up and I was unable to respond to him.

Frank eventually made some money in a big drug deal and wanted to go to Reno for a couple of days. The allure of booze, gambling, decadence and, of course, cocaine was irresistible. We left for Reno on a Friday afternoon. But the six-hour drive took 10 hours because we stopped so often to snort a line or have a shot of whisky at a bar. Once at our hotel we collapsed onto the bed, scarcely able to see through the veil of drugs.

The next morning we hit the casinos. Frank got involved in a poker game, while I played the slot machines. Already I felt resentful at not having snorted any cocaine that morning. So I took out my anger on the machines and drank innumerable free screwdrivers served by waitresses in bunny costumes.

By late afternoon I was drunk. Frank rescued me from my stool by applying a few life-saving lines of coke up my nose. That enabled me to at least grab the drinks from the tray without falling off my chair. Time ceased to exist. Day and night merged into one. Frank went back to his poker game and I reentered the phantasmagoria of ringing slot machines, blinking red and white lights and bunnies offering me an endless supply of screwdrivers.

Finally, Frank wanted to go back to our hotel and sleep for a few hours. I would have preferred to stay at the casino, but I reluctantly accompanied him. In our room he tore off his clothes and fell into bed with a raging hard-on. I made love to him quickly, riding on top of him and coolly observing his face convulse when he climaxed. When he fell asleep I took a bath. All I could think of was cocaine and casinos. Frank was still asleep when I finished bathing. I dressed quietly, then rummaged through his pockets until I found the package of white powder. Guilt crept up my back like the first chill of coke in the morning. But I took it and left anyway, trying to comfort myself with the thought that there is no such thing as free cocaine.

All night long I sat at the blackjack tables, feeling guiltier by the minute. I had never taken Frank's coke without asking him first. Now I felt like a junkie, desperate for a fix, who would even steal from a friend or lover. Hours later Frank suddenly pulled me off the stool with a face red more from hurt than anger. It was then that he realized I liked his cocaine more than him. I was surprised. Did he think that I loved him all this time?

We drove back to California at a furious pace, never stopping once for a drink or some coke. Frank had calmed down by the time we got home and almost seemed his good-natured self when he dropped me off at my apartment. He never even mentioned the coke that I stole. Perhaps he had reconciled himself to the fact that I regarded him not as a lover but my drug supplier.

But I seldom saw him after that weekend. Nor were we ever lovers again—for a simple reason. He never offered me any more cocaine.

I SLEPT WITH A GANGSTER

By Katie O'Shaunessy

All through my adolescence I entertained fantasies of sleeping with bad guys and making them good. It must have been my Catholic upbringing, with the extra emphasis on the value of the sinner. Or maybe it was a book I read—by a Jesuit, I think—called *You Can Change the World*. By my mid-twenties I had begun to live my fantasies. The time coincided with the opening of *The Godfather*, and the most fashionable bad guys in town had Mafia connections. I, being au courant, found myself lying naked next to a gangster one wicked winter evening. His mother-of-pearl pistol sat in its holster next to the bed. He was young and Italian and healthy and virile, and I combined the erotic primitivism of a nubile Sicilian with the external good looks of the classic blue-eyed blonde. But nothing was happening. What could be wrong? How had I gotten there? Would I get out unharmed? It had all started about five hours earlier, on a snowy Saturday night in New York City. I was high on some wonderful Thai stick and had just stopped at a deli for a roast-beef-on-rye. As I stepped back out onto the pavement on East 72nd Street, I heard wheels spinning futilely on top of the ice. One man, cursing and grunting, was pushing a creamy Eldorado; a second man climbed out of the car and stood with his hands in his pockets by the first one. Both had on identical camel-hair coats, both wore Gucci loafers, but there the similarities stopped. The driver was tall and thin and extremely good-looking. His friend, thick and flat-faced, looked like a thug. I'm a good reporter and a beautiful woman and I use both these attributes to get around town. Of course it doesn't hurt that I have a sprinter's body—long, muscular legs, broad shoulders and a chest that doesn't weigh me down in the dash. But that night I was dressed for the weather, and my face and body were cloaked in a parka. My legs were lost in overalls and my feet ensconced in hiking boots. Maybe because I felt protected by my outfit and emboldened by the grass, when the thug said, "Goddamn weather," I came to the defense of the weather.

"What's so bad about the weather?" I asked, looking at him.

"It's a fuckin' mess, what else?" He spoke with a very broad, almost flat native Brooklyn accent.

"I think of it as quite lovely," I said in my very finest English.

"And what's so lovely about it?"

I kept on walking until the tall handsome one stopped me.

"Wait a minute," he said. "How would you like to have dinner with me?"

"I've got a sandwich in my bag," I informed him.

"Eat it tomorrow," he said convincingly. I, anyway, was convinced, and so I climbed into the front of the creamy Eldorado, where I sat in between the two of them. I looked to the left at the lovely features of the driver. His brown, curly hair, brown eyes, beautiful mouth and jutting chin. He wore horn-rimmed glasses, which made me think he must be smart.

Then I looked to my right, at the flat nose of the other one. The heavy breath, the unappealing, heavy jowls, the thick fingers that were constantly twitching.

"Are you two gentlemen with the Mafia?" I asked. In my business you learn that the best way to get an answer is to come right out and ask. They both laughed.

"What makes you ask that?" said the burly one, whose name was Ron. He looked straight at the other, whose first name happened to be Michael.

"Instinct," I said. "Where are we going for dinner?"

"Where would you like to go?" Michael inquired.

I looked out the window and saw Daly's and said, "Daly's." He swerved over and pulled into a tow-away zone, and I knew that he had connections when he didn't bother to lock the car. I thought about grabbing my sandwich and running, but I didn't think I'd get too far. Besides, I felt like having a medium-rare cheeseburger just then.

It's disconcerting to sit down at a restaurant table with a couple of hoodlums you met on the street. It was a decent restaurant, but the male waiters were too pretty and seemed to be snickering about our trio behind their pads.

I ignored them and focused instead on Michael. Though his conversation had been as banal as singles' bar shoptalk, his mouth was as eloquent as a Rhodes scholar's. He had full lips colored in a deep rose flush. As I fantasized being grazed upon by these two gates to heaven, he put his drink down and blew a kiss through the air. Suddenly my own lips began to tremble. Fortunately, the medium-rare cheeseburgers arrived, giving me something to do with my mouth.

At the end of the meal, Michael paid the check. I was glad to see that it was he who had the money. He asked me if I'd like to go with them to a discotheque. I always try to take advantage of unusual opportunities. After a moment, I accepted the offer.

At that time, discotheques were exclusive dancing clubs on the East Side of Manhattan where the rich and famous hung out. The place was exclusive, all right. The sort of fancy defined by understatement and the newest fashions in black and white. We were met at the door by the manager, who did not look twice at my jacket or once at my boots. Instead he looked me straight in the eye and introduced himself as Roger.

The dance floor was small. Half-naked women and glamorous

men dodged the flying squares of light that spun the room around the dancers. The wonderful thing about narcissists is that they pay no attention to what anyone else wears or how anyone else dances, so when Michael and Roger sat down in the corner, I accepted Big Ron's offer to take a spin on the floor. I stood right out there in the center of the music, feeling quite groovy and not the slightest underdressed. My giant shoes grounded me securely to the floor and the joint I had smoked earlier added a nice sway to my hips.

Ron, however, was easily distracted. He kept leaping aside with undue exaggeration every time one of my clodhoppers landed on his dainty loafer. I had the unmistakable feeling that he thought *I* was the oaf, and after a couple of spins we returned to the table.

There, he and Michael left me alone with Roger while they retreated to the inner room.

"What are you doing hanging out with these guys?" Roger asked. It was a brotherly question; he was Irish, so was I.

"Should I get out while I can?" I wanted to know.

"If you stick with the younger guy you'll be okay. But stay away from the other one. I think he's bad news."

"Who are they?"

"Michael's the son of a Godfather."

"Which Godfather?"

"A big don from Brooklyn."

"And Ron?"

"I don't know who he is. I'm not too interested in finding out."

The information on Michael made him more appealing than ever. I thought intently about what I might say or do to arouse his attention and insure future contact. When he returned from the inner room and slid into the booth next to me, my thigh pushed against his; the seams of our pants kissed right down the line.

"Come here often?" I asked very casually.

"Couple times a week."

"Seems pretty exclusive."

"It is."

"And expensive."

"I don't pay."

"How come?"

"A lot of places are like that. If a guy's young and handsome he'll attract pretty women. If a place has pretty women, it will draw the rich men."

"What's my function?"

"You can be my bodyguard," he said.

"What's wrong with the one you already have?"

"He's gone."

"Lucky me."

"Let's go home."

"Where's that?"

"By the ocean."

We had crossed the Brooklyn Bridge before I asked where we were going. He told me to be patient, that I'd see soon enough. I had visions of a Tudor mansion looking out onto a vast lawn, ending at a sea wall overlooking the ocean. But he pulled onto an ordinary neighborhood street and parked in front of a small split-level home.

Inside, the carpeting was red. The French provincial furniture was new. There was a crystal chandelier over the dining room table. On a smaller table under a mirror in the entrance hall sat several color photographs of a wedding in white frames.

"Who got married?"

"My sister."

I thought it was strange that he would keep pictures of his sister's wedding in the entrance hall of his bachelor pad, until I found out that it was his mother's house. His mother was in Miami.

"You live with your mother?"

"No. I sometimes stay here when she's out of town."

I had mixed feelings about being seduced in his mother's bed, but it seemed that seduction was not exactly what he had in mind. Michael probably wasn't used to going to all that trouble. He was the type who stepped out of his trousers and women begged for the rest.

He stepped out of his trousers while I sat on the bed pressing the soles of my combat boots together. Then he took off his jacket. A lovely ivory-handled pistol sat snugly in his shoulder holster. He slowly removed the holster, keeping his eyes on me all the time, and laid it on a small, delicate end table in front of a goldframed picture of Our Lady of Perpetual Help.

The unbuttoned buttons at the bottom of his shirt were the next stage of his conscientious undressing. When the two front panels of his shirt fell apart, I admired the neatness with which his briefs cradled his cock. It's a neatness I've admired in magazine ads and on street posters, but I had never had the pleasure to see it so enchantingly duplicated in real life.

He stepped closer. His stockinged feet covered the toes of my boots. There was nothing to look at but the enlarging in front of me. Without thinking twice, I cradled his nuts through his bulging nylon briefs.

He backed up a few steps.

"Kneel," he said.

"No," I answered.

"I could put a gun to your head," he warned.

"I know, but you won't."

He stood there a little longer, then took off his shirt and his drawers and tossed them both on his bed. Then he walked into the bathroom and put on the shower. Michael had left the door to the bathroom open, and the full-length mirror on the back reflected the full length of him. He had a high-jutting ass. I wanted to take a bite from the back and nuzzle up to the front. "Do it," demanded my body beneath the multiple layers of clothing. I kicked off my boots; I shed my parka and overalls, my sweater, my panties and even my argyle socks.

Michael's body, exquisite when dry, hard, lean, angular and tan, was irresistible when glistening with water. He was soaping his armpits when I joined him in the shower and took the washcloth from him. I went right to work on tightening his loose genitals, which showed their appreciation by jabbing me firmly in the belly. I reached around with both hands to the rear, where my fingers enveloped the full curves of both spheres. I noted that he, like a woman, enjoyed having his pubic mound rubbed.

I knelt down and pulled at his pubic hairs with my teeth, still holding out on taking his cock into my mouth. I wanted to make sure that his alpha was not my omega, so I waited for some indication that my lovemaking would be reciprocated before sucking him.

But none was forthcoming. He got out of the shower, dried himself with the only towel and left it crumpled on the floor in a puddle of water. I shook myself dry while using a tigerskin toothbrush, then hurried into the bedroom to be beside him under the covers.

He had his back to me. I stroked his neck and his shoulder blades and counted each vertebra with the tip of my finger, but I might just as well have been playing with a smooth piece of wood. I stopped and lay with my head on my elbow, refusing to believe this was happening to me. I didn't understand the game he was playing. I certainly didn't understand what I was supposed to do all alone. Did his icy detachment turn some women on? Fuck him, I thought. So I decided to turn over and at least pretend to fall asleep.

According to the bright red numerals on the digital clock, I had been playing possum for ten minutes when his fingers woke me. They were gliding down my sides, up and down my body, along the peripheries of my hot points, the outer curves of my breasts, the edge of my pubic hair, taunting me, teasing me. When his hand slipped into the tight, wet place between my thighs, I locked it there with my tightest grip, as if I'd been riding the slimmest of horses for thousands of years.

He stopped struggling. My legs fell open. His lips retraced his fingers' path and landed, quivering, between my loose thighs. Or was I quivering? By then the mere radiation of his breath brought such an orgasm to my clitoris that it boomeranged along my body, bounding off the top of my head, the soles of my feet and back to my vagina, where it coiled hotly, finally settling down in anticipation of the next one.

His tongue outlined all intersections of my curves and, in an extremely complicated maneuver, he rotated my body in order to follow those intersections into deeper, darker chasms. My ass rose to meet each gliding kiss. He turned me over again and lifted my mound to within inches of his cock. My lips opened to lure him in, but he remained centimeters beyond my desire, kneeling, stroking himself, one hand on his cock, the other on his balls. I wanted him so badly, but he stayed just far enough away from my complete satisfaction. As I thrust up to meet him, he leaned back to avoid me; all the time watching me, all the time stroking himself, as he knelt between my legs, making inaudible statements through his trembling lips.

I threw myself around and began devouring his cock; he grabbed me by the hair, pumping my head, sometimes faster, sometimes slower, to intensify his pleasure, to prolong his excitement. But I was so angry that he had postponed my own pleasure that I had no desire to prolong his.

I overcame his slowing down with my own speeding up. Running my fingernail down the seam of his balls, I stroked the skin on his penis with the lightest trace of my teeth and teased his urethra with a heavy battering of my tongue. He screamed against the surging inevitability of his orgasm and I bit down hard with my lips at the base of his cock. He shot come down my throat, and I sat back on my haunches like a put-upon cat. Angrily he leaned forward and pulled my nipples to bring me closer. He brought me right up to his face, whose planes shifted from passion to cruelty, then released my nipples and shoved me back by my shoulders. In a matter of minutes he was stretched out and snoring soundly.

The next day Michael drove me into the city. When he dropped me off he surprised me by asking for my phone number. I made one up quickly, though I later regretted it. In fact, I thought of him fondly for several months after that strange winter night.

Unfortunately, the incident didn't cure my propensity for danger. On the contrary, it made me hungrier than ever. I now felt that I was invincible and had Houdini-like powers with which to exit tight situations. I continued seeking out shady characters and ominous sets of circumstance. It wasn't until that time in Alaska that I began to question my judgment. But that's another story.

THE LESBIAN EXPRESS

By Christina Tagliari

"We gotta get these Boy Scouts outta here!" Wanda muttered as she walked through the bottle-littered car of the "Gay Disco Party Train" to Montreal. Amtrak had positioned our group in front of the club car. A travelling Scout troop had just wound its way through a carful of 65 gregarious lesbians.

Three business executives in pin-striped suits also sat in the club car. A Humpty Dumpty look-alike in man's clothing, Wanda complained to the conductor, "This is a private party." While she approached the Scoutmaster, the conductor asked the three businessmen to leave. They snickered, exchanging meaningful smiles. One of them said, "Well, we want to be with the women."

"Not these women, you don't," the conductor replied.

I wondered if I liked being with them myself. Hearing of a trip to Montreal for gay women, I had envisioned numerous opportunities for a lesbian orgy. Though primarily heterosexual, I occasionally enjoy a fling with one of my "sisters."

The ethnic make-up of the group surprised me. Of the 65 participants, about 50 were black and more than half in their 40s and 50s. Most were nurses. The older black women played cards, smoked cigars, wore wigs, chomped on chicken wings and sat on each other's hefty laps.

"Watch out, hot stuff is comin' through!" one black woman yelled as she sashayed down the aisle.

"Hey, cutesie-poo!" a cigar-smoker called out mischievously when a gay man boarded the car.

Almost all of the older participants had children and grandchildren. A factory worker told me that she married to please a strict grandmother. Now her mother, aunts and uncles had come out of the closet, too. "Everyone in my family is gay," she said proudly.

Music blared from a loudspeaker ensconced in the luggage rack. Women danced in the aisles as the group leaders dispensed wine from a jug. Wanda returned to announce that the Scouts would not be coming through the car again.

"Then can we get down now?" asked a woman.

"You better get down!" Wanda shouted. But no one did. Although women cuddled and kissed, not even a Scoutmaster would have disapproved of their behavior.

Suddenly, the train stopped. Looking out the window, we saw the conductor walking across the tracks.

"He can't stand the idea of women loving women," proclaimed one of the Amazons, hugging her lover.

"Let's get the Boy Scouts back in here and have a sing-along," another suggested.

"Yeah. We can sing, 'It's great to be gay.' "

Glancing around the car, I surmised that only five of the group members were single. The others were obviously mated. Each duo seemed comprised of a butch and a femme. The only attached person who appealed to me was Betty, a Jewish editor. She seemed interesting and witty, but also angry. At Penn Station, when a male official had asked her, "Where's the rest of the group?" she rudely snapped, "What am I, my sister's keeper?" And as the disco music pounded on, Betty clamped her hands over her ears and bemoaned ever having boarded the train.

I wondered if I would ever find a friend, much less a lover, on this trip. Feeling lonely, I headed for the club car, where I sat drinking Scotch and thinking about fucking men.

I felt nostalgia for the tension between men and women that can make lovemaking incredibly exciting. Women together are unthreatening, and gay female sexuality tends to be more sensual and drawn-out. The atmosphere on the train was cozy, intimate and non-competitive.

At customs I passed four Hispanic nurses, who invited me to join them that evening. Their tone was platonic. They seemed concerned that I was alone. I felt immensely grateful. And I was especially attracted to Maria, who had a sensual mouth, beautiful bedroom eyes and large breasts. Her friend Petra had long brown hair, but was not as hot-looking as her lover. The other couple consisted of Griselda, a middle-aged woman who had left a husband and three children at home, and her younger friend Inez.

When we arrived at the hotel in Montreal, everyone went up to nap. Waking at 4 P.M., I paid a visit to the editor. She declared that she disliked all of the women on the trip and was flying home the next morning.

At 6:30 I joined the group in the lobby. Greeting me like an old friend, the nurses invited me into their cab. We proceeded to an exclusive disco where the bartenders and the d.j. were all gay men. Maria, Petra, Griselda, Inez and I congregated at a table.

In a low voice, I confided to Maria about the perils of being single.

"We're all single here," she answered provocatively.

I asked if she and Petra were a couple. She nodded, but added that they were no longer relating. I inquired whether they planned to sleep together that evening. Maria shrugged.

"Aha," I thought, "then maybe I'll get lucky tonight."

"Have you and Petra ever engaged in a threesome?" I wondered.

"Only with another man," Maria answered.

All four nurses turned out to be bisexual. Each was extremely feminine and sensual. Like myself they were connoisseurs of sensuality rather than man-haters.

When I danced with Maria, she put an arm around my waist and touched my cheek. Petra boogied over and whispered in her ear. "She says we're getting too wild," Maria told me. "Don't worry. Just give her time to think about it. She just likes to be in control of everything in her life."

The new "gay anthem"—the song "I Am What I Am" from the Broadway musical *La Cage Aux Folles*—came on over the loudspeakers, and everyone in the club cheered. I was constantly startled to see men on the dance floor—only to realize after a moment that they were masculine-looking women.

A young black lesbian named Denise called out to me, "Hey, little fresh girl."

Unfamiliar with lesbian etiquette, I could not imagine how to respond to this appellation. First of all, I was about five years older than she. Secondly, what did she mean by "fresh"? Was I supposed to act little-girlish? I decided to ignore her.

Finally, we went to a seafood restaurant. By now everyone was tipsy. I sat with the four nurses, and with Cecile and Denise. As we waited for our dinners, Inez told a string of dirty jokes. Cecile related how her mother had cried upon discovering that her daughter was gay. "She cried for what she was missing," Griselda quipped.

When our lobsters arrived, Cecile asked how to extract the meat from the claw. Maria winked lasciviously. "Just find the hole and suck it out," she advised.

Suddenly Wanda had an asthma attack. The other group leaders took her to the hospital after giving us a list of gay bars in town. Denise quickly whisked Cecile into a private cab.

"Gotta get this little girl home and back to bed," she stated. The other two nurses returned to the hotel, citing fatigue. Maria, Petra and I decided to sample Montreal's lesbian scene.

The first bar was called Babyface. The proprietor, a stern, mannish-looking woman with gray hair, held a toy poodle in her arms. A crowd of 15 or so women sat around talking and drinking. It looked too tame for our taste and we left. The next two bars on the list had closed down. We decided to go back to the hotel.

"Let's just have drinks in the lobby," Petra suggested.

We stopped off at Petra and Maria's room first to get some money. Petra turned on the television. Maria and I sat on a bed, watching it.

Suddenly Inez burst into the room, followed by Griselda. Inez carried four thin belts in her hand. She tackled Maria and pushed her down on the bed.

"Okay, I've always told you I was going to do this and now your time has come!" she cried half-jokingly. "Help me hold her down, girls."

Maria did not resist. Soon her arms and legs were bound together.

"What should we do now?" Inez asked. "Beat her?"

I picked up a copy of *The Joy of Lesbian Sex* that lay on the bed.

" 'Lesbians do not usually partake in bondage and flagellation,' " I read aloud.

"In that case, let's paint her," Inez suggested.

Maria rolled her eyes. She seemed quite blasé. Since I had identified myself as an artist, Inez handed me lipsticks and eyeliners.

"Paint her tits," she cheerfully commanded me. Unbuttoning Maria's blouse she removed her bra to expose her large, black-nippled breasts.

"This is so boring, you guys," Maria sighed.

I painted psychedelic flowers around Maria's nipples. I longed to suck her tits and pull down her panties, but hesitated, still unsure of how Petra was feeling. Inez took some snapshots; then she and Griselda exited, hand in hand.

"That was really lame," Maria complained. "You call that bondage? Untie me." We did so. Petra suggested going downstairs for drinks.

"I feel too lazy," I said

"Me too," Maria confessed. "I want to watch *The Exorcist*."

Petra offered to go downstairs and bring back the drinks. As she walked out the door, she added, "It will help relax us." I turned to Maria and murmured, "It looks like she reconsidered."

"She just needed some time," Maria replied.

We started kissing and feeling each other's breasts. On the TV screen, Regan masturbated with her crucifix. As Maria and I lay down on the bed together, I felt that sweet, calm sensation of being with another woman.

"You're really sensual," I told Maria.

"So are you," she answered, sucking my nipple. "God, your breasts are so sensitive. Can you come from having them sucked?"

"Yes," I said.

We stroked each other until Petra returned. She silently undressed and climbed into bed with us. Suddenly, Maria was sucking my left breast and Petra my right. Having extremely sensitive nipples, I soon reached fever pitch. Moaning and crying, I stroked their hair and breasts. Then Maria moved down to lick and suck my clit with artful abandon. It was exciting to watch how passionate she could be. Her eyes were half closed with pleasure as her tongue skillfully flicked in and out of me.

After I came, Maria kissed Petra. I went down on Maria. Her cunt, like her nipples, was almost black against her dark tan skin. Her clit seemed to be the size of my thumb. I relished her firm, voluptuous body, but also liked Petra's. She had small breasts, wide hips and a large ass. As she sat on Maria's face, I admired how womanly and beautiful she looked.

Maria did not come from my oral ministrations. She got up and lay on top of Petra. They kissed with the poignancy of lovers. Then Maria went down on Petra, who had an orgasm with soft little moans. Petra began sucking Maria, who asked me to sit on her face. After Maria finally climaxed, the three of us lay side by side.

"Making love with women is so out of sight!" Maria exclaimed.

I could have remained in bed with them, but I sensed that they needed time alone. So after a few moments I returned to my room.

The next morning we went sightseeing. None of us even mentioned the previous evening's activities. Petra and Maria appeared to have resolved their differences and were a serious couple again. I felt like an outsider once more. But the sexual tension had vanished. We were now just three girlfriends.

During the train ride home the atmosphere was considerably more convivial. Everyone danced in the aisles. Maria changed into a leopard-skin bathing suit and tight jeans. Denise yelped like Tarzan and carried her off over her shoulder. A mannish, middle-aged black woman kissed my hand. No one disturbed us. This time we had the last car on the train.

THE LESBIAN WHO LOVED MEN

By Donald Jackson

I met her after a sex famine—one of those stretches of weeks and months when females seem like alien, incomprehensible beings. Sex seemed no more than a treasured memory not likely to come my way again. Having just taken a job as a disk jockey in a small town, I felt very much on display.

Leslie was my immediate boss. She looked plain at first glance because she hid her figure beneath neutral gray suits and tweeds. But she had beautiful, out-of-style long blonde hair and flashing slate-gray eyes. A colleague confided that she was a friendly and fair boss, informal most of the time and firm only when crossed—

and that she was a lesbian who lived with a feminist singer named Cynthia. Everyone knew about her relationship, but that had not stopped her rise to the position of station manager.

It took me a few weeks to realize that she was in the midst of great trauma. Her easygoing nature seemed forced when I studied her face and hands. She made too many jokes and put herself down too often. Finally it occurred to me that she was flirting—with men; with Frank, a fellow jock—and girlishly sizing us up like forbidden fruit.

Meanwhile I got laid occasionally, when old girlfriends came to visit me. But I wanted someone new and different. Yet every pretty girl I met was part of a couple. I started to feel quarantined.

Then one night I was working late on some promotion spots. Leslie came back after dinner, claiming she had to go over programming for the coming week. But I noticed that her eyes were red and rimmed with tears.

"We're breaking up, it's final," she told me. It was the first time she spoke of her personal life to me. "It's really been dead for a long time, but now it's official. I'm moving out."

The next morning her professional guard was up again. But now I was determined to see what her bland business suits were hiding. Fucking my boss was probably the dumbest thing I could do, but the job wasn't really that important to me.

No sooner had I made up my mind then she did too. She wanted Frank. I knew it before he did. The dope didn't even realize that her eyes followed him around the station as if he had a homing device in his pants. At my first office party, a barbecue at a nearby state park, Leslie got a little high and blurted, "Frank's so cute," after he gave her a beer. Everything came easy to Frank—that was one reason why I disliked him. But I decided to sit back and wait for Leslie to discover that I was the quality item.

It took three months and another office party, this one at a beach house. Leslie looked incredible that evening. Her eyes sparkled and her long hair covered her breasts mysteriously. Cynthia seemed the farthest thing from her mind. We were drinking wine and talking when I lightly touched her elbow. The spark seemed genuine.

We went home together that night. First we walked the beach for miles. When I tried to put my arm around her, she pulled back sharply.

"I've never kissed a man," she said. I assumed she was putting me on. But back in my apartment she insisted on wearing her slacks and blouse to bed. And she would not let me touch her. I thought I had won the prize, but had only been allowed to join the race. Thus began the slowest seduction between two basically consenting adults since the sexual revolution.

The situation improved a month later when we were in my bedroom watching television. Leslie sat behind me on the bed with her arms circling my chest. It was the farthest we had gone so far. Without thinking, I turned and kissed her. Her tongue met mine unafraid. The dam seemed to open. I pushed her down, ground my cock against her cunt, and reached inside the back of her blouse to unhinge her bra, fearing she might panic.

We lay on the bed, kissing wildly, and she returned the pressure from my cock. I explored her ass for the first time, pulling it toward me. She made no move for my cock, but bucked against me, legs spread, and I started to feel a wild, unwanted orgasm. I hadn't come in my pants since high school. It felt good, as if we were dry-humping in her parents' living room, afraid that her pop would walk in. Leslie was taken aback by the sticky wet spot on my pants. She thought that could only happen when a man was inside a woman. But at least she was becoming intrigued by the penis and its capabilities.

The next night, when we started to kiss, I slid my hand down inside her panties. Her clit was dripping wet. She did not resist. Pushing me on my back she unzipped my pants and freed my cock.

She took one look at it and said, "My God, it will never fit."

I was in heaven but for the lack of a tape recorder. My cock measures five and three-quarter inches or six and one-quarter inches, depending on where the tape measure is placed. I was the ultimate average, for years persecuted by pictures of Johnny Wadd and his foot-long cock. Never had a gorgeous, horny young woman pulled back in fright at the sight of my own equipment. It's an experience that I highly recommend to every man at least once.

Using my finger to explore Leslie's cunt, I discovered the reason for her apprehension. To describe it as tight would be an understatement. Her sex life had apparently focused on oral and anal lovemaking, with a minimum of penetration by anything even as large as a finger. This was unexplored territory! This was a certifiable virgin eager to have me captain of her maiden voyage!

"You'll have to teach me how to suck it," she declared. "I won't let you put it in yet."

I found it in my heart to teach her how to administer a blowjob. Lying on my back with my head on a pillow, I encouraged her to first rub her breasts over and around my cock, then slowly lick the bottom of the balls and the entire shaft before gently taking the cock into her mouth and sucking it while tonguing the head. I thought she would rebel at this explicit, paint-by-numbers drill, but she had no hesitation.

After bringing me to fever pitch, she strapped my legs over her shoulders while she crouched over my cock. Wolfing it hungrily, she stuck her finger deep into my anus with more gusto than any woman ever had before. She certainly was not interested in "being gentle." Meanwhile she increased the speed of her sucking. Just before I came I glanced up. Her eyes looked crazed with pleasure. She swallowed my come eagerly.

"You're a natural," I moaned, exhausted and drained. "You know how to make a man feel terrific."

She smiled. It was a smile I saw more and more of as our closeness grew. We worked toward fucking slowly by stretching her cunt with my fingers and tongue until she decided two weeks later that she was elastic enough to deal with my cock. After that, her sexual appetite became voracious. She wanted to try everything, as if making up for very precious lost time.

I shied away from anal sex, thinking the initial pain might be too much for her. But she bought the Vaseline on her own and insisted that I take her. We did it gently the first time, hard and piercing the next. She relished the mix of pleasure and pain. Sometimes I fucked her up the ass standing up, or with her lying on her back on top of me. And she often put me on all fours so she could lick my anus. Then she would plunge her fingers deep inside while alternately cupping my balls and stroking my cock with her other hand. That posture gave me an unreal combination of feeling hot, vulnerable and pleasured at the same time.

I began to think we would be together forever. Her lesbianism never bothered me; it seemed at first like an odd ethnic trait, no more meaningful than if she had been Irish or Venezuelan. Politically, I knew that lesbianism was a choice, not a disease, as our parents thought. I never felt it was something to be ashamed of.

When she moved into my place, I quickly discovered that Leslie, despite her untraditional sexual past, was the most conventional of women. My women friends even thought she was unliberated and my male friends figured I had struck it rich. She thrived on cooking for me and making our home look wonderful. I was waited on hand and foot by a sexy young woman who only wanted to make me happy and comfortable.

And so our problems began. Our sex life flourished, but boredom set in elsewhere. I became critical of her for having no ambition. Her work at the station slacked off and the general manager rebuked her for taking too much time off. Formerly a workaholic, she now rushed home to prepare dinner. Our being together at the station further complicated matters all day long. I started snapping at Leslie far too often.

After a year, she asked for a commitment. She wanted us to always be together and for me to be faithful. Soon afterwards I began paying more attention to other women. I also felt guilty for not giving this wonderful person what she deserved. I even started to rethink Leslie's gay past and found myself, for the first time, filled with doubts.

Could I tell my parents that she had been gay? If we had a family, would our children ever think their mother had a dark secret about her past? Was I facing a lifetime of deception?

At bottom I knew such thoughts were mere excuses. But I also felt that our passion had soured. Even if I were living with the world's most beautiful blonde, I would worry about the inevitable day when her breasts sagged, or convince myself that she must be dumb since she was so gorgeous, or that she was too flashy to be faithful. I was not proud of myself.

I also developed a hypocritical definition of fidelity. I went home with other women, unbuttoned their blouses, feasted on their breasts, then blithely informed them that I could not fuck because of my "commitment" to Leslie. However, I would permit them to go down on me. After coming in their mouths, I went home to Leslie, relieved that I had not violated her trust.

These liaisons convinced me that I was hot stuff. I envisioned a wild sex life if I only broke up with Leslie. The details are uninteresting, but we finally parted. She decided to leave town and start fresh.

My friends predicted she would go back to women. I hoped not, then wondered why. Originally, I had believed that gayness was just as viable as heterosexuality. But now I no longer felt quite the same way. Rather I had come to believe that straights in general were more fulfilled than gays and lesbians.

My friends were right. After about four months of being alone,

Leslie began seeing another woman. They moved in together and even bought a house. I was relieved. Making love with a woman who cared for her was at least better than being alone or entangled with a man who left her unhappy. But I was still baffled by the basics. What made Leslie prefer women? I had no answers.

Meanwhile I entered one of those famines most men go through periodically—a time when sex, especially during those first halcyon days with Leslie, was no more than a treasured memory.

THE STUNTWOMAN:
HIGH SENSATION SEEKER

By Ginger Fahey

I perform movie and TV stunts for a living. I drive cars, spinning and skidding them, stopping on a mark, executing a near miss or an actual hit. Or I jump out of high windows, fall down stairs, get thrown across rooms and appear to have the daylights beaten out of me. I do all this for money and I enjoy it.

Being a stuntwoman means that I have to keep myself in perfect physical shape. Though amply proportioned, my physique is muscular, and living in Los Angeles has given my hair that sun-streaked-blonde look. I often favor jeans, boots and a cowboy hat, and while I take risks for a living, I am no tomboy.

I always get a jolt of fear before doing a stunt gag. My adrenaline is pumping, my sense of space and time is a little unreal, and my breathing accelerates. Fear creates a state of hyper-awareness. Half of me is filled with terror, while the other half is concerned with the cool, mechanical execution of the stunt. Sex is like that for me, too. I like the element of high sensation in both.

Stunting also satisfies my desire for power. To a large extent, men's opinions run everything. As a stuntwoman I jam their circuits. They don't know what to make of me. For certain men that makes me very, very desirable.

I work in a macho field. That makes my relationships with my male colleagues highly charged and often difficult. If a stuntman doesn't accept a woman as a stuntwoman, he'll try to fuck her.

He'll want to see if she'll fuck for a job. I get tested all the time by stuntguys who don't know me.

Taking risks all the time makes me especially aware of how precious things like sex are. I won't waste my time on men who bore me. I want them to be risk-takers like me. An athletic body is a plus; so is a large cock. But I am most interested in men who abhor the ordinary.

Occasionally I get involved with stuntmen. Most of them have been very special men. I particularly like those who act as professional mentors to me—who are willing to train, teach and protect me, but who still regard me as an equal.

Sam, a New York stuntman, is one of my best lovers. Since I am based on the west coast, the geographical limitation is considerable. But the arrangement allows us to keep emotionally unentangled while preserving a sense of camaraderie! Making love with him is always a major event—a *battle*.

I had been introduced to Sam through proper stunt channels and was hoping he would give me some pointers. I spent an entire day with him and he taught me some driving tricks and gave me tips on getting a job I wanted. Though not looking for a sexual encounter, I was quite aware how attractive he was. He has black hair and green eyes—a hard combination to resist. After we parted I returned to my place and the phone rang. It was Sam asking for a date. He made it very clear that he didn't want to talk business. I was caught completely off-guard. Sam is one of the hottest stuntmen in the country. He lives on the edge and does very dangerous things. A lot of younger stuntmen revere him. It put me in an awkward and heady position. I said yes.

He took me to an expensive restaurant and over dessert pressed a vial of cocaine into my hand. Coke is it in the movie business, but stuntmen use it with great discretion. I could have refused his offer, but felt it was a sign of his acceptance of me; I knew that it did not compromise how he felt about me professionally.

The best way to describe fucking with Sam is that he is a tornado and I am the state of Kansas. What happened between us is an interesting illustration of how I approach sex. I love a man to be stronger than I am. I admit it. Sex, when consensual, can be violent. And you can interpret violent to mean anything you want. Lovemaking provides no thrill if that dangerous edge in my sexual encounters is lacking.

Sam drove us back to my place after dinner and I found it hard to concentrate on anything but the palpable tension between us. Once inside and after some wonderful kissing, he picked me up so I was facing him. I locked my legs around his waist and he carried me up the flight of stairs to my bedroom.

I left to get candles and when I returned Sam had stripped and was lying *flat* out on the bed with an immense hard-on. He didn't say a word. I lit the candles and with deliberate slowness took off my outer blouse, shoes, stockings and underpants. In my white gauze dress, I climbed onto the bed and straddled him. Sam reached up, pulling loose the shoulders of my dress, freeing my breasts. He looked me up and down and told me that he was going to talk me into an orgasm! I almost lost my breath. No one had ever done that to me before.

Sam undid the rest of my dress and pulled it off. I was sitting on him, his thighs locked in between mine. Sam ordered me to look at his cock. He told me to imagine how his hardness would feel inside of me. I felt that twinge of a contraction inside my cunt as Sam entwined his fingers in mine, holding me still. He had beautiful hands; broad and brown with square fingernails. I felt the strain of his muscles through his grip. He told me that his cock was to be the center of all my attention and pleasure, and that orgasmic release depended on my acceptance of that. I couldn't speak.

Then Sam described my arousal and that is exactly how my body responded. He said my breasts were made to be sucked and that their roundness and softness demanded a hard cock in between them. My nipples grew hard from his voice. He saw that and told me to slowly describe what his cock would feel like fucking my breasts. I couldn't get the words out but Sam insisted. I told him that the humid warmth of his cock made my mouth want to suck it. Sam told me to imagine that it was in my mouth.

I looked down. His thighs are beautifully muscled and his cock was straining. The balls were drawn up tight. I didn't want him to shoot. I said so but Sam smiled and replied that it wasn't about to happen. He told me how soft my thighs were and that as I thought about his stiff cock, the lips of my cunt would part and the muscles inside would contract as if around his shaft. I felt it happen. I struggled against the grip of his hands because I wanted to fill up my cunt with his cock. He wouldn't let me do it. He described his super-heated tongue teasing my clitoris and opening the folds of my cunt.

A drop of moisture from my extreme arousal fell on Sam's cock.

He said he was pleased that I was giving him what he wanted. A spasm rippled over me, an indication that I was going to explode. I begged Sam to enter me. He refused. He told me to be as still as possible and listen to the sound of his voice. I wanted to please him more than anything.

"What do you want?" he demanded. He pulled me sharply when I didn't answer. "Your cock," I finally said. Sam countered, "You could have anybody's cock, because all the men want to fuck you, they want to feel your pussy grabbing their cocks. What do you really want?" "Your stiff, hard cock," I spat at him. He replied slowly. "I'm only going to let you imagine that now, baby. Do you still want it?" I could only nod, and Sam whispered, "Fuck me with your mind."

I watched the hard, lean muscles of his body strain toward me and I felt very weak. Control was disappearing rapidly and I was radiating from my clitoris. I was shocked by the stunning power of the orgasm I was having. My body jerked. Sam's hands were still entwined in mine and held me firmly above him. I wanted him inside me and the ache within my cunt was intensified by the rush from the orgasm. I was dripping on Sam. The last shock wave subsided and he eased me down. I wanted to make his stiff penis part of my body, absorb it inside of me. He finally let go of my hands and I slid his cock in between my breasts. He pulled my head up gently by the hair so he could watch. Seeing it sent him over the edge. I closed my mouth around his cock when the first foam of semen appeared. He came for a long time, like a little river, and it was sweet as honey.

Making love like that was a supreme example of total control on both our parts. As I often say, a man's mind can be his sexiest organ. However, I am not always so compliant. I had a very sweet young lover once, Billy, who adored me. That is a statement of fact and not a boast. He was a sexual technician, handsome and well hung. But we fucked only when I said so, and he came inside me only if I allowed it. The sexual dynamic was entirely different from what it was with Sam. He was nicer to me than Sam, but I didn't desire him as much. It's strange, but if a man's sun rises and sets on me, I'm not all that interested. Billy didn't make me hungry. I became satiated sexually with him easily. With Sam, the more he fed me, the hungrier I became. That's why it's a good thing we don't live in the same city.

I am a voracious consumer of sex. Though I can always find

someone to fuck, I do believe in quality over quantity. I sometimes make mistakes and end up with men I shouldn't have bothered with. Sometimes they perceive me as a threat and almost have to dare themselves to get into bed with me. If I have had a bad string of affairs, I'll swear off men for a while and try to get my center back.

Here is an example of how stuntwork has changed me. I was in New York, visiting a few film sets to make some new connections. I dressed to impress—in shocking pink cowboy boots, a mini-skirt and my perpetual LA tan. On the last set I saw a producer I knew named Fred. A little thrill of fear ran through me because he often worked with a director named Anthony with whom I once had a tortuous affair. Anthony was also married. His temper, my lack of focus and the ever-present thought of his wife had ended the physical affair, but for me some emotional baggage remained. We had not spoken to or seen each other in quite some time. Fred saw me and said, "Guess who's here!" I didn't have to. I could see Anthony, his back turned, discussing the set-up of a shot with the cameraman. I shrugged to Fred nonchalantly, then went about my business of talking to the stuntguys. As I was giving my phone number to the stunt coordinator, I heard footsteps approach and Anthony's familiar voice say, "So, how many men have you given your phone number to today?"

Barely looking up, I finished writing, smiled and said, "Fuck you!" Anthony laughed and continued walking. I laughed, too, but my heart was hammering and a moment later Fred came over and "borrowed" me from the stunt coordinator. He brought me over to Anthony. The three of us joked around and I suddenly realized that the dynamic between Anthony and me was now different. Previously, I had been woefully unsure of myself and he had controlled all the strings of the relationship. But now I sensed that he was clearly excited by my presence and, oddly, sort of shy! I asked about his wife and he told me that she was back in L.A. It was an awkward moment because chance was beckoning. I realized that it was up to me whether or not to become involved again. That was a wonderful feeling. He asked me to dinner. I said yes but asked him to call later to set up the time.

That night, a stuntman I knew phoned and wanted to introduce me to some people worth meeting. I agreed, aware that Anthony was expecting to see me. As I was walking out the door to my appointment, the phone rang. I told Anthony that I had made other plans and he was enraged. He hung up on me. He used to behave just that way when I had been in love with him—letting that Italian temper hold sway, assuming he had a "right" to me. He was wrong this time. I kept my other plans.

When I returned at two in the morning, Anthony was sitting in his car in front of my place. With unusual humility he apologized and asked if we could be friends. I felt a little guilty, knowing that I had been a bit of a cock-tease when I cancelled our date and that we both deserved better from each other.

The house was dark when we got inside. I took off my shoes and got a bottle of wine from the kitchen. Anthony lit a fire in the potbelly stove. I sat down opposite him and put my legs up on the table. I was not sure which way I wanted the evening to go. We were no longer encumbered by the immediacy of our affair and there was a wonderful freedom between us.

When he told me about his deteriorating relationship with his wife, I felt a twinge of sadness. He was not looking for passion. He just wanted to feel alive. Sixteen years older than I, though still striking and dynamic, Anthony looked his age.

I put my wine glass down and sat beside him. Opening his shirt I saw how grey his chest hair had become. He kissed me and joked that maybe he was too old to handle me now. But the feel of his hand on my ass, as he worked his way under my panties, assured me otherwise. Anthony undressed me. I sat quietly on the couch, almost childlike. That had been a powerfully exciting dynamic in our relationship and was still. He knelt down and slowly ran his hands over my body. Now I was stronger, slimmer and tighter. He remarked on the firmness of my muscles. I ran my fingers through his hair. It had definitely thinned.

"My little girl," he said simply. Anthony stood up and pulled off his shirt. I reached for his belt and unbuckled him. Then I pulled his cock out of his jockeys. I could see that even his pubic hair had begun to go grey. He stopped for a moment and said, with a measure of uncertainty, "You want this old man again?" I did.

Instinctively I knew that we weren't starting something again, but finishing the affair we had never ended properly. He lay me down in front of the firelight of the wood-burning stove. I saw his reaction to the sight of my body, more beautiful than he remembered. He brushed the curls of my pubic hair and tasted the moisture on the lips of my cunt. My breasts looked rosy in the light and my customary flush of arousal appeared. He smiled at the familiarity. Anthony entered me very carefully. The slow opening of my cunt was the gentlest of feelings. He fucked me slowly for a very long time. We hardly looked from each other's eyes. I cried a little, but it was the most proper of resolutions. Anthony and I have now worked together a few times since. The closeness and camaraderie is there, but it will never get sexual again.

I am a physical woman. I need the physical release from tension, whether in stuntwork or in sexual adventure. I doubt if I will pursue this line of work forever, but right now it complements my unrestrainable nature best. To me the important thing is to live life the way you want, with only you deciding what is too risky and what isn't.

And when I'm old and grey, I want my grandchildren to know that I used to be one hot number and that it's all up there on the screen in living color to prove it.

Oral Histories

*

THE WOMAN WHO CRAVED CUNNILINGUS

By Petula Pauling

Even in a pair of jeans it is impossible to camouflage Jenny's small, well-proportioned figure and magnetic femininity. But Jenny is a woman with the sexual psychology of a male chauvinist. She likes to get head—exclusively.

Her greatest bedroom pleasure dates back to her very first orgasm. Cunnilingus was her open sesame to the world of carnal satisfaction. Ever since then, she had single-mindedly orchestrated her sexual experiences so that they culminate with her being licked and tongued into ecstasy. Even when she was completely heterosexual, she avoided intercourse while making love. She saw it as a challenge to climax through oral sex without giving men their sexual release through fucking. While her male partners were often apprehensive about her unusual demand, intimacy with Jenny seldom left them unsatisfied.

Jenny now feels that she has a more enjoyable sex life than most women. Not that she is in competition: Rather, she thinks the majority of women sexually shortchange themselves and that most men will not help a woman explore her erotic limits if their own needs are fulfilled. In her eyes, it is the rare man whose desire to give is greater than his desire to get.

Finding her sexual niche was a long and often frustrating road. Like most women, Jenny did not always know what she preferred in the bedroom and, initially, she was more than willing to make sure that her man was satisfied first.

Jenny's first orgasmic experience is the key to her unique psychology because it incorporated elements of what is usually perceived as a "male" sexual orientation. Very early in her erotic career she found out that male passion scared her. Intercourse was so intimate and overwhelming that having a man inside of her was literally too close for comfort. A man's powerful sexual needs seemed to stand in the way of her own path to orgasm. Jenny believes that only about 10 percent of men really enjoy giving head to a woman. Half would much rather not, and perhaps 40 percent comply because they expect the same in return. But a member of that elusive 10 percent is what Jenny hopes to find every time she ends up in bed.

Jenny's predilection for cunnilingus began only when she met Sandy, a widower 15 years her senior. He was able to convince her that he would go down on her all day, and did not care if she fellated him or if they fucked. If it felt good to her, he was happy. She tasted and smelled wonderful to him and he made her moan and whimper. What more could he ask for than to see her sexy little body in a fever of delight? Jenny began to trust him and his expert mouth. But she could not tell whether the pleasurable twinges she felt were the real thing. Sandy told her that when orgasm happened, she would know it.

One steamy afternoon, Sandy and Jenny took a drive into the country. Jenny fell asleep in the car and woke from her doze because of Sandy's gentle touch on her thigh. She felt very relaxed, with the seat back as far as it could go. Sandy did not know that she was awake. He just wanted to touch her.

Jenny wondered if the drivers of the giant semi-trucks whizzing by could see Sandy's hand working its way under her skirt. The idea of all of these macho truckdriver voyeurs caused an unaccustomed twinge in Jenny's cunt. While pretending to be asleep, she saw from the corner of her eye the familiar bulge in Sandy's crotch. Removing his other hand from the steering wheel momentarily, he unzipped his fly to let his hard cock loose. Still feigning sleep, Jenny shifted and opened her legs.

Sandy slowly worked his way under her damp panties. In her fantasy, Jenny saw the truckdrivers pulling their own cocks out to play with themselves. She also added a crucial element to the fantasy: The horny drivers were watching Sandy go down on her. His head was between her legs while his tongue explored her cunt. The sight made the truckers mad with lust and they ejaculated all over their steering wheels and windshields. With this image in mind, Jenny stretched her legs wide open and Sandy's fingers entered her cunt. But in her fantasy, it was his tongue.

As he flicked against her clit, Jenny slipped over the edge for the first time. Her body arched with blinding pleasure and Sandy almost lost control of the car. In keeping with Jenny's fantasy, he actually ejaculated all over the dashboard. The next day Sandy sent her a card that said, "Congratulations: May you have many more!"

This enormously erotic experience set the stage for her desire for orgasm through cunnilingus. Either in reality or fantasy, it had to predominate.

After her affair with Sandy ended, Jenny had a series of lovers who fell into the category of men who simply did not enjoy giving oral sex. Not that they minded her overtures to fellate them, of course. Then came a period of time when being alone seemed preferable to sleeping with a boor. That was when she discovered that she could give herself an orgasm through fantasy cunnilingus without having to please a man first. Initially, she bought a dozen or so erotic magazines. Once home, she began leafing through them. Some were vaguely exciting but most left her unaroused. One story entitled "A Snatch of Pepper," however, had possibilities. With scissors and tape she amended it to make her own unique version. The new story went as follows:

Pepper is a poor Mexican girl who lives in a pickers' shack on a farm in the Southwest. She has stayed home this particular hot and dusty day to sweep out some of the workers' quarters. Pepper wears a thin peasant blouse and skirt and the effort of sweeping makes her sweat and her clothes stick to her breasts and legs.

Unexpectedly, two young men who live in one of the shacks come home in the middle of the day. One of them collapses on the bed and teases Pepper. She tries to ignore him. The clothes sticking to her damp skin arouse him and he slowly fondles himself. While continuing to ignore him, Pepper is alarmed to feel the stirrings of powerful first arousal.

When he suddenly frees his cock from his patched linen pants, Pepper is stunned and stops in her tracks. Then slowly she feels two large calloused hands slide around her waist. It is the other young man. Unknown to Pepper, he has been watching the scene from the doorway, and now he brazenly kisses her neck.

As he slides the peasant blouse down, his work-hardened hands cup her ample breasts and she feels the pressure of his hard cock through his clothing. The man on the bed walks over to Pepper and pushes up her skirt. He rubs his erect cock against Pepper's bare thighs and she leans back against the other man as he eases his penis between the damp cheeks of her ass. Then the first man gently opens the folds of her cunt with his fingers. Pepper looks at his strong brown hands against the curls of her pubic hair. His fingers are wet with her juices which he rubs over his cock. Then he slowly licks and nibbles her cunt, working his mouth toward her now taut clitoris.

Jenny's perfect masturbators fantasy culminated as she lay on her living room floor atop the pile of erotic literature. The image of the young Mexican men pleasuring her caused the most explosive orgasm she ever experienced.

While masturbation continued to be a source of erotic pleasure, however, it did little to ease her loneliness. Jenny craved the closeness of skin-on-skin intimacy. But it never occurred to her until it actually happened that her next sexual breakthrough might be with another woman.

Jenny had joined a woman's task force during an election year, and in that way came to meet the kinds of women she had never known before—avowed lesbians and bisexuals. The all-female atmosphere seemed rarefied and exciting. While she did not shun men, or take on the sensibilities of a lesbian, Jenny now found male company simply uninteresting.

One of the women whom she became good friends with was Elena. Tall, fair, frail and shy, she was Jenny's opposite. Through the grapevine Jenny heard that Elena had considerable sexual experience, both straight and bi. Jenny felt an attraction to her that was disconcerting and persistent. Yet the possibilities of an erotic encounter with a woman was unnerving and she did not press it.

Circumstances intervened, however, at a party when the election season was over. The staff presented Jenny with a book of erotic stories, and Elena jokingly began to read some of them aloud. Emboldened, Jenny asked Elena to come back to her room and continue reading the book with her. Elena blushed and stammered, but said yes.

Taking the unaccustomed "male" role of pursuer thrilled Jenny. Yet seeking out this sexual encounter only made her feel more feminine, if anything.

Alone in the room with Elena, the pretense of reading was dropped and in silence Jenny sat on the bed as Elena slowly undressed for her. The taller woman seemed like a fragile bird, her heart beating quickly under Jenny's tentative hand. Now Jenny realized that she wanted to know what it felt like to give a woman head. She touched Elena's body slowly, very aware of the differences between her pliant, soft form and the lean hardness of a man and the rough abrading touch of his five o'clock shadow against her face. Yet Jenny was not comparing. Now, without haste and with an unusual sense of wonder, she languidly explored Elena's vagina, doing for her what she so often desired from men.

Cunnilingus was so different from fellatio. Jenny lost herself in the unusual texture of the folds and the moisture and scent of Elena's cunt. Jenny proceeded as slowly as she wanted her men to go with her. When Elena finally reached orgasm, Jenny rubbed her own clit against the rough bedspread and came, too. Although their affair would not last long, Elena did reciprocate a few days later. She invited Jenny to her apartment and when Jenny arrived, she found the bed sprinkled with rose petals and encircled with burning incense and candles. Elena catered as exclusively to Jenny as Jenny had to her. The experience was as near sexual perfection as Jenny could ask for.

But while accepting their lovemaking as a facet of her sexuality, Jenny did not feel homosexual. Further, the consequences of pursuing that kind of lifestyle outweighed the attractions of the affair. And however wonderful the sex was, Jenny still desired the forceful, uniquely masculine touch of a man. About six months after her affair with Elena, Jenny called New York on a whim. Kevin was an actor with whom she once had an intense affair. He and Jenny made passionate (though inorgasmic for her) love for an entire summer. Then he left Jenny's life as unexpectedly as he entered it. But she had never forgotten him. Finding his phone number in New York was easy enough.

Kevin was surprised to hear Jenny's voice. And it was clear that he also remembered that extraordinary summer. When Jenny asked if he would like a weekend visitor, he did not say no.

After meeting her at the plane, Kevin took Jenny to an upper west side cafe. Getting reacquainted over a bottle of wine proved that their long dormant attraction to one another was easily rekindled. When Kevin's hand touched her thigh under the table, Jenny told him about her Pepper fantasy and how important it was to her ability to reach orgasm. It was the first time that she ever confessed a fantasy to a man. But she felt she could trust Kevin. Quietly absorbed by her rendition of "Pepper," and without taking his eyes off her once, Kevin led Jenny out of the cafe.

Inside his apartment, they barely spoke a word. Jenny's uncertain expectations only heightened her sexual desire. She could see that Kevin's pants were straining from his erection. So she walked over and slowly went down on her knees in front of him. As her hand touched his zipper, he stopped her. "Not yet," was all he said as he led her to a pile of throw pillows on a soft rug. As he slowly unbuttoned her blouse, freeing her ample breasts, he called her by name . . . "Pepper."

For a moment Jenny was taken aback—no man had ever entered her fantasy. But then a delicious sense of abandon flooded her and the Pepper fantasy began to unreel in her mind. Kevin flicked her dark nipples with his tongue and kissed her neck and ears. Jenny pushed his head urgently down to her belly, but Kevin was in no hurry and emphatically pressed her arms down at her sides. Jenny was beside herself and arched like a cat, but Kevin was going to play the fantasy for all it was worth. Jenny closed her eyes and began to see Pepper sweeping the floor of the shack with beads of perspiration gathering between her breasts. The first young man entered the room and stared at her, much to her discomfort. As Kevin ran his hand down Jenny's belly to her thighs, the man watching Pepper stroked himself and lay down on the bed with an immense hard-on showing through his thin pants.

Kevin suddenly parted Jenny's legs. In her mind's eye the man on the bed freed his cock and Pepper stopped, not knowing what to do, but shivering with unexpected arousal. The second man then glided his hands around her waist. Pepper was incapable of doing anything but lean against him as he grasped her breasts with his work-calloused hands. Finally, Kevin moved his mouth down to Jenny's cunt and parted the aromatic folds, tasting her moisture. The rhythmic moving in and out of his tongue almost sent her over the edge. But he stopped and began to tease her ever so gently.

In Jenny's fantasy, with one man holding Pepper from behind, the first man got off the bed and pushed up her skirt, pressing his cock against her thighs. The man behind her began to slide his cock up and down between the cheeks of her ass.

With one of his hands pressing against her clit and the other massaging her breast, Kevin whispered in Jenny's ear, "They're both taking you at the same time, Pepper." Then he expertly returned his tongue to her clit.

Jenny could only cry out and completely give over to the sudden waves of orgasm that Kevin elicited. When she finally opened her eyes, she felt a warm spreading sensation on her belly. Kevin had freed his ample cock from his pants and the sight of Jenny responding to his touch made him come in a surge of powerful rhythmic bursts.

Jenny smiled at the thought of traveling half a continent just to have a great sexual encounter. But then the road to orgasm had never been simple or short.

SUSHI SEX

By Erica Kaplan

I have had French kisses and Latin lovers. Italians, Jews, Irishmen, Wasps, Blacks, Eastern Europeans and Scandinavians have shared my bed and captured my heart. Yet not once in the 15 years since I lost my virginity have I ever encountered an Oriental on a social or sexual basis. Then, last month, my friend Estelle met a Japanese man at a San Francisco rock and roll club. Like me, Estelle has had an adventurous and versatile sex life. So when she told me that Toshi knew astonishing sexual techniques, I was intrigued. I began to closely observe Japanese waiters and sushi chefs in the New York City sushi bars I frequent.

In the past, I had always regarded the Japanese as being excessively polite and formal. Most Japanese people seemed so tidy and impeccably groomed that I couldn't visualize them in the sweaty heat of passion. Now, I wondered whether Japanese sushi chefs ever daydreamed about women while they skillfully rolled those moist pieces of raw tuna and giant clams in their slim, delicate fingers.

I remembered that a gay friend of mine had once worked as the only American sushi chef in a Japanese restaurant. I asked Fred if his coworkers discussed sex.

"Are you kidding?" Fred replied. "They reported to work every morning reeking of cunt. They were really funky, like they'd been partying all night. First they'd prepare their vegetables and rice, then they'd shower and shave. Even though they knew I was gay, they asked me every day, 'You wanna meet Japanese girl? Velly tight pussy.' ''

"How could I get to meet a sushi chef?" I asked.

"Just go to a sushi bar right before they're closing," Fred advised. "Look hot, and flirt."

So one evening I dressed in ultra-sexy black lace stockings, red leather miniskirt and heels, and doused myself in perfume. I headed over to a local Japanese restaurant that featured a young and handsome sushi chef. I had never conversed with Fuji before. That night I discovered that he barely spoke English. Whenever I asked him a question, he consulted a Japanese-American dictionary. Doubting whether he would be able to translate, "Do you want to fuck?" I deemed him unseducable.

The next night, I took myself to another restaurant. The sushi chef was a middle-aged man with a severe expression. I downed a sake and split.

Someone told me about a hip Greenwich Village sushi bar where the waiters wore punk attire. I made my entrance an hour before closing time. Rock music was blasting and the walls were covered with abstract fiber sculptures.

The sushi chef looked to be in his early 20s. He had a trendy New Wave haircut and wore a gold earring. I greeted him with the expression "*Komba-wa*" that Fred had taught me. The sushi chef introduced himself as Shoji, and gave me a friendly smile and a wink.

After placing my order, I informed Shoji that I was a journalist writing an article on Japanese men.

"Can I interview you later?" I asked.

"Okay. We go bar across street when I finish work."

I studied Shoji as he prepared my sushi. His elegant fingers deftly squeezed the wet rice balls and slivers of tuna as he created artistic, brightly colored arrangements. He seemed to take extra care with my order, adding an extra slice of avocado, a sliver of cucumber, arraying it all with precision.

An hour later, we were sitting over drinks at a fern bar. Shoji drank American whiskey and smoked Parliaments. He told me that he was 22 years old and had lived in the United States for two years.

"What do you want to know about Japanese men?" he asked.

I decided on a straightforward approach.

"Is it true that you are the best lovers?" I asked provocatively.

Shoji dropped his cigarette, then picked it up and regained his composure.

"That depend person to person" he replied. "But Japanese peoples loving sex."

I nodded and sipped my wine.

"But I must tell you," he continued. "Japanese men have complex. Compared to American guys, we have little dicks."

I couldn't think of a proper reaction, so I changed the subject to rock and roll. Shoji asked if I had cable television. I suggested that we go to my apartment to watch music videos.

We sat on my sofa, but Shoji was too polite—or too shy—to sit close to me. So we quietly sipped from a bottle of wine. Finally, I asked Shoji, "Can you give a massage?"

"Oh yes!" he eagerly replied. "I give excellent shiatsu massage."

I led him into the bedroom and dimmed the lights. Then I lay face down on the bed. Shoji lifted up my blouse, and pressed gentle fingers up and down my spine and neck. As he unleashed the tension and loosened the kinks with a professional quality massage, I moaned.

Suddenly, he was licking my neck and shoulders. He kissed and licked every inch of my back. I blissfully allowed him to.

His mouth and tongue worked their way to my shoulders. He kissed and licked each arm from shoulder to fingertips. Then he sucked each finger.

From my hands, he segued to my buttocks. He kissed and licked them as I cried with ecstasy. He must have kissed me for five minutes before turning to my cunt. I came instantly, and kept coming as Shoji treated me to the most divine head I have ever experienced. His tongue lapped my labia, sucked my clitoris, tickled my mons, penetrated and devoured my cunt, kissed my thighs. His movements were so quick and skillful that I couldn't keep track of what he was doing when.

He ate me for a few minutes and then lifted his head.

"Please turn on light, Erica," he asked. "I want look your pussy."

"It's too bright!" I protested.

"Please!" he begged me. "I want look your American pussy. I look American pussy in magazines—big and beautiful. Japanese pussy very little, very wet, not so beautiful."

How could I turn down his request? I turned on the light and watched him watching me. His expression was reverent.

"You like Venus," he declared, diving down between my legs again. I lay there passively, letting him pay homage to my large American labia. When I had come for the fifth time, Shoji completed undressing me. He sucked my breasts briefly. Then he undressed himself. He wore navy-blue cotton boxer shorts decorated with a batik design. I started to pull them down when he covered my hand with his.

"I embarrassed," Shoji admitted. "I drink too much wine. My dick not stand up. I have little boy dick."

I slipped his shorts off and scrutinized his member. Indeed, his Nipponese knob measured only about three inches long and two inches wide in its soft state. I tried to erect it with my mouth.

"Good blowjob," said Shoji. "But my dick not standing up."

"It's okay," I said wistfully, attempting to be mature and understanding. "It's really okay."

"Do you have vibrator?" Shoji asked enthusiastically.

I pulled out the magic wand I store beside my bed and handed it to Shoji. Zestfully, he moved it over and inside my cunt, and around my ass and thighs. He licked and sucked my cunt, clit and thighs while he maneuvered the instrument. He made an art of playing with the vibrator. His fingers, too, penetrated me. Soon, he had provoked me to another shrieking, screaming orgasm.

As soon as my spasms subsided, Shoji turned the vibrator back on. He gave it to me again and again until I couldn't stand it anymore. For the first time in my multi-orgasmic life, I felt satisfied.

As I lay gasping and shuddering, Shoji whispered, "I must go. I have early morning appointment. You sleep. I come back tomorrow and fuck you. I promise my dick standing up then. I sorry I not fuck you tonight."

"Sayonara," I whispered.

I spent the entire next day thinking about Shoji. His sexual expertise would have been remarkable for any man—but it was especially so for someone his age. I was also impressed by the fact that he wanted only to please me, and demanded nothing in return—not even a touch. In my experience, most men didn't develop that selfless approach to lovemaking until they reached their early 40s. Shoji was a natural-born lover, a genuine woman-wor-shipper. Only one question remained—how large would his erect cock be?

The next night, Shoji took me to his favorite sushi bar. He ordered in Japanese, and then fed me luscious, sensuous pieces of raw shrimp, eel and avocado with his fingers. I sucked the morsels into my mouth and kissed his lips.

"You so beautiful," Shoji murmured. He fed me a slice of tuna sashimi and then sniffed his fingertips. "It smell like you—deli-cious."

We made out in the taxi going towards my house. As he pressed against me, I could feel a hard bulge in his pants. This time we didn't bother with any preliminaries but proceeded directly to my bed.

Again, Shoji licked and sucked my entire body without requiring me to reciprocate. Again, he devoured my cunt juices and ran my vibrator all over my breasts, mons, slit and ass.

Only this time, when he pulled down his shorts, Shoji revealed a hard, slender cock that looked to be about 6 inches long. Happily, I fellated him. As my lips slid over the head of his penis, I pinched his nipples.

"Good, good," he moaned. "Erica, why you so sexy?"

Then, finally, we made love. Shoji gently maneuvered me into innumerable positions. I moved my hands over his slim, muscular body while he lifted my legs onto his shoulders, gave it to me from behind, penetrated me from the side.

We had a dynamic mutual orgasm, and then lay together, hugging and kissing. I felt that his only desire at that moment was my happiness and pleasure. He was so sweet, so adoring.

He whispered, "You my first American lady. I never forget you."

I whispered, "And you're my first Japanese man. I'll never forget you either."

I lit a candle and studied Shoji's smooth white body. His chest was hairless, but he had a bountiful, silky pubic bush and his legs were covered with black hairs.

"You should wear black kimono," said Shoji. "And put clips in your hair."

I began to imagine myself as a Japanese lady. Suddenly, I wanted to have long hair piled on top of my head. I wanted to make up my face as a geisha. Walking over to my closet, I pulled out a silk kimono someone had once given me as a birthday gift. On my way back to bed, I grabbed the fan displayed on my dresser. Climbing back to bed, I slithered around in the kimono and waved the fan in front of my face.

"How does a Japanese lady make love?" I asked.

"Japanese lady love to give blowjob," Shoji replied. "My dick standing now."

"Do Japanese girls have big tits?" I asked, opening the kimono and cupping my breasts in my hands.

"Some Japanese girls big tits. I had a Japanese girlfriend 17 years old, very big tits."

"Do Japanese girls have tits as big as mine?" I asked.

"No, nobody have tits like you. Nobody have pussy as beautiful as you. Nobody coming like you. And now, please, blowjob."

I wanted to give Shoji as much pleasure as he had given me. So I began by kissing his lips and cheeks. Then I stuck my tongue into his ear and blew into it. I nibbled on his earlobes, and began tonguing his neck.

"Good, good," moaned Shoji. "Erica, you so good."

I worked my way down to his nipples. I squeezed one and sucked the other.

Shoji grabbed my vibrator. He ran it all over my body as I gently bit his nipples.

I felt completely uninhibited with him. I knew that he thought that sex is beautiful, women are beautiful, and anything sexual was permissible.

"Lie still, I'm going to fuck you," I said.

Still wearing my kimono, I climbed on top of Shoji's hard cock. I opened the fan and spread it over my face so that he couldn't see me. Like a savvy geisha, I flirted and teased. I coyly covered my breasts and then my cunt with the fan. Whenever I withdrew it, he touched me in the spot I had hidden.

While I pumped up and down, he ran the vibrator over my clit.

"I want you come very strong," he whispered.

Squeezing his cock with my cunt muscles, I orgasmed repeatedly. While I came, I imagined myself as a Japanese geisha. I fantasized that I was serving my man. When he finally shot into me, I experienced an Oriental serenity.

The next day I gave my battered old sofa to the Salvation Army. I replaced it with colorful tatami mats. I stocked my cupboards with plum wine and sake. I hung a set of tinkling windchimes in my window.

Shoji came over to cook for me last night. We ate our tempura sitting barefoot on the tatami mats. Then he carried me into the bedroom and initiated our lovemaking with another shiatsu massage.

Today I bought the complete works of Yukio Mishima. I rented "The Seven Samurai" and played it on my VCR. I borrowed Shoji's Japanese-American dictionary. I'm studying up for my trip to Japan.

FEAR OF LESBIANISM

By Marcy Seeger

I no longer remember why she was stripping, outside, late at night, on the quiet street near the parking lot; only that she was. I held her clothes, watched her raise her arms under the streetlight, shake herself and say how good it felt to be naked. Shyly, I stood there and let her taunt me.

Over a year before we had gotten drunk together on the stairs of my lover's apartment. Mark was hosting a Christmas party and Annie and I, still strangers, wound up with a gallon jug of wine and each other. We sat close together, brushing shoulders, laughing as the conversation turned into mist. Through the alcohol I saw that she was beautiful in an antique way, with mellow skin, large eyes with perfectly symmetrical brows and a long, aquiline nose. Her body was slender but wide-boned and full.

She got sick that night and we spent the early morning hours sitting on the bathroom floor. Annie leaned over the toilet and I stroked her back and whispered to her. With Mark's help, I put her to bed in the spare room. She kept whispering, "Thank you, thank you" and, still drunk, turned on her side toward the wall. I covered her with a blanket and went to my lover's bed.

We were juniors that year at a small school in New England. Three years earlier I had fled a conservative high-school for a college campus that boasted a large gay minority and a strong feminist community. I met my first gays and my first feminists and began to embrace the thinking of the latter.

As a young straight woman, feminism presented me with real problems. I had always been saddened by my relationships with

men, including those with my father and my brothers. I felt weak
with them. And behind the as-yet-unnamed feeling of vacancy I had
when I was with a man, I was angry. My freshman year was full
of slow realizations about my and all women's lack of freedom. I
saw that women had always been forced to choose compromising
affiliations with men, whether husband, lover or boss, that put us
into competition with each other. To fight our own oppression, to
emerge from the very sorrowful, frightened and angry solitude in
which we found ourselves, we had to find each other. Salvation lay
in other women. Thus, we no longer wanted to say to women friends
that they were secondary to male lovers. In philosophy, even in
reality, women came first.

But love and sex were not so neatly packaged. As long as men
provided me my sex life, I would give greater importance to them
even though they were the source of the problem. But how could
I, how could I still date, fuck and fall in love with them? With
women I was strong and honest. Why wasn't I able to make the
leap from emotional to physical intimacy with women? Why couldn't
I really love them, why couldn't I sleep with them?

To be honest, I didn't berate myself with these questions. I was
new to feminism and, as much as I was learning, I still liked men.
I liked the way they looked, smelled and moved. I liked the way
they felt against my body and under my fingers. I liked them in
much the same way men have historically liked women—as sensual/
sexual experiences. I wasn't pleased with my schizophrenic uses
for the sexes. I wanted a man who would treat me right or I wanted
a woman in whose body I could revel.

Throughout my first years of college these boundaries kept shifting
and crossing but were never eradicated. I fell in love with men,
several of whom were working diligently against their own sexism.
And in the middle of my third year, I fell in love with Annie.

Annie and I shared similar backgrounds and similar misgivings
about our intellects, our relationships with men and our beauty. As
I grew to know her better, I began to have dreams about her in
which our names were confused. Slowly I realized that I felt differently about her than I had ever felt about a woman. We hugged
a lot, aware of each other's body through our clothes, safe with our
clothes on.

In the front seat of my car one evening after dinner Annie opened
the conversation by saying she'd been thinking about lesbians. For
a silent moment we looked at each other and then I started talking

fast about Denise, a woman I had recently met at a party. Denise was a campus legend, famous for both her brilliance and her brutishness. She liked soft, beautiful women and she came onto me with aggressive and obsessive machismo.

For weeks Denise followed me all over campus. She appeared throughout my days as though she had memorized my schedule. I was afraid of her but even as I spoke I was more, differently, afraid of Annie.

When I stopped talking, Annie was silent, looking at her hands clasped in her lap. I was shocked at my reaction to her—shocked at my fear. We said goodnight; she kissed me and opened the door. I waited for her to reach the dormitory entrance before pulling away. She did not turn and wave.

I thought I had lost her, but the ensuing days proved that I hadn't. The issue had just been opened; it rested between our words when we spoke. We started to tease each other; Annie openly began to seduce me. I fantasized about her, touching myself as though my body were hers.

In fantasy I am still wary, but not afraid. I lie in bed. The night feels alive the way summer nights do, but for me, the excitement is Annie. Her skin is white in the dark. She lies down on top of me, breasts to breasts, toes to toes. I am curious about her body. My hands stroke her length, trying to find out what she is like. Her breasts are bigger and differently textured than mine. I slide down, still beneath her, licking her breasts, sucking the nipples. I run my palm down her stomach, over the slight outward curve of her belly and touch the hair just starting there. And stop. Even in fantasy I can't quite bring myself to her cunt.

I told Mark about it one night as we lay next to each other in bed. He was holding me, running his fingers up and down my belly, as a prelude to his mouth. "I've been thinking about Annie," I said as his fingers circled my breasts. "She wants to sleep with me." I paused.

"Are you asking me for my permission?" he said.

"No, I just want you to know and that it confuses me."

He started to squeeze my breasts and pulled me on top of him, my legs straddling his hips, his tongue in my mouth. He ran his hands down to my ass, pushing our hips together. "Well, you've got to know that it turns me on," he said, "you and Annie."

His cock was rigid. I bit his neck, walked my mouth down his body, felt the tensing of his muscles, his cock wanting me. I bit his stomach, I licked around his hip bones, teasing. Taking his cock into my mouth, my mind a blank, I felt only the need to fill my mouth with him. Suddenly, the image of making love to Annie became impossible, a fantasy removed from the actuality of her real body. It was something I didn't think I could do, or even wanted to do.

But when I was alone with Annie I wanted her once again. It was as though I was two women with two different sexualities, the boundaries of which refused to meet.

When I thought back I realized there was a precedent for this. The feeling was familiar. In my sophomore year I had roomed with a woman whose name was Janice. Though not sexual we had an intimate physical relationship. Jan loved massage and was practiced in its subtleties. I was less generous and far less interested, but Jan never tired of giving backrubs. She would light candles, close our curtains and heat oil on our hot-plate. Naked, I would stretch out on the bed face down and, with warm, oily hands, Jan would begin the massage. My relaxation was total, and Jan was uninhibited about touching me. Her hands would slide to my inner thighs and my ass and the sides of my breasts.

When Jan slept with a woman for the first time and came to me the morning after, her face shining with pleasure, I wasn't surprised. And when she added that it was the first time she had felt love for the person she was having sex with, I was happy for her. And while I did not wish I'd been the other woman, I was jealous. I envied the closeness she had shared with someone else.

Shortly thereafter, without warning or discussion, she moved into an all-women's dorm, leaving me utterly crushed. The magnitude of my hurt was that of a lover's betrayal, and I knew, though I have never been attracted to her, that I had trusted her implicitly, as one does a lover. I also began to understand why I was always bored and strangely guilty with my boyfriends. The same dynamic was happening again with Annie, complicated by Mark and by the fact that when I masturbated it was Annie's mouth I imagined pressing on my cunt.

One night after an exercise class, Annie paraded naked around the empty locker room. She had an elegant bearing, long-legged and unself-conscious. Her hair slapped her hips. Her breasts were very large and round. She said she was getting her period and her body was swelling up. She came over to me and leaned against the lockers, touching my hair. As I pulled my sweater over my head she stopped me with my arms in mid-air and ran her fingers down the middle of my back. She did it again with her nails, softly.

I let the sweater drift off my arms and drop. I turned to look at her. We were the same height and our eyes were exactly level. Hers were sad and full. She reached out her hand and touched my ear then traced the side of my face with her fingers. "We are just alike," she said. "We should not be afraid of each other."

Fantasy: This one begins where Annie left off. We go to my room, running. She is in my room, my bed, next to me. My hands reach for her crotch and part the lips, touching wetness. She has pulled my mouth against hers, slid her tongue inside. I slide my finger into her cunt. I think that this is what men feel, this strange opening in the body. I slide in two more fingers and it is a tight squeeze. My thumb finds her clitoris, she presses her pelvis into my hand and comes so easily, like breathing. My hand is soaked, I run it up her body, making a wet trail until it reaches our mouths, still touching. She darts her tongue around my fingers. And then she slides between my legs. She rests her elbows in the crooks of my knees, pushing my legs apart. Slowly she slips her thumb into my cunt then plants her lips between them, licking.

But it never happened. We fucked our boyfriends. We masturbated thinking of each other. And we graduated. It took time for me to get over the feeling of loss I had about Annie and to put it into perspective. I have still not slept with a woman and don't fully expect to because it wasn't any woman I wanted, it was Annie.

The Comedy of Sex

✳

A GIZMO NAMED DESIRE

By John Garside

My wife and I like to spend our yearly tax refund on something wild and, preferably, erotic. We call this windfall our Intimate Recreational Savings, in honor of the IRS. The king-size water bed with the mirrored canopy was our first extravagance (big refund *that* year). Next we treated ourselves to the sensuous "honeymoon suite" in a Poconos resort. The third time around, Pam, my wife, splurged on a dozen naughty nighties from the Frederick's of Hollywood catalogue.

But this year we wanted something more daring and less likely to be tomorrow's fad. Water beds are now standard bedroom equipment, and the Poconos place advertises in *Redbook*. A local Frederick's outlet has moved into the same end of the mall with J. C. Penney.

Then I saw an ad for Accu-Jac in *Penthouse Variations*. Intrigued, I glanced down the copy: "Lubricated flexible sleeve feels just like a woman." "Add suction for oral sensation." *All right!* "Hey, honey," I called out, "*you'll* like this. A machine with variable speed and depth of stroke on the 'amazingly lifelike erect penis.' *And* . . . 'choice of bellows or piston-driven dildo.' " I read the last part to her word for word: " 'Can handle up to four people at the same time.' "

"Yes," said Pam, peering at the photo of the two dildos. "But we don't know two other people that well."

"Just in case," I reminded her. "Isn't it nice to know that in a

113

pinch, we always have the two extra outlets? Four fuckers. No waiting.''

I sent $3 for complete details. By return mail we received the packet of particulars, plus photos and quotes from reviews (''Futuristic eroticism''; ''The apex of sexual technology''; ''A hot item''). The Accu-Jac promised to be a male-female, super-masturbation, fucking, sucking, come-one-come-all pleasure machine, with more attachments than our vacuum cleaner. After careful deliberation, Pam and I decided to spend every penny of our $850 refund on this Electrolux of sex, convinced that it was going to change our sex life forever.

While Pam wrote a personal check, I struggled with the most intimidating order form a man can be asked to fill out.

Measurements. ''Be as precise as possible,'' the instructions read, ''in submitting the *erect* penis measurements. The sleeve fit is important.'' A diagram on the order blank showed how to measure for topside length and circumference near base.

It was my moment of truth. I got out my tape measure and the latest copy of *Penthouse*. With a little finagling I could *just* manage six inches. On the circumference I was a trifle under five, which translated into a diameter of about an inch and a half. ''Not too impressive,'' I mumbled to my wife, imagining some well-hung hulk in the mail room opening my order form and reading it to the gang for laughs.

But I remembered that the standard Accu-Jac dildo was the same size. Men, I told myself, worry *too much* about *too little*.

Out of curiosity I called Funways, the California company that makes and distributes Accu-Jac, to see how precise my measurements had to be.

''A lot of men overestimate slightly,'' said spokesman Charles Boynton. ''I always laugh, because they'll have to give us the correct measurements eventually, even if they don't the first time.''

All penis sleeves must be custom-made, since only a snug fit ensures a proper air seal. I asked Boynton for the smallest penis measurement on record. He recalled a fitting for less than an inch in diameter and about three inches long. The largest is a matter of debate. Funways once made a sleeve to accommodate a cock seven inches long and four inches in diameter. The customer who requested it must have mounted fire-plugs before Accu-Jac came along. Another order specified a sleeve eleven inches long—obviously for a man who had never worn swimming trunks.

The standard Accu-Jac unit, consisting of console, two dildos and two penis sleeves, had a base price of $695. I decided to order all eight sleeve models, plus extra tubing for four people and a few spare sleeves in various sizes. I would take my change in lubricant. Boynton recommended Astroglide.

Two weeks later the UPS man was stacking up boxes outside our door as if it were Christmas. That night, after the children went to bed, we returned to our bedroom and began ripping open the cardboard cartons. The console was about the size of a four-loaf breadbox and weighed in at just over 40 pounds.

"Will it be hard to set up?" Pam asked, pulling off the plastic wrapping. "It's not going to be like the high chairs and the bicycle, is it?" Over the years we have bought various easy-to-assemble kits that still sit in our basement, missing step, screw or widget.

"No," I assured her. "The man told me it came ready to use. Just plug it right in."

"It or us?"

"Both," I replied, unwinding the cord and finding a socket nearby.

Pam suddenly burst into laughter and waved a brick-red dildo at me. "Look!" she exclaimed. "Aztec dick."

"Or sunburned lifeguard," I said, taking it from her. Flexible but firm, it looked like a cock with a round rubber plug, about two inches thick, at its base. Pam grabbed it back and slapped it in her palm like a black-jack. "Assault with a lively weapon," she teased, feinting at me with it.

I soon located the piston cylinder for the dildo. The instruction booklet stated that the apparatus, operating on air pressure and suction, was easy to set up. It was. Within moments we had the eight-foot-long plastic tube connected to the console and the plug end of the dildo lubricated.

The "gold-anodized" control panel was a marvel of simplicity. Dead center were a large on/off toggle switch and a dial for setting the speed. On either side of the speed dial were metal tips marked "external" and "internal" respectively.

We switched the dildo tube to "internal" and put another tube —my tube—on "external." Above the tube connection on my side of the machine were two knobs marked "suction" and "stroke length." Pam's side had only one knob—"stroke length." The manual stated that stroke length varied from half an inch to three inches and that the speed could be moderated independently. Stroke combinations included long/fast, short/fast, long/slow, short/slow or anything in between.

"Shall we get started?" I asked, waving my plastic sleeve. It looked like a soft, oversized test tube with a nub at one end.

"Not yet," Pam replied, unwrapping the bellows dildo and plunking it down on the water bed. Obviously heavy, it bobbed gently and settled in. A block of rubber with concave sides for the thighs, it was powered by a round, accordion-fold plastic tube.

Reading from the booklet, I informed Pam that the bellows model was designed exclusively for vaginal sex. The piston-driven dildo, whose speed and direction could be more precisely controlled, could be used anally as well. The dildo came with a belt-and-ring harness to hold it in place.

I hadn't been this excited since I got my first Lionel train.

By now we were at Step 8 in the manual, which suggested a "dry run" for beginners. "Okay, let's get going," I urged. "Hold the dildo-driver."

"The what?" Pam asked, looking around frantically. "You said this would be easy."

I pointed to the piston dildo. "*That*," I explained, "is what the book calls a dildo-driver, and you are supposed to keep it in with one hand while I turn it on."

Grimacing, she inserted it while I set speed and stroke length to "minimum." The directions said the dildo would "pulse gently." I flicked the toggle switch.

The machine started wheezing like a dirty old man. My wife began to giggle.

"It sounds like a horny respirator," she quipped as the dildo began to move in and out in slow motion.

"This is great!" I exclaimed. "There's a pump somewhere in that machine, and it sounds like a heartbeat."

I slowly increased the stroke length and turned up the speed. The rubber cock began to slide in and out with a solid, rapid stroke that brought a smile to my wife's face.

"It's powerful," Pam murmured, curling her hands around the dildo, letting it slither back and forth through her fingers. She was still smiling.

I swallowed. "Maybe we should, uh, take our clothes off." She set the dildo-driver on the bed, where it tried to copulate with our comforter. We undressed about as quickly as we had on our honeymoon night.

I shut the machine off long enough to slap some more lubricant on Mr. Aztec Dick. (The instructions suggested fitting it with a condom to ensure both sanitary and anti-irritant protection.)

"Could you start slow at first?" Pam asked, reminding me again of our honeymoon.

I lowered the settings and she reinserted the disembodied cock. Enraptured, I watched it gliding back and forth. It was almost, but not quite, the fulfillment of a lifelong fantasy—seeing her making love with another man. But when I saw the glow of pleasure on her face, I felt a curious, surprising twinge of jealousy.

I had assumed Accu-Jac would be a good, nonthreatening way of indulging my fantasies. Instead I found myself thinking: Who is this *intruder* in my bed? What is it *doing* with my wife?

"How is it?" I managed to ask, keeping my voice neutral.

"Ummmmmm," she murmured. "Turn it up."

"The length or the speed?" I asked briskly.

"Both," she sighed.

"Right." I complied with her request.

"Honey," she moaned. "Do you know what I've always wanted to do?"

I did know, and scrambled up beside her on the bed. Moments later she was sucking my cock. Pam's favorite fantasy had always been to get fucked and give head at the same time. Mmmmmm. Big Chief bring peace.

The sensation at first was like getting head in a moving car—both of us were too distracted to enjoy it. But Pam soon began to respond to the steady thrust of the piston-cock, opening her legs and arching her back while undulating her pelvis in a sensuous dance that made me tremble with excitement.

Suddenly Pam abandoned her usual "dainty" style of giving head —a combination of gentle licking and tentative nibbles that rarely brought me to climax. Now she was sucking my cock as though she were famished. Writhing and squirming with each thrust of the Accu-Jac, she pressed her mouth deeper and deeper around my penis.

When I came, she hungrily swallowed every drop, something she had never done before. A moment later she began to moan, pounding her head back into the pillow in the throes of an orgasm that seemed to go on and on. Finally she relaxed and gestured feebly toward the machine. I shut the Accu-Jac off.

After getting our breath back, we discussed the experience like two rational adults.

"Was it okay?" I asked, (Translation: You liked it better than me, didn't you?)

"Oh, it was pretty good." (Especially the part where my eyes rolled back in my head.)

"Did it feel . . . authentic?" (Does this mean you don't need me anymore?)

"It had the heft and feel of a real cock. But I'd rather have the real thing. After all, it was *just* a cock. You haven't tried your side yet." (Don't be too eager getting around to it, either.)

I set the controls to slow speed and heavy suction, lubricated my limp cock and stuffed it into the opening of the sheath. *Fwoop!* went the machine. Three seconds later I had the fastest and perhaps biggest erection of my life.

(In my conversation with Accu-Jac spokesman Charles Boynton, he said Accu-Jac would probably produce an optimum erection. He added that some customers reordered sleeves in a larger size, or even two or three sizes larger over a few years.)

"That was quick," Pam exclaimed, turning up the stroke length and speed. After experimenting, I found that I could make the tube barely clear the end of my cock and then grab back on for the downstroke. The sensation was a lot like getting head. The tube was even making loud sucking sounds. As I got closer to orgasm, I lowered the air supply to allow the sheath to approximate "deep throat" sucking.

Then, just as I began to come, I drew the tube back, increasing the speed to get a series of "grab-on" sucks, one right after the other, until I climaxed.

During the next few days, we put Accu-Jac through all of its paces. I found that the tighter sleeves simulated intercourse, and that the ribbed and expanded-end sleeves felt like a hand or a thumb and forefinger stroking me. Some of the sleeves reminded me of past girlfriends, because of either their fit or the slick, soft or rhythmic sensations they produced. I named a few of them, though I never said to my wife: "No, not Vivian. Give me Gina and, uh, Patty-Anne."

Pam was turned on not only by what Accu-Jac did for her, but by the sexual rejuvenation it was causing in me. Overnight I had once again become the horny, hop-in-the-sack-anytime male she had married a long time ago.

She was especially intrigued by how quickly my cock got hard—

and how big. Within a few days it seemed to grow noticeably. I liked being able to get good sex with little effort whenever I wanted it. Since I could depend on the sleeve to always give me an erection, I found myself wanting sex about five times a day.

Within a week Pam was too sore to sit down and the end of my cock looked like it had terminal sunburn. Skin was beginning to peel. Just like old times, I reflected, as I gently applied the Vaseline. The only cure was to leave the machine alone for a week. We sent away for more Astroglide, which is expensive ($9.95 per bottle) but worth it. The lubricant was easy to clean off the equipment and ourselves, and was not only flavorless but harmless if ingested.

Over the next few months we tried all of the variations. Pam preferred the bellows dildo for a slow, comfortable screw. As it was held between the thighs, any movement caused the dildo to slip out.

The piston-powered dildo was usable either with or without its harness. Occasionally I made love to Pam by holding the plastic cylinder between my legs and letting her control the speed and depth. At other times Pam and I made love and then she continued with the machine after I came. Occasionally she started with the machine, came to orgasm and then invited me in for "seconds." On some nights she switched back and forth from me to Accu-Jac. She also never had "enough" anymore.

I used all the sheaths: ribbed, tapered-in, tapered-out, bent, tight fit, vibrating, coke bottle and standard, which was supposed to simulate actual intercourse. I gave them names of my own: handjob, oddjob, blowjob, humjob, loose shoes and, of course, tight pussy.

I also fantasized about women I knew. The 19-year-old college girl across the street worked her way from the ribbed (handjob) sleeve to the loose (mild blowjob) model to humjob (vibrating sleeve). Eventually I used tight pussy (a tapered sleeve) to relieve sexy little Janice of her virginity.

I also discovered a pleasant way to get off while holding up the latest Pet of the Month centerfold with *both* hands.

Other advantages of the machine were that it never got tired or complained of sore wrist or aching jaw. Afterward I never had to whisper, "Was it good for you?" or "Did you come?" It could give an unrivaled 30-minute handjob that kept me exactly a degree below my boiling point for as long as I could stand it. Its steady, unvarying rhythm was perfectly tuned to Pam's inner harmonies for hours at a time.

"It's not as good as a cock," Pam said, when I asked her what she really thought about Accu-Jac. "But it sure is better than a vibrator. I prefer a man, but the machine does give me a sense of absolute pleasure. No matter what happens—if the phone rings or there's a knock on the door—this cock isn't going to go down. And it isn't going to come before you do or tell you that your orgasm is taking too long and making it tired.

"The dildo moves with so much of the rhythm of real intercourse that it is just the most incredibly luxurious masturbation you could imagine. Plus you're completely in control of your own fantasies. You control angle and depth of penetration, intensity and perfect placement, without asking your partner to be a contortionist."

One time I came home early from a business meeting to find my wife in her underwear. "Hi," she said nervously, trying to hide something behind her on the bathroom sink. I peeked. Oh, looky! It's Mr. Dildo. And Mr. Cylinder! "I was just . . . washing a few things out," she added, shrugging. "You never said we had to use it *together*."

It was a damned funny feeling; but why shouldn't she use the Accu-Jac alone? It was the perfect *harmless* affair. What was I going to do? Shoot the machine?

"Can I have seconds?" I asked.

She dropped Aztec Dick into the sink and winked. "I was hoping you'd say that."

A few nights later I asked her if she wanted to try anal sex with the Accu-Jac. In the past we had never had much success with this form of lovemaking.

"You know what would really put me at ease?" she said. "For you to do it first."

I consider myself fairly liberal sexually, but never would I let any man stick his cock up my ass. I can't even look my proctologist in the eye afterward. So again I passed. This was one barrier Accu-Jac did not help us get over.

Eventually we mentioned our acquisition to our closest friends. Some jokingly asked whether we would rent it out or bring it to the next company picnic. When we told a gay woman friend about Accu-Jac, she said it was a shame it did not have an attachment for female oral sex. "Never mind," she said. "You let me at that machine. I can get all the female oral sex I want. But a stiff dick

—without the actual hassle of dealing with a man—is something else again. I like what men can do. I'm just not crazy about what they put you through before and after." When we went on vacation later, we loaned the machine to her.

I wondered if we would miss Accu-Jac, since it had become a regular—though by no means constant—part of our sex lives. I got my answer the third night in our lakefront cabin. I had a sex dream. About the machine.

FOAMING AT THE MOUTH

By Adrian Buffet

My first date with Linda had gone surprisingly well—much better than a Horny Guy could expect after six weeks of bad luck. Not only did I wangle a nightcap at her place, but I soon found myself wrapped around her naked body on the brink of some serious love-making. Considering the circumstances, I paid little attention when Linda excused herself and slipped into the bathroom. For all I knew, she was rearranging her mascara or flossing her teeth.

The mood quickly returned as soon as Linda bounced back onto our four-poster playground. As the foreplay shifted into high gear, my old skills resurfaced with amazing swiftness. I slid down Linda's smooth body, caressed her stomach, ran my tongue tantalizingly around her light brown pubic hair, and then buried my nose in her crotch as forcefully as possible without deviating a septum.

Surfacing for air, I noticed a slight medicinal odor between her legs. But Linda was wriggling, cooing and moaning so contentedly that my normal street-smart instincts had gone on hold. I began to snake my tongue into her vagina again. In the heat of passion, I was unaware of the mouthwash tingle numbing my tongue and neutralizing my taste buds. Like the average dumb Horny Guy, I probably would have ignored herpes to make the Big Score.

I put the pieces together afterward. Linda's little trip to the bathroom was not to freshen up. She had inserted a plastic syringe into her vagina and fired a round of contraceptive foam onto her vaginal walls. Dwelling on that image, I wondered what the foam could do to a man who slurps down a mouthful like whipped cream and comes back for seconds. If the contraceptive is potent enough to wipe out a few million sperm on contact, how does it affect a fellow's taste buds or digestive tract?

I was mad. Linda should have warned me about the spermicide. If the foam was safe to swallow, why did she turn her head when I kissed her goodbye? I called her the next day.

"How would I know it tastes terrible?" she replied indignantly. I protested that she should have read the label for warnings and informed her partner. We were having our first fight. She dropped the phone and got the package.

"There's nothing on here about eating the stuff," she reported, "but I'm sure the government would not permit the company to make the spermicide if it were dangerous to eat." I asked if she ever heard of Red Dye No. 2, and told her that my taste buds had nearly short-circuited. "So what's the alternative, bimbo?" she huffed. "Fatherhood?" Linda hung up, ending the conversation and our relationship.

Nevertheless, my quest for the truth about foam continued. When I complained about my encounter to the guys at a local pub, I was surprised to learn that quite a few had felt the same confusion. Like me, they were riled. All of them agreed that a woman should tell the man when she has foamed up. But none had considered the possibility that swallowing spermicide was dangerous. After much speculation based on total ignorance and fueled by a few more rounds of Lowenbrau (the official Horny Guy brew), my friends charged me with the task of investigating the dreaded foam.

My first stop was a local apothecary. Pharmacist Paul Perniciaro escorted me to the "Feminine Needs" section and explained that the active ingredient in contraceptive foam is nonoxynol. The spermicidal property of this common emulsifier—belonging to a class called surfactants normally used to hold a mixture of oil and water together—was discovered in 1961. No one knows exactly why it destroys sperm cells. The different brands of foam included Koromex, Because, Emko, Delfen and Semicid. Actually, as Perniciaro pointed out, Semicid is not a foam, but rather a suppository that "effervesces like Alka Seltzer" when inserted in the vagina.

There were no references to oral sex on the packages. The only warning was on a box of Emko: "If vaginal or penile irritation occurs and continues, a physician should be consulted."

"My God," I said to Perniciaro, "if it can irritate skin, what would it do to a tongue?" He suggested I talk with Dr. John Zuzack of the St. Louis College of Pharmacy, where the first foam—Emko—was developed.

When I explained my purpose, Dr. Zuzack laughed. "That's a new one on me," he said. "But I imagine that if you ingested enough foam, it would serve as a laxative. Foam is chemically related to laundry detergent, and would lubricate your G.I. tract. Eating the foam might be a problem only for someone with a delicate or nervous stomach." However, Dr. Zuzack noted that research on the ingestion of foam was not extensive.

Next I telephoned Leonard Naeger, another pharmacologist at the St. Louis College of Pharmacy, who also assisted in the creation of the first foam. He wryly observed that his fellow researchers had discovered an alternative use for the spermicide. "We also found it effective for athlete's foot," he informed me, "and that's what we used it for." I remarked that anything that kills fungi could not be too wonderful to swallow. But Naeger disagreed. "You could probably eat the whole thing without causing any irreversible damage to your taste buds," he said. "It may desensitize them for a little while, but so what?"

I asked Naeger why manufacturers did not produce flavored foam. "As a joke," he replied, "when we were students, we were going to use fruit flavors. We even came up with a name—Statutory Grape." I thought about the possibilities. Maybe even a flavor of the month—Penis Colada in June; Harvey Ballbanger in July.

The manufacturers apparently do not want to acknowledge that women, God forbid, submit to cunnilingus while using the foam. This attitude explains why oral sex is not mentioned in brochures or on labels—nothing about terrible taste, numb mouth or laxative effects. "We know it's not toxic," said a spokesman for Schering-Plough Corporation of Kennelsworth, New Jersey, which bought Emko in the late 70s, "so why should there be a warning?"

Contraceptive foam was invented by a company that makes sharpening tools. Emko was the brainchild of the late Joe Sunnen, founder of the St. Louis-based Sunnen Products Company, known the world over for its quality honing machines.

Joe Sunnen was a prominent industrialist and philanthropist in his day. He owned 50 patents in the automotive field and perfected the modern hypodermic syringe. With financial success came Sunnen's desire to help the poor. Population control became his passion. During a visit to a wretched barrio in Puerto Rico in 1957, Sunnen had an idea that he thought would revolutionize birth control: a simple, inexpensive, mass-marketed aerosol foam that would act as a barrier to conception. When he could not interest pharmaceutical companies, he decided to produce it himself.

Sunnen commissioned the chemists at the St. Louis College of Pharmacy to fulfill his dream. Professor Arthur Zimmer, one of the analysts, noted that the foam was originally intended as a barrier alone and that the spermicidal action of nonoxynol was a complete surprise. Zimmer explained that nonoxynol invades the spermatozoa and blows them to bits. "They literally swell up and burst," he said. Why this chemical has this effect is still a mystery.

But, stressed Zimmer, just because the foam detonates sperm cells and knocks out athlete's foot does not mean that it lays waste taste buds or digestive bacteria. "I have never ingested foam myself," he said, "but I'm willing to bet that it is not much different from eating shaving cream." Which is not a Horny Guy's idea of fun on a Saturday night, either.

Dan Becker, a former Sunnen Products employee, was also eager to tell me foam stories. "When they first got into birth control," he recalled, "the scientists were using samples from male prostitutes, seeing what would kill sperm. They found this one guy who had sperm that wouldn't die . . ."

After Emko went on the market in the mid-60s, the biggest problem the company had was designing illustrated instructions. "They couldn't devise a simplified graphic, so people misused the product," Becker said. "We'd get letters saying, 'I took three teaspoons and still got pregnant . . .'"

Having completed my research, I reported the news to my friends. The only thing we have to fear from foam is fear itself. It probably is no worse than eating escargots.

IF IT'S MIDNIGHT, IT MUST BE JERRI

By Clark Gristus

Like most young men, I fantasize about having feverish, spontaneous sex with every woman under 40 who crosses my path. But the memory of a recent streak of luck still causes my penis to shrink and my balls to crowd up close.

Three of us had answered an ad in Chicago seeking riders to Denver. I quickly allied with the only female in the car, an attractive girl from Boulder named Sandy. By Kansas City we found common interests; near Abeline we were laughing; in Salina we bought beer.

Somewhere near the Colorado line at about 2 A.M. Sandy nestled under my down jacket and took my cock deep into her mouth. The Air Force cadet and the redneck in front talked about football while Sandy used her hand to pump my come down her throat. One of my countless fantasies had finally come true and I was enthralled —at the time.

Sandy gave me her phone number when we dropped her off in Boulder, 25 miles north of Denver. She invited me to visit her after I attended the wedding of a friend. She worked nights as a word processor and even offered me the use of her car. It was a mildly attractive proposal, but I remained noncommittal.

That night in Denver I went to the opening of an avant-garde art gallery. Standing before a decaying exhibit called "Interesting Food," I was approached by a startling young woman who, counting the heels and spikey hair, was nearly six feet tall. She wore a black leather skirt, dog collar, studded bracelets, leopard-spotted sweater and lipstick that looked like it had been applied with a razor.

Jerri played bass in a Boulder punk group called Dogs in Heat. We went into another room where the band was playing. I expected her to pair off with someone like the lavender-haired fellow in the corner. But she stuck by me as we elbowed through the crowd. A few minutes later, I felt her hand kneading the crotch of my jeans. I suggested, in a pathetic I-wish-this-happened-all-the-time manner, that we go for a walk.

As we emerged in the freezing night air, I pondered what had transformed me from the retiring young man back home to an apparent sexual magnet. Perhaps higher altitudes cause women to crave sex with oxygen-rich men from nearer sea level.

Shortly we found a dilapidated house trailer on a construction site across from the gallery. I spread my coat on the floor. Jerri pulled out a faintly pink tampon. It dangled from her fingers, steaming, before she flicked it into the shadows. We screwed hard and fast in the cold shed, with most of our clothes still on. When we finished, panting warm, white breath at each other, we laughed. She said she lived in Boulder with her parents and gave me her number to call if I was ever there.

Boulder, it seemed, beckoned. The prospect of having Sandy free during the day and Jerri at night gave me an exhilaratingly nasty feeling. I was going to soak this gift from the gods for all it was worth.

Sandy and I went to bed within an hour of my arrival on a Thursday afternoon. As I sucked one of her little pink nipples and prodded her thighs with my penis, I took a deep breath, ready to fire the first shot of a three-day campaign. After savoring the exquisite feeling of a snug cunt, I started to thrust. Then Sandy screamed.

"Does that hurt?" I asked, surprised.

"No, it feels so good."

I moved again and she started yowling as though she had learned to fuck from a cat. Apparently her outburst denoted excitement. I buried my face in the pillow to hide my laughter. When I came, I was sure her wailing would bring the police.

"I haven't had a man in a long time," she whispered in my ringing ear.

After dinner we went back to bed. There was nothing else to do. What had passed for interesting conversation along hundreds of miles of highway wore thin across the salad. I was barely into Sandy again before her low moaning shortly gave way to bona fide screeching.

"Hey," I said, suspending operations, "let's try this."

Wheeling around, I gazed into her vagina and put a stopper in her mouth. I felt bad shutting her up like this, but her neighbors must have thought someone's fingernails were being pulled out.

A sense of grimly digging in on the Sandy front made me look forward to seeing Jerri. When I dropped Sandy off at work she paused at the car door, smiled wickedly and said, "I'll be thinking about you all night." I tried to grin as winningly as I could.

Jerri still had her prickly hair collected under a McDonald's paper cap when I picked her up at work half an hour later. Inside the apartment, the tenancy of which Jerri never questioned, she immediately took off her uniform.

"These are the ugliest fucking clothes ever made," she muttered, slipping out of the McDonald's blue polyester pants. She was wearing tube socks, panties and no bra.

I was undressing on the couch when Jerri took my cock in her mouth. Straddling my legs she swung in rhythm with her sucking and stroking. Although I had been screwing most of the day and it hung in the balance for a while, I finally came. As I shook with orgasm Jerri breathed hard through her nose while taking the jolt of semen deep into her mouth.

"Let's keep this hard," she urged, kneading life into the subsiding erection. I was pleased with what I had managed so far, but now felt I had been given an ultimatum. After a few minutes I simply could not thrust again, much less make either of us come. She settled for having me stroke her off with my hand.

The action apparently over for the time being, I smiled helplessly to myself. This was pleasure beyond satiation, but my entire body felt as enervated as my dick. I groaned something about taking her home. She suggested that we sleep for a few hours and then I could drop her off at her high school at seven. She had clothes in her locker.

"High school? Your locker?" I yelped.

"Yeah," she laughed. "I'm 17. Don't worry. My parents don't fuck with me or my hours."

Later I watched miserably as Jerri trotted off to her classes and the kids walking by the car stared at me quizzically. Then I remembered that Sandy was just getting off work. She was waiting outside when I pulled up. I apologized, saying I overslept.

Back home Sandy wanted to sleep and asked if I'd come back to bed with her. No, I did not. After a nap Jerri and I had had a long fuck. I was not feeling anywhere near the top of my form and was disinclined to be on top of Sandy's. But when she pulled her sweater over her lacy white bra I felt a glimmer of excitement and my penis began to stiffen. Whether guided by hormones or instincts, I shortly found myself rutting away toward my seventh orgasm in 15 hours. Though no doubt not even a regional record, it was protested by every inch in my body save six. Sandy, on the other hand, was shrieking in ecstasy, "Oh yeah, baby; oh, baby; yeah, yeah, yeah."

"That was unbelievable," she sighed after the din subsided and I slipped out of her. "God, please go down on me."

She pushed my head down to her soft brown hair. I was relieved: now I could relax. It was not much of a respite, though. Seconds after my mouth closed on her swollen labia, she started kicking and squealing with renewed vigor. She finally reached a plateau of hysteria which I took to mean orgasm, and we fell asleep.

I awoke from a nightmare in which I was trapped in a dairy farm, trying to escape from a gang of roving milking machines. As my head cleared I discovered that Sandy had my penis in her mouth. She took it out long enough to say brightly, "Hi! I've always wanted to wake someone like this."

I laughed hollowly. Then, feeling like a punchy lab rat, I glimpsed a swaying nipple and a tuft of pubic hair. Soon I was guiding her head into my eager thrusts.

It was only noon. My body craved eight hours of sleep. No matter how thoughtful Sandy was to rouse me with oral sex, my testicles were ready to have a word with the shop steward. Fair was fair, though, so I lowered my face to her vagina and tucked into the job to be done.

When we were done I was frantic for more sleep. But in a playfully scolding tone, Sandy declared that I could rest when she went to work. We spent the afternoon touring the town.

That night Jerri was in a stormy mood. "Fuck the cheese on a Quarter-Pounder, and fuck the assholes who eat it," was her opening remark.

Something like fear shot through my loins. I had been hoping for a fairly quiet evening. If we had to have sex I wanted to vote for something slow and sensuous, preferably beginning with a long backrub. Jerri was ready for war.

"Tie me up," she demanded.

I dutifully found some scarves in Sandy's dresser. After securing Jerri on the bed I started in on her, taking care to dodge the snapping teeth. Afterwards, as I untied the last scarf, she growled, "Now you."

I soon found that bondage is liberating because it frees you from having to *do* anything. I was on my knees. Jerri started roughly, scratching my back and adding the occasional slap with one hand while with the other she stroked my penis. I had just resolved to beat her up at my earliest opportunity when she dove into my ass with her tongue. All was forgiven. She kept pumping me and I came with a shuddering, utterly satisfying orgasm.

"What are those marks on your back?" Sandy asked as I crawled, a broken man, into bed the next morning.

"Oh, you know. You get pretty wild sometimes," I answered vacantly.

"Wow! I didn't know I did *that*."

"It's okay," I generously replied. Naturally, I felt a little guilty about using her car and apartment, but I was not a shirker. My incredible luck at the beginning of the trip had turned into a Sisyphean ordeal. Was I doomed to fuck one girl all night only to find her place taken by another horny young woman by day? Would I have to invent increasingly fantastic explanations to cover up my "unfaithfulness"? Would I get bedsores?

I fled town the next day and for weeks turned a venomous eye to any overly friendly woman. I may have even been unfair to the teller at my bank. But now I'm beginning to wonder if I will ever get lucky again.

Girl Talk

*

THE EROTIC CONFESSIONS
OF A ROMANCE WRITER

By Susanna Beaulieu

I have good news: The Land of Happily-Ever-After does exist. It is a place where men are bold, brave and godlike in their strength and wisdom. Women, vulnerable and lovely, are their counterparts. They meet—electricity passes between them. Yes, there are complications, *sturm und drang*. But sooner or later they take that arm-in-arm stroll right into the sunset. It happens every time.

But I have bad news, too: Mostly, such happy endings occur in books. Romance books. Last year more than 200 million were sold. So lots of people do believe in a perfect-love-there's-a-right-man-for-every-woman world.

As one of the creators of these books, I have a confession to make. The stuff is strictly fiction. The last time a man took my breath away, he was driving the uptown bus and I just could not catch him in time.

Do romance writers create by reclining on chaise longues, wrapped in pink organdy gowns and nibbling chocolate truffles whilst spilling out passion-filled prose onto the dictation pads of young, lustful male secretaries? It never has been that way for me. I was neither popular nor conventionally pretty while growing up. My mother was harshly critical. At the age of five, when I developed a mind of my own, I stopped being Daddy's little girl. To keep myself amused I developed a skill for introspection and an observant eye. These were necessary survival skills that later merged and gave birth to a talent for fantasy. By thinking and writing down those thoughts, I could construct a perfect world where mothers adored their daughters, fathers were button-popping proud and beaus abounded. Even if I could not physically live in that world, it was my refuge during a lonely adolescence.

Then I grew up and fell in love. Alas, the romance was nothing like my well-constructed fantasies. The exigencies of real life, work and my lover's feelings were surprising intrusions. Lying in bed next to him, how often I wished I could write a script of passion and undying love for him to enact with me. But those words were only to be spoken by men I had created in books. *They* always knew when a woman needed to hear the "I love you" that heals, confirms and secures.

Even sex was a let-down. Could anything ever be so heady as making love in a tropical paradise with a bronzed stranger who had just saved my life? It happened in one of my books, with yours truly as the surrogate heroine.

In a way, though, I am lucky. I have two lives. When the real one disappoints me, I go back to that beach, cave or mountain top for another fix of Mr. Right who, unlike my friend Wayne, always knows just what a woman needs.

"Do you still like me?" Wayne asked, easing the car into gear and pulling away from our therapist's office.

At the first meeting with Phyllis, our couples counselor, Wayne and I had trotted out our enmity for one another in a most civilized and adoring way. An onlooker might even have mistaken us for characters in a romance novel, seeing Wayne touch his manicured, stockbroker fingers to my cheek and tenderly confide, "Susanna is a wonderful companion—emotionally, sexually and intellectually." Then reality vitiated romance as he added, "But I'm not sure I love her. Bells don't ring."

Although we were not married, four years of comfortable domesticity peppered with tears, walk-outs and angry silences had more than qualified us for these sessions. I merely wanted to get rid of the bad feelings, but I suspected Wayne was almost ready to get rid of me.

While we sat on the couch in Phyllis' office, Wayne's hands clasped lovingly around mine, the prosecution went to work. He revealed that, besides failing to play Quasimodo to my amour's chimes, I neglected to share his enthusiasm for sports. My crimes were these: I didn't like boxing; hated football; wouldn't even play catch in the park.

Guilty as charged, I admitted, not realizing that the way to Wayne's heart was, literally, through his balls.

"Perhaps you should take up a sport," ventured Phyllis.

I glared. "And perhaps you should stop dispensing the kind of advice even *Seventeen* magazine hasn't dared print in years. Don't quote *me* '10 Ways to Catch and Keep a Boy.' I used to write that stuff before I started selling romance novels. And frankly, the only time I break into sweat is when I can't meet a deadline."

Later, after Wayne and I got home, he repeated his question. "Like you, darling?" I echoed. "You know I *love* you." Although I spoke more out of practice than passion, it still took two to pay the rent, and I had no immediate plans to look for a new lover.

I headed for the typewriter to begin Chapter One of *Strangers on the Beach*, and to escape my aggravating Pele in pinstripes. I would start the book with another victim of love. Like me, she would know what it meant to suffer from a man's betrayal. But there would soon be another to soothe all that pain . . .

A harsh and frigid wind froze the tears on Vivianna Bartholomew's pale, beautiful face as she stared into the ebon sea. The high, tumultuous waves beckoned to her like fingers, coaxing her closer, closer. Above the roar of the taunting tides was the thudding of her own anguished heart and the mournful litany: If I cannot have love, then death I choose.

"Gregory!" She sobbed his name on the deserted beach. It was an epithet as well as a paean to the man who had loved her and then died before wedded bliss could entwine them. The tragedy of his death in the small, single-engine plane he piloted was agonizingly fresh yet incomprehensible to her. How can you press your lips to a man's mouth one moment and witness his death in flames the next?

Since Gregory had perished, then she must, too. Their union now would be one of death, not marriage. And now all that was left in this life was her lonely ceremony by the sea.

"Gregory." Her tone was softer now as she readied herself to yield to fate's dictum. "I'm coming to join you, darling. We'll soon be together again." Her determined footsteps brought her to the water's edge. The impervious tide washed around her small black

boots, yet she was numb to the cold, numb to all mortal feelings. Looking up at the sliver of moon, she awaited a sign that her betrothed was prepared to receive her.

A cloud passed in front of the sky's only source of light, and she took several resolute steps forward. Her wet skirt now clung to her body, revealing the curves more men than Gregory had noticed and admired.

"Miss! What do you think you're doing?" a male voice screamed from behind her.

Two strong arms began to pull at her, wrestling her from the water's grip. "Are you insane? Come out, you foolish woman!"

Vivianna struggled to be free of him, but in her weak and grieving state, she was no match for this man. He lifted her wet, frail form into his burly arms and began to carry her up, away from the sea, toward a cottage wherein a soft light shone.

Inside the wood-hewn edifice, he brought her blankets and tea. He was a large man with a brooding, dark mien, yet he moved gracefully in his familiar environment. As he took away the untouched tea from her shaking hands, their eyes met. His revealed something more than curiosity, something untamed, and it frightened her.

Quivering from the cold, she stood up and let the blanket slide from her shoulders. "I—I must go," she said.

Catlike, he strode to the exit, blocking her passage. "No, miss. I won't let you leave. Not yet." His lips were only inches from hers, and she cringed from the implicit threat they had issued.

I was in bed editing the pages I had written earlier. Wayne sat on the armchair nearby watching a baseball game on television, to my unspoken annoyance.

"Susanna, this is it. I've decided to move out. I'm just not happy. It's not going to work."

His announcement hardly took me by surprise. For an instant, I actually felt relief. I had known we were heading nowhere—yet I had come to treasure the journey. Being half of a couple was so cozy and safe—and I still did love Wayne. I was about to lose my lover, roommate and sustenance in one swoop.

I wanted to tell him no, he could not leave. But that would not stop him. I started to cry, then soon felt the weight of his body next to mine on the bed. Looking up I saw that he was crying, too.

"Telling you that was one of the hardest things I ever did."

"Hearing it was one of the hardest things *I* ever did."

"We'll still be friends—see each other, have dinner, talk on the phone, sleep together—if you want to," he said.

"Of course, that's what I want—I don't want you to leave at all."

"But I'm going to. I have to."

I fleetingly thought of offering to take tennis lessons, but I said nothing. That was not why Wayne was leaving. He loved me—but not enough. He cared about me, worried about how I fared—but not enough to stay. I wanted to shout that no relationship is perfect and that no person can be everything to another. Wayne had embraced some romantic ideal of togetherness and I was its victim.

"Hold me," I pleaded, hoping to stretch that moment to cover all the loneliness ahead. My cheek went to the spot on his shoulder where it had lain countless times. He hugged me and kissed my neck. I cried harder.

My hand moved down his body to caress him, and it was no different from the way we had always begun to make love. His fingers found my breasts inside my robe and cupped them. My body felt numb to the touch. Physically we were getting closer, but all I could think about was how soon he would be gone.

Our lovemaking was interrupted by tears and talking, but desire was missing. We went through the motions to reassure each other that we were beyond anger and above the pettiness of other couples.

"How soon will you go?" I asked.

"A couple of days. I found a nice apartment."

I curled into a ball on my side of the bed. Wayne got up to shut off the TV. The game was over. I was certain his team had won.

The next day, rereading the pages I had written the day before, I laughed at the irony. In *my* scheme of things, the heroine yearned to leave, but the wise hero stood in her way. Oh, why couldn't Wayne understand that the only reason lovers separate is so they can experience the sweetness of reuniting?

Vivianna's breasts rose as she took in a breath. The outline of her nipples was evident against her thin, wet sweater, and Nicholas' eyes rested there. "Step aside," she said.

He folded his arms across his wide chest and stood rooted to the bare wooden floor. "I won't let you go now."

"But I must leave!" she cried. "S—someone's waiting for me."

"There's not a soul on that beach," he stated, staring through

*the window. "A storm's coming up. If you go now in those wet
clothes, you'll fall ill. Stay the night here with me."*

*Vivianna glanced at the room's only bed and then at her insistent
host.*

*"Don't worry about that," he assured her. "I can sleep on the
floor." The wind howled around the small cabin, making it a lone
refuge in a frightening world.*

*Nicholas slipped a long robe off a hook near the door and handed
it to her. "Take those wet clothes off and wear this." Slowly her
hand reached for the garment. "Turn around, please," she said,
unanticipated tears filling her eyes. She stepped out of her skirt,
pulled her sweater over her head, and hung the items over the
bedpost. She slipped on the robe. Sobbing quietly, she sank into the
downy mattress and put her weary head in her hands.*

*He walked toward her slowly, instinctively aware that any quick
move might cause her to flee. Kneeling by the bed, he took her
small, childlike hand in his and whispered, "What makes you so
sad?"*

*She turned her face away from him. "Why did you have to find
me? Why couldn't you have left me alone to die?"*

*"So there was no one waiting for you on the beach," he con-
cluded, gingerly taking a place next to her on the bed. Compared
to her chill, the heat radiating from his body was like a fire.*

*"But there was," she insisted. Her tears came faster now, drip-
ping from her luminous eyes and down her cheeks.*

*"A companion to die with?" he replied, puzzled. "That's one
thing we all do alone, and I can't understand why a beautiful young
woman like you would want to do that now." He touched his finger
beneath her chin and made her look at him. In her eyes was a heart-
wrenching mixture of fright, sadness . . . perhaps even insanity.*

*"Let me hold you," he gently commanded. She did not resist
when his arms went around her narrow shoulders. Ever so slowly
she grew aware, in a not unpleasant way, of the warmth his body
brought.*

*Each time she sobbed, he held her tighter until her cries subsided.
Now in her eyes was a tired gratitude. His rough fingers caressed
her dark hair. "Perhaps there was a reason why I looked through
my window and saw you by the shoreline earlier," he mused. "Perhaps I was meant to save you." His lips pressed down on hers,
softly at first and then increasingly more forceful and hungry. In-*

*stinctively she responded by opening her mouth to his and savoring
the hot, full-bodied pleasure.*

*A moment later she abruptly stood. The robe fell open to reveal
her perfectly shaped breasts topped with nipples the color of pink
rosebuds. "You must not touch me!" she hissed, stepping backward,
away from him. "Gregory, dear God, Gregory, what is happening
to me. . . ."*

Shock. Denial. Anger. Acceptance. According to the latest literature on the subject of loss, those were the four emotional stages
following separation from a loved one. I was stuck somewhere
between shock and denial. I stayed at home in my nightgown and
cried. I talked on the phone to Wayne and cried more. I called my
friends and, in tears, bored them.

Meanwhile, the all-new, emotionally healthy, self-directed
Wayne was busy making a new life, furnishing his apartment and
getting plenty of physical and sexual exercise.

"But it didn't mean anything. Being with her was nothing like
being with you," he reported after his first sexual conquest. I took
the liberty of assuming that this statement was some sort of compli-
ment, although I would have phrased it much more elegantly. Something along the lines of: "My darling, I am *sick*, and just half a man
without you beside me. How my loins ache with desire for you."

To be fair, I had to admit that Wayne attempted to be supportive
and understanding. On several occasions, he responded to frantic
middle-of-the-night calls by coming over to hold me in his arms.
But soft words and tender assurances did little to quell my panic. I
did not want to be alone. I was alone all day, writing. And with
most of my advance payment for *Strangers on the Beach* already
spent on tissues and therapy, money was becoming a problem.

"Try to be positive," counseled Wayne and my 14 next-closest
friends. "You're young, attractive and successful. Not living with
a man, you will get that book finished much sooner."

I almost bought that—until Mother called from Florida. "As far
as I'm concerned, that Wayne ruined your life," pronounced the
peroxide sage. "Forget him and find someone else to marry."

"Haven't you heard a word I've said? I've spent the last six
weekends alone or annoying my women friends. That hardly qual-
ifies me for the bridal registry at Bloomingdale's."

"But you should get married," she replied, undeterred. "After
all, you need *someone* to take care of you."

My shrink and my friends thought otherwise. They wanted me to use Wayne's departure as a steppingstone to becoming a strong, independent, self-sufficient woman.

Crying, I went back to the typewriter. You want to see happy endings, Ma? Well, so do I, damn it! But the only one I can manufacture at the moment takes place between two people who only live in a book.

"I'm sorry," Nicholas said, looking up from the bed. "I never intended to force . . ."

"You never intended! What do I care what you intended—or even who you are?" Vivianna shrieked, her dark eyes flashing.

The chill she had felt was gone and now, in its place, was a fire of rage—at this stranger, at Gregory, at life itself for bringing her such loss and pain.

"My name is Nicholas Powers," he stated in quiet dignity. "And if I'm not mistaken, I've saved your life—for the time being, at least. So if I were you, young woman, I would lower my voice and show some appreciation."

Chastened, she grew quiet, yet a world of emotion was swirling inside her. "You don't know anything!" she protested. "My fiancé died less than 10 days ago. I've no parents, and no place to go. There is nothing left of my life."

"You're wrong," he murmured, slowly coming toward her. "You've got life itself. No need to rush death or run to its arms—it will take you soon enough. Only a coward—or a scared child—would make such an irrational choice."

"Perhaps I am both," she whispered.

"Then let me be your strength," he earnestly beseeched. "I live alone and have little money, but I offer you my home and all that I have."

This time it was Vivianna who brought her face close to the stranger's, her eyes begging for a kiss. Nicholas complied, his arms reaching out to embrace her. She began to tremble, but this time it was neither fear nor cold that motivated her—it was desire. It was life.

"That's good. Thanks for showing it to me," Phyllis declared, handing the manuscript pages back to me. "I like happy endings."

I shrugged. "It's required."

Her soft, blue-gray eyes assessed me. "When are you going to admit the real reason why you write these romance novels? I know—you write well and it's an easy way for you to make a living. But why do you choose to write these kinds of books?''

I drew in a breath and looked at her. ''Because I still believe in love, romance and passion. God, I'm embarrassed to admit that.''

We both laughed. Then she said, ''If you believe it's there, maybe it is. So why don't you begin to let go of Wayne and try to find those things with someone else? Not because your mother says so, not because you can't care for yourself, but because you feel it will enrich your life.''

''And even if it doesn't,'' I added, ''at least I'll have some new material to work with.''

I FALL FOR BASTARDS

By Natasha Sarnoff

I remember the precise moment I stopped having affairs with bastards and switched to men who were good for me and I'm going to tell you why I did it and how it changed my life. I didn't stop dating rotten men because I had a fabulous insight in therapy, been to est, lost every member of my family in a plane crash or gone to India to work for the Peace Corps and seen the light. No. My conversion came about because I couldn't get in to see *Annie Hall* in a Manhattan movie theater on a Saturday night in August. It was the sixth day of a record heat wave and I got to the box office right after the last ticket had been sold. I was real upset even though I had already seen the movie.

The reason I was left to wander the scorched streets of Manhattan was a creep named Marvin Goldman. If that doesn't sound like a name you would ordinarily associate with a bastard, that is exactly the point I'm going to make.

I was once asked by a man why rotten men get the best women and nice guys have trouble scoring (at least that's what he observed). If anyone else is considering going into the bastard business, let me say that bastards are not what you expect them to be. They are

definitely not mean, macho, insulting or ostensibly cruel. The true
bastard, the guy born to the role, the one who can really hurt you,
is usually a very nice human being with a name like Marvin, Harvey
or Clifford.

My Marvin, the bastard who forever changed the course of my
sexual destiny, was not wearing a black leather jacket, boots, or a
Hell's Angel's t-shirt when I met him at a party, nor did he walk
with a swagger. He was standing on the fringe of a lawn party in
Southampton in a pair of blue jeans, white Adidas and an alligator
shirt. He looked shy, ill at ease and frightened. A few inches shorter
than I, he had a sunburn that made him look like a strawberry ice
cream cone with glasses. I returned his "Hi" because I felt sorry
for him and thought he was grateful to me for answering him.

Marvin wasn't rare. Before Marvin I'd known other bastards who
were not only shy but capable of acts of generosity and gentleness
you'd never expect from a rat. They genuinely wanted to make me
happy. Lloyd made love to me as if I were a piece of fragile crystal,
parting my legs and licking my clitoris so softly that it was like
being aroused by a butterfly—though he knew when to metamor-
phose into a man.

Terry liked to raise my t-shirt, free my breasts and circle my
nipples with his fingers as if he were worshipping at a shrine. He
also wrote poetry. It is very easy for a normal woman to fall in love
with a bastard because he is usually warm, loving, vulnerable and,
at first, emotionally accessible. Often what he gives her is something
she could not get anywhere else.

But I wasn't thinking about all this when I returned Marvin Goldman's "Hi." I was thinking of how to get away from him. It was
the first singles' party of the season. I had rented an alternate share
in a group house and hoped to meet someone. Marvin Goldman
was not what I had in mind.

"So do you come here often?" he asked.

"No," I said, deadpan. "This is my first time."

"Me, too," he said. "I have a friend who comes here all the
time. He said he met some fascinating people here."

"No kidding," I replied. "Like who?"

"Oh," he shrugged, "Lauren Hutton . . . Christie Brinkley . . .
Golda Meir. He liked Golda Meir the best but her career was too
much. Israel this! PLO that! I mean he's not a male chauvinist pig
at all. He thinks women should work. But there are limits."

"So what happened?"

"They decided to be friends. In fact, he flew over for her funeral and felt lousy for months. He thought maybe he had been too demanding. Perhaps if he'd been a little more giving they could have made it."

"He shouldn't blame himself. You can't change your basic nature."

"I guess you're right," he grinned. I grinned. His sunburned cheeks glowed.

"So listen," he said. "What's your sign?"

I saw Marvin Goldman twice that week and twice the next. Two weeks after we met, on my next alternate weekend, we made it together on a blanket in the dunes. It was not a passionate, romantic occasion with me ripping off a pair of bikini panties soaking wet with the juices of my desire. I liked Marvin. He made me laugh. But he did not turn me on. However, I'd been out with him six times and it was now or never. Marvin may have come on like a nebbish, but he was not a jerk. I could either fuck him or lose him. I didn't want the latter.

And so I slipped off my jeans and dry underwear and lay beneath Marvin while his thin, short body in its pale, freckled skin writhed on top of mine. The best thing about the sex was that it didn't last long. And only after it was over did I begin to fall for him. The bastard rolled off me, put on his glasses, pushed them up the rim of his nose with his finger, propped his chin in the palm of his hand and said, "That was the worst sex I ever had."

"No kidding," I exclaimed. "Worse than the first time?"

"A lot worse. The first time at least I was curious. This time I knew how it was going to turn out."

"Worse than Miriam Skolnick?" (Miriam weighed 207 pounds. He had told me about her.)

"A thousand times worse than Miriam Skolnick. At least I was doing a good deed with her. I felt charitable. I could have taken it as a tax deduction."

"Worse than all the women you were angry with, hated, couldn't say no to, but didn't want to do it with?"

"Worse than every single one of them," he answered solemnly. "Of all the lousy lays I've ever had," he went on, looking at me tenderly, "you were the worst."

I began to feel a stirring of desire. Who can explain it? "Do you really mean that?" I asked. "You're not kidding me?"

"I swear," he said. "You take the cake. You are the rottenest fuck I ever had in my life."

A warm rush went up through my thighs and I moved closer to him.

"Are you sure? Absolutely sure?"

"Positive," he whispered softly. "Without a doubt."

We were both grinning now. I pulled off my sweat shirt, which I'd left on during our amorous encounter, and pressed myself to him. My nipples were hard, my hands roamed his body. I ran my tongue over flesh that five minutes earlier I'd managed only to tolerate. I moved past his stomach toward his groin.

"Are you serious?" he said. "What do you think I am, Superman? I haven't been able to do that since I was 20."

"If I'm the worst lay you ever had," I said mischievously, "who knows what other records we might break? I'll take my chances."

I licked his thighs, balls and limp penis, then took him in my mouth and swirled my tongue around his glans. As I kissed the base of his cock where it sprouted from stiff, wiry red hair, I felt a flicker of interest, but I wasn't sure.

"Well, what do you know?" I said.

"Don't get cocky," he replied. "It means nothing."

I kept working. He began to moan. "Oh God," he cried. "Oh God. Oh God." He became erect. Mounting him, I galloped, his body arching to meet mine, my buttocks slapping against his thighs.

The night air was chilly, but we were damp with sweat. Marvin was grinning wildly as I pounded on top of him. His hands wandered over my body and cupped my ass. I came and fell on him. Moments later he rolled me over and began to fuck me. His eyes were closed and his head flung back. Finally he shuddered, then slumped on top of me. I pulled the blanket over his shoulders.

"Am I still the worst lay you ever had?" I inquired.

"Not that time," he answered. "That time you were the best."

"The best?" I repeated. "You don't really mean that?"

"You're right," he admitted. "You weren't really the best. I was just being nice. But the first time you were definitely the worst, and the second time you were really good."

"Who was the best?"

"Kathleen O'Dougherty. My uncle's bookkeeper. We used to do it on the back stairs of his clock company in Fall River. She was the best. I'm sorry," he said. "But you were definitely the worst."

"I believe you," I whispered tenderly. "I'm glad you told me the truth. I trust you now."

There was an uncomfortable pause—the kind of pause that is the identifying mark of the bastard. A chill wind blew on the beach. I looked at him, waiting.

"Don't trust me," he murmured.

Another pause. I knew what I had heard.

"Why not?"

"Just don't."

He rolled off me. The moment passed. I could have pretended that it never happened. Marvin put on his glasses, propped his chin in his hand and asked, "So what's your sign?" Could such a person be a bastard?

I began spending weekends at Marvin's, where he had a full share and only two roommates instead of eight. We made it together often; in the dunes at night, on a sailboat in Gardners Bay, and in Marvin's bedroom, which opened onto a deck with a view of the ocean. During the week we ate dinner together in town and went to the movies. (I'm a school teacher and was off for the summer.) One of the movies we saw was *Annie Hall*.

"You remind me of Woody Allen," I told him after the movie. We were walking up Third Avenue toward Marvin's apartment. "You're funny like he is, confused and sort of shy. You even look a little like him. Just a little bit."

"Women have told me that before," he informed me. There was another one of those pauses. I was getting better at ignoring these long moments.

"Especially about the confused part," he added.

There was another pause. Mine. And then I asked, "What do you mean confused? How?"

"I get scared. I run. I don't want to. I feel like a louse. But things get to a certain point and then I have to cut out. My shrink tells me I'm not a little boy anymore, but so far I haven't stopped."

"Will you do it to me?"

"I hope not," he responded. "I like you. Sometimes I think I even love you."

"Sometimes I think I love you too," I confessed.

"Don't," he warned. "Just don't."

"Why not?" I asked. I knew the answer but felt exasperated. "We have so much fun together. And we have great sex. So why not?"

"You said yourself. I'm confused."

That night I made love to Marvin more passionately than ever before, as though I were trying to blot out his confusion. But in the weeks that followed, we discussed his problem with increasing frequency. He told me about all the women he had left and how he did not want to spend his life "going from woman to woman." Sometimes his eyes filled up with tears. But by late August it became apparent he was not going to change. One Sunday night at the end of the weekend Marvin dropped me at my apartment and said, "I'd like us not to see each other for a while. I have to get my head together."

"What about next weekend?" I pleaded wistfully.

"Let's not."

"But it's not even my alternate weekend," I joked. "Besides, I was going to tell you my sign."

"Please," he said. "Don't."

I waited all week for the phone to ring and it didn't. I couldn't believe it. We had made love on the beach, gone sailing and cooked lobsters. By Saturday I had to see him. I took a train to Southampton, planning all the way how to tell him I would live with his confusion. He could stop seeing me for a few days every month. When I arrived at the house Marvin was leaving for the beach with a French designer we had met at a party. Marvin turned red and said, "Hi." At least he had the grace to look ashamed.

"I was just in the neighborhood," I said, "and wanted to pick up my hair dryer."

I caught the next train back to New York. En route I saw in the papers that *Annie Hall* was playing at the Festival Theater. I decided to go because Woody Allen would remind me of Marvin. The city was a steaming canyon, but when I reached the Festival it looked as if every human being in town had come to see the movie. The last ticket was sold just as my turn came. So I stood on 57th Street feeling worse than I had in a long time. At that moment it occurred to me that Marvin Goldman was a bastard. It made no difference that he was confused, shy, scared, neurotic or hated doing what he had done. He was a creep. As long as I permitted people like him a foothold in my life I would be at the mercy of their confusion. Marvin had screwed up my weekend for me and it was his fault that I did not get to see *Annie Hall*.

Since then I've stayed away from people who didn't seem to

know what they wanted. Two years later I married my husband Hal, who has never been confused for more than 10 minutes, and that was in the hospital, when he was given a large dose of Demerol after his hernia operation.

LOUSY LOVERS: A REPAIR MANUAL

By Christina Tagliari

The other day I had lunch with my girlfriend Sheila. Quickly dispensing with the preliminaries—jobs and families—we moved on to more important topics—men and sex. Sheila mentioned that our mutual friend Felicia had broken up with David whom I had once dated.

"Felicia said he was cheap and a lousy fuck," cracked Sheila.

I was surprised. David was a tightwad all right, but a lousy fuck he was certainly not. In my arms he was a sensuous, passionate and energetic lover. On trips to the country David brought along massage oils, leather whips, velvet ropes and a stack of erotic novels. In short he was a splendid fuck—like most of the men in my sex life. Not wishing to appear boastful, I kept my recollection of David the Swell to myself. If I had been totally honest, I would have told Shelia that I had never had a bad lover, that is, not for long.

When I was in my early twenties, I was pretty wayward. My friend Arlene and I dressed up in evening gowns and went to Philadelphia's snazziest hotel.

In the cocktail lounge we ordered daiquiries, hoping to lure some wealthy businessmen on expense accounts. A handsome pair quickly claimed us. We had a few laughs and were soon persuaded to go upstairs with Herb and Andrew to get stoned.

They shared a room with two double beds. Herb passed around a joint and immediately went to town on my body. Not unexpectedly Arlene had her hands full on the other bed. The moment Herb's mouth touched my cunt, I came—again and again, in my usual multiple fashion. A few minutes later I heard Arlene's meek little orgasm. Andrew came quickly and rolled off Arlene. But Herb kept pounding away on top of me for another 10 minutes. Then we all switched. I reacted the same way with Andrew. He had a thick, hard cock that he used adeptly. "You're so goddamn sexy," he whispered hoarsely.

The next morning after a room-service breakfast, Arlene and I quit the premises. Walking home, we compared notes. "That Andrew was really lame," she griped sourly. "He could hardly even keep a hard-on!"

Apparently, Arlene has endured many similar disappointments at the hands of men. Even though she is more attractive than I, with long, honey-blonde hair and cover-girl looks, I get far more satisfaction. I think our sexual styles make all the difference. She expects men to perform for her, whereas I *challenge* men to prove themselves.

Once a friend dragged me to a feminist consciousness-raising session. Many of the women present were attractive, even sexy. But when the topic of male performance arose, the majority castigated men as selfish boors concerned only with their own pleasure. "The day I meet a man who doesn't just want to put it in and come," groused an olive-skinned dancer, "is the day I throw away my vibrator." Her comment gained a round of applause.

My heart pounding, I raised my hand. "If women could only teach men to be perfect lovers . . . ," I started to say. But I was booed into silence. These foolish women did not want to hear about rehabilitation. They preferred to let their drippy faucets drip.

If they had let me speak, I would have spelled out my ten rules for fixing lousy lovers. And here they are:

1. I never play games with myself. I do not pretend that a dinner date will conclude with a good-night kiss. I allow for the possibility that every encounter will end up in bed. So I come prepared—impeccably clean, smelling sweet and carrying my diaphragm in my pocketbook.

2. I take great care of myself. Being a desirable sex object is extremely important to me. Exercise keeps my body firm and muscles toned. I also lavish attention on my skin to make it smooth and soft. I want men to like touching me.

3. The environment and accoutrements of lovemaking are crucial. My apartment is always clean. I light candles, dim lights, put satin sheets on the beds. I dress in lingerie and utilize vibrators,

K-Y jelly, massage oils and whatever else will enhance the experience.

4. I frankly appraise men as potential lovers. If I am attracted to a man, I immediately fantasize about him as a lover. I am curious about the size and shape of his cock. If he seems uptight, rigid or unimaginative, I do not encourage our friendship. The qualities I admire are a good physique, self-awareness, intelligence, intensity and humor. Body language is always revealing. And I like to share a meal with a man before he eats me. If he is blasé about food, or dumps salt on his steak before tasting it, I suspect that he is equally crude as a lover.

5. The role of sexual aggressor suits me just fine. When I am interested in a man, I call him up, ask him out and in general pursue him. I do not sit around waiting by the phone for calls that will never materialize.

6. I disassociate my ego from lovemaking. My aim is mutual satisfaction. If a man hints that I am sucking him too eagerly, or stroking too passionately, I immediately accommodate him. In fact, I often inquire beforehand about how he likes to be licked, touched and kissed.

7. I say sexy things. A man gets incredibly excited when he hears me whisper, "I'd like to sit on your face and come all over your mouth."

8. I give guidance when necessary. If a man is licking my clit too hard, I tactfully tell him to ease up. Most men respond favorably to this kind of openness.

9. I will experiment with anything that does not cause serious physical pain.

10. I come a lot. I am multi-orgasmic and have long, sensuous, expressive orgasms. Men usually try to give me as many as they can.

Some men do not rate a "10" or even an "8" during our first encounter. But if a lover seems willing to please, I give him another chance. A majority of males are nervous the first time they make love to a different woman.

John was typical. We met at a rock-and-roll club. A videotape editor, he was very poised, handsome and self-assured. We danced and he charmed me with his sense of humor. Afterward we shared a few lines of coke. The sexual tension between us was hot and highly electric.

We closed the club. John suggested that we leave together. After a visit to an all-night diner, we decided on my place. In the taxi, John kissed me. I was disappointed. He had a small, stubby tongue and he scarcely pushed it into my mouth.

"We'll get down to some real kissing later," I thought. Once in my apartment, I put on a reggae tape. The sexy, sensuous beat may have annoyed my neighbors at 5 A.M., but it turned me on. We huddled together on my couch and did some more lines.

This time I took the initiative in kissing John. Thrusting my tongue deeply into his mouth, I tried to excite him. But he still did not respond. I wondered whether I had misjudged his potential as a lover simply because he looked sexy.

"Let's go to bed," I whispered.

He hesitated, then followed me. Though dawn was coming in, I lit lots of candles. They cast an exotic glow around the room. When he began tearing off my clothes, I felt disappointed. He was depriving himself of the pleasure of admiring my breasts encased in a black lace teddy.

After some brief but skillful foreplay, John penetrated me. He did not perform cunnilingus. We fucked. He rolled over and fell asleep soon after.

His performance showed all the signs of first-night nervousness. I decided that if he was to be upgraded from a "7" to a "10," I would have to take the initiative.

A few days later I invited him over for dinner on a Friday night. This gave us the opportunity to sleep late the next day. I prepared a five-course Italian dinner. John brought wine and champagne. Both of us enjoyed the meal immensely. For dessert John lit up a joint. Afterward we drifted toward the bedroom. As we embraced, I whispered, "Let's do this nice and slow, okay?" We kissed.

"Kiss me deeper," I requested. He stuck his tongue an inch deeper into my mouth.

"No, deeper, deeper," I urged.

Soon we were engaged in a passionate, earthy kiss—the necessary preliminary to a great fuck.

"Do you mind if I take off my clothes?" I asked coyly. He laughed. In the dim candlelight, I slowly stripped for him. When he saw my garter-belt and black stockings, he moaned with delight.

"You're so sexy," he murmured.

"And I want you to really give it to me," I replied. "I want you to fuck me all night long." I unzipped his stiff cock and took it into my mouth.

Only a wimp would refuse such a challenge. John performed admirably and has remained a lover for more than a year—one of many.

But my girlfriends are still complaining about their Mr. Wrongs.

A Fly on the Locker-Room Wall

*

THE PROFESSOR OF SEX

By Jack Martin

Whenever I hear stories about coeds trading sex for grades I have to laugh. I have taught for 12 years at various colleges around the country and talked to dozens of colleagues about making it with students—and guess what? Few of us would even think of risking our careers by bartering bodies for grade points. Why should we? Getting laid on campus is more a matter of selection than seduction.

A lot of good old-fashioned romance and affection springs up between a student and a teacher. With men and women both interested in the same subject and spending a lot of time together, inevitably some of them are going to fall in love. I know. I've been there—often.

Perhaps the odds favor those of us who teach creative writing. We have more reason than our colleagues in the sciences to sit over coffee and bare our secret hopes and deepest feelings. The kind of soul-talk that ordinarily grows *out* of sexual intimacy can also grow *into* it.

The first day of class in September or January is always special. By the end of that session I have had enough suggestive eye contact with two or three students to know that my only problem is to separate the mere teaser from the serious pleaser. The former have come on to me in class or in my office with as much subtlety as your average B-girl. Wanna buy me a Coke, *professor*? Wink, wink.

Take them up on it and these teasers plead total innocence. Or they write nasty editorials about sexual harassment in the campus newspaper.

During my first semester at the Midwestern university where I now teach, I was sleeping with a female student from *each* of my three creative writing classes. In two instances I was the initiator, but in the third I was chosen. While walking back to my office after a brief, get-acquainted lecture I felt a tap on my shoulder. A tough-looking, street-wise girl from the class asked what my sun sign was. I told her. She nodded. "I thought so," she said and gave me hers.

"Don't you know what that means?" she asked as we continued walking. "Those signs are a dynamite sexual combination. If you and I have an affair, which I expect we'll do before the semester ends, it'll be *fantastic*."

"I don't really believe in astrology," I informed her, hoping she was not as dumb as she sounded.

She smiled as I pulled out my keys to open the office door.

"But," she inquired sweetly, "do you believe in affairs?"

What could I do? I let her in ahead of me and locked the door. I've had some fast approaches from students before, but this one took my breath away, it was so totally unexpected.

As soon as I got inside, she turned and I slipped my arms around her, pulling her close, running my hand down to her firm, blue-jeaned buttocks. She'd looked almost tom-boyish sitting in my classroom. But as she pressed against me in a long, hungry kiss, I knew right away she had a voluptuous figure.

I ran a hand up underneath her sweatshirt and was pleased to find she wasn't wearing a bra. Her breasts were large and her nipples became erect as soon as I touched them. She undulated her hips against me and began pulling her jeans off.

We separated for a moment so I could drop my trousers and clear a space on the edge of my desk. In a moment she was naked from the waist down and sitting among my papers, breathing hard and staring at my stiff cock as it popped out of my shorts.

"God," she whispered, "I'm glad we didn't have to play games all semester. We could have wasted so much time."

I moved close and she seized my cock in one hand, squeezing it hard.

"I want to fuck you this time," she said, guiding me into her cunt. "But next week I'm going to give you the sincerest blowjob you've ever had in your life."

Two students walked by the door, talking about a literature assignment. In the office across the way one of my colleagues was pounding on his old manual typewriter. The 19-year-old girl on my desk lay back among my scattered papers and wrapped her legs around my hips as I thrust into her. Here I was fucking someone, and I didn't even know her name! But I sensed that this was not the proper time to ask.

Never before or since have I made love to a woman within half an hour of meeting her. Most students are far less aggressive, although a shy, good-looking friend of mine seems to bring out the boldness in his Texas coeds. One simply drew him a naked picture of herself, added her phone number, wrote "Would you like to see the real thing?" and included it with her short story. He even gets calls at home from amorous women.

More often I run into women students who ask to see me after my regular hours ("when you are less likely to be disturbed") or after an evening class ("to go over my story in depth"). Or they invite me to dinner before my evening class. Not infrequently, they submit poems and short stories with characters who seem a lot like me and a lot like her. And the characters are making love in unusual places, like offices or seedy little apartments in which "she" and "I" discover unlimited sexual fulfillment.

Students who write such *roman à clef* stories can often cause their professors a few hair-raising moments. I will never forget the night a fellow writing professor brought a short story over to my place to read after dinner. He was agitated. It seems that a pretty student had written about a tender love affair with an older writer, presumably a teacher. And the apartment she described, although not precisely like his, was what a writer would have around him. "I think," he confided, raising his eyebrows, "she's trying to tell me something."

My wife said she would like to hear the story as soon as she finished making the coffee. While she was in the kitchen I suggested to my colleague what I'd do to him with a steak knife if he read the manuscript. That "apartment" was my off-campus study. We talked football all through coffee and my wife finally said, "I guess I'm not going to hear the story, am I?" She shrugged philosophically.

"It's about a student-teacher affair," I shrugged. "You don't want to hear about things like that. It makes you feel suspicious."

"I'm suspicious about what happened when I was out in the kitchen."

"See?" I exclaimed. "Even mentioning a story like that gets you upset. I just hate to add to the myth. Everyone thinks teachers are trying to jump in bed with their students all the time and it's just not *true*."

Not entirely true. And not entirely a matter of males chasing coeds. A female professor I knew was so angry at her husband for spending his sabbatical at a faraway writers' colony that she systematically fucked every willing male student in three different classes. And when she finished off the kids, she started hitting on single male colleagues.

The sad thing about the story that almost got read over dinner was that the girl who wrote it had left me for another student. And getting through the rest of the semester, trying to smile and not notice the two of them leaving together, was almost unbearable.

Once I fell into a serious discussion at a conference for English teachers regarding the likeliest courses that get one laid. There was a certain amount of bragging, but we came to the same conclusions. Literature was the worst. Essay writing was okay. But the best was fiction and poetry writing. Upper division poetry seminars were absolutely tops. Several of those present immediately decided to revise their fall teaching plans.

Since then I have discovered that evening magazine writing courses do at least as well as poetry. Magazine writing attracts mostly women, including several divorcées and bored housewives looking for something interesting to do—and someone interesting to do it with. One such woman was Susan, a copywriter in a local advertising agency, who invited me out for a drink after class. Over a beer she complained about the difficulty of meeting men, the general horniness of women over 30 and the limited sexual opportunities available to them.

"Well," I assured her, running my hand up the arm of her expensive silk blouse and patting her lightly on the shoulder, "maybe you'll meet someone in class."

She slipped off a shoe and ran her toes up the inside of my leg, softly kneading my groin as the waitress came by and picked up our empty bottles.

"How would you like a ride to your car?" she asked when the waitress went away.

Susan was tall and slender with small, sharp breasts, the kind that are visible only in certain positions so that you end up watching for that moment when they suddenly made a delicate imprint on her blouse. She had long, dark hair and was always shaking her head to make it fall in different ways over her shoulders. I loved her hair the first time she walked into class. But, as I was to discover, I was going to love it even more for what she could do with it. We went to her car, which was parked in a deserted lot high above the sidewalk.

"I can't wait to see your cock," she whispered, sliding the front seat back. It was a mild night and I eased out of my sports coat. She didn't start the car, but instead asked me to take my pants off. I didn't argue. A minute later I was squirming bare-assed on the slick vinyl seat, my trousers down around one ankle. We hadn't even kissed. She sat behind the wheel for a moment, smiling down at my limpness.

"You're not aroused?" she queried playfully. "What's the matter? It doesn't like me?"

"I think I may be too uncomfortable to have a hard-on," I answered. After all, I told myself, we didn't kiss, I hadn't touched her, this was all very sudden, I was very nervous about having my pants off with her sitting there still dressed. I could have thought up more excuses, but she was suddenly on her knees with her tongue deftly licking the head of my now very interested organ.

"We'll see about that," she murmured, flicking her tongue over my cock tip and turning her head swiftly from side to side so that her hair began to trail over my thighs. I was boulder hard in seconds.

"Ummmm," she sighed, kneading my ass with one hand while with her other she swirled her hair over my cock and balls. "Is this good?" she asked and I groaned. Moving her head back and forth, she brushed that wonderful dark hair up my thigh, over my cock, up my belly and back down the other leg. She whipped me with her hair three or four times in succession and then plunged her mouth down over my cock and began sucking as though she meant to draw marrow. Running her tongue crazily in and around and under with each stroke, she used her free hand to drop a cascade of hair onto my balls and slowly, deliciously, pull it away.

As I came she popped me out of her mouth and jerked me off

by hand so that my come spurted over her face and the seat and—especially—into that dark mane of hair.

"I hope we can do this again sometime," she said as we drove the three blocks to my car. We did. In her car. In my car. In her apartment and on a hillside above and, of course, in my office.

I don't know why most students, insist that we do it at least once in the office, no matter how near my apartment is. I've made love to maybe 40 or 50 students in the last 10 years, some only once, others often, but nearly every one has ended up on my desk or flat on the floor, or on top of an air mattress (which I keep in my office closet along with a pillow and blanket), sitting in the swivel chair, standing against the office door or kneeling in front of me as I sit at my desk. Office blowjobs are obviously the easiest way to have quickie sex, especially if I'm between classes.

I have no illusions about the purpose I serve for many women. I'm grist for the mill, experience, something to write about. This is not conjecture, but fact. Several have told me so.

One student, when we went to a "no-tell motel" rentable by the hour, actually brought a notepad and wrote down details. "Smell of mildew and disinfectant. Air conditioner noisy. Long blue dress, sexy bra and panties. Him: Harris tweed, blue shirt, olive tie. Leaves wristwatch on table, in ashtray. He's done this before, you can tell."

She showed me her notes only about the room, though. I never got to read them after dropping her off at the dorm. "Don't worry," she murmured. "If you turn up as a chapter in my book I'll change your appearance and name."

Other women just want to check off one more category of sex partner. "Sure, girls, I made it with a professor back when I was in college. Don't tell me you didn't?"

But one teacher's pet stands out. She came to see me for all the reasons I list above, and for a better one. She was in love with me and, for a time, I was in love with her. But she was 29 and wanted to start a family. I was nearly twice her age and wondered if I could make it through the last few years of raising my own. Ultimately, we knew our affair would have to end.

Her name was Kirsten and she was a redhead with startling green eyes and a lovely body. When she wore her glasses she looked like a librarian above the neck and a Penthouse Pet below. The first time I saw her I thought she was a teaser. She came to all of the poetry readings and flirted with most of the male teachers. One night she flirted with me and, since we were off in a side corridor, I slipped my arm around her waist, kissed her and then waited to see her reaction. I don't know what else to do with teasers.

"Let's go to your office," she suggested. Classes were over for the day, the building was deserted and I looked forward to it. But all she wanted to do was kiss, which she did very sincerely and expertly. When I put her hand on my cock, she pulled away. "I don't know you, not really, not yet," she protested. "I have to get used to you."

She was so incredibly attractive, she smelled and felt so good, she kissed so passionately, that I decided to give her three days. And at the end of it, I was in pain. "This is not a line," I complained, "not a game. *I have blue balls.* I am too old to have blue balls. At 19 I would make out with you for a month and not complain. Now I'm a grownup and necking has lost its charm—charming as you yourself are. So if you want to make love to me, don't make me talk you into it or somehow seduce you. Take some responsibility. Come back here and ask like a grownup. Otherwise don't come back at all—unless it's for class someday as a student."

I watched her walk away without saying a word. When she was gone, I collapsed into a groaning, miserable heap. What if she didn't come back? I would go crazy!

Two days later she returned. "Where will we go when we make love," she asked, "and how would you like it to be the first time? Don't you think it should be special?"

I told her I would tie her naked to a bed, play with her breasts and cunt, kiss her, let her suck my cock, rub her everywhere until she couldn't stand it anymore and then, only when she begged me to put it inside her, would I fuck her.

She stood for a moment, staring at me. I wondered if I had overplayed my hand, if she would run screaming down the hall or hit me. Finally she smiled. "What will you use to tie me up with?"

For a semester and a half, until her fiancé came back from his stint in the Peace Corps and married her, Kirsten and I made love all over that campus. We met in empty classrooms, lecture halls, secluded benches, the roof of the science building, between stacks in the library, the elevator of the student union and, best of all, in my office. We played out every fantasy about student and teacher that we could think of. Once Kirsten was walking down the hall and I grabbed her, dragged her into the office, shut the door and pushed her against the file cabinet.

"Why, *Professor*, whatever are you doing?" she cried.

"You little prickteaser." I grabbed her face in both hands and kissed her roughly. "I'm going to fuck you."

"No," she whimpered. I shoved her on the floor, driving my hand up under her dress, throwing my weight on top of her, covering her mouth with one hand. She struggled, but not too hard. Kirsten could probably have broken away easily, but that was another game. In this game Kirsten, the sexy little coed picktease, was getting what she really wanted all along.

I let go of her mouth as my hand closed on her crotch and my fingers worked in under her panties.

"Oh, my God," she exclaimed. "Oh, Professor, *please* don't do this."

I yanked her panties down and unzipped my pants, pulling out my cock and grabbing her hand, forcing her to touch it.

"I'm going to fuck you now, baby, I'm going to put my dick right up inside that hot little pussy of yours and fuck you good."

"Please, Professor, no . . ." We fought, but a moment later I had buried my cock deep in her cunt. "Please," she begged. I pinned her arms to the floor and fucked her deep and hard, holding both wrists with one hand and rubbing her breasts roughly with the other. I came, grunting and moaning, triumphant.

She also liked me to tell her she was flunking, and force her to give me a blowjob. Or she would love to sit beside me at my desk and seduce me.

Occasionally the phone would ring while we were fucking, and I'd move to my office chair and she'd straddle it, a leg on each arm of the chair, so she could raise and lower her pelvis on my cock, leaving my hands free for the phone and message-taking. I talked to my wife, other students, the chairman and my colleagues dozens of times while Kristen slowly fucked me in the swivel chair or sat under my desk, contentedly sucking my engorged cock.

When her boyfriend was due to come back, and with the semester at end, we had one last day together. We spent it in my office with a sign on my door that said: "No hours today, leave papers in faculty mailbox." We lay naked on the rug as the sunlight poured through my upperfloor window, licking each other, screwing very slowly, kissing, holding each other and saying goodbye and good luck. When she left I found a card on my desk that thanked me for teaching her more than she expected about things that really mattered.

Teachers learn from students and students from teachers. And often we end up making love. And it has damn little to do with grades. I have 25 years of teaching ahead of me and I'm looking forward to every golden year of it. As they say in the profession, all you need is one good student in each class to make the job worthwhile. And I've sure as hell had that.

THE DEFLOWERING OF A LESBIAN STRIPPER

By Clark Gristus

Terri, a delicate, attractive 24-year-old woman, straddled me and guided my penis into her vagina. Then she rocked mechanically back and forth on her hips. From the beginning of foreplay her lovemaking had been passive almost to the point of disinterest. I was incredulous. The last place I had expected to find prosaic sex was in a stripper's bed.

I was a rock musician on tour. Earlier that evening a mutual friend had introduced me to Terri in the Houston nightclub where I was playing.

"I'm not an exotic dancer," Terri informed me. "I'm a stripper." She affected a world-weary, matter-of-fact monotone. But occasionally when recounting a bizarre detail in her life story—how her agent doublecrossed her or how a girlfriend had been murdered—she would suddenly burst into a giggle. And I would smile back to show that I sympathized with her often harrowing line of work.

Naturally, I found her lovemaking later that night not only lackluster but incongruous. Terri made her living as sexbomb April Magnolia. Yet she was a bad fuck. While performing she was ogled by sleazy businessmen and horny truckdrivers. Afterward she circulated among the crowd, inviting men to share a bottle of champagne with her in a back room for $50. I naively assumed that Terri would welcome uninhibited recreational sex as a change of pace.

Terri's place was off limits. Whenever she was in town a middle-aged man put her up for a few weeks so long as she occasionally slept with him. So we went to bed at her girlfriend's apartment.

Drawing Terri toward me, I nipped at a breast while reaching down to play with her clitoris. Her body was lithe and athletic, though uncannily white, as if untouched by sunlight. Delicately pink, hard nipples crowned her small breasts. My erection reasserted itself as my fingers ran through her tuft of pubic hair. I wanted her even more when I realized she shaved the edges of her cunt to make it look attractive on stage. I was sucking on a breast that thousands of men paid just to look at.

Yet her vagina was not wet. Her dry labia bunched up as I ran my finger along them. Cupping some saliva with my fingers, I slid a finger into her, then gently rubbed her clitoris with my thumb. But I observed no twitch of excitement and heard no soft moan of pleasurable enjoyment.

Terri's unresponsiveness was confusing. She had suggested that we spend the night together. She had also smiled mischievously and grabbed my erect penis while I was undressing. Now she seemed to be only enduring what she had precipitated. I felt both seduced and unwanted at the same time.

I mounted her and we screwed almost cursorily. Terri clung to me, but her fingernails did not dig. She moved her hips in rhythm with mine, but her head barely moved. Her snug vagina remained fairly dry thoughout. Mercifully, I came before long. "This isn't exotic," I thought. "This is like being married."

Afterward we lay together on the bed, neither of us feeling any post-coital revery. Terri stared at the ceiling, looking out from under the curly brown hair that hovered just over her eyes, framing her face and falling to her shoulders.

"I was a lesbian until last year," she said, still staring at the ceiling. "But I've gotten to know a few guys lately—mostly musicians—so now I just go to bed with people I like. I don't care what sex they are.

"I got started on girls with Kim," she continued, referring to the girl whose bed we were in. "I've been on the street since I was 12. My mama kicked me out because she didn't like the boys I was running with. Things were pretty bad for a while—these old guys hitting me up with junk and sending me out on the street. Then I started dancing go-go at this club when I was 15. I'd been living in a car off and on, but Kim—she was dancing at this place—had me move in with her. She was my first girlfriend, and after that I just kept going with girls I was working with. About every stripper I've ever met was a lesbian.''

I realized that Terri's stiffness in bed was not incompetence. She was just tentative about having sex with men she liked. Oddly enough, she did not know quite what to do with a guy if she was not getting $50 to sleep with him.

We talked a long time before falling asleep. Terri told me how she wanted to stop dancing before she got too old to strip, and before the business finally succumbed to peep shows and massage parlors. When we awoke after our first night together, we felt more at ease with each other.

Taking my penis in her hand, Terri looked at it in a tentative way. Then she straddled me and eased herself onto my erect penis. She held it firmly at the base, pushing the head against her clitoris as she ground her thighs into my ribs. Her pink labia were slightly swollen and easily visible beneath her mat of cropped pubic hair. She was wet now, too. Abruptly she shoved me inside her, dropping down with all her weight and gasping. As she began to move she slowly drew her right hand up her thigh, feeling her own soft skin, stroking her own firm muscles. She rolled her nipples between her thumb and forefinger. Then she began to strum her clitoris, starting slowly, then getting faster as her rocking increased in speed.

Terri masturbated for a long time as we fucked. Sometimes she anxiously pushed her finger into her vagina, sliding it in with my penis in order to get it wet. Then she would resume masturbating. I writhed under her as she rubbed herself, but she never seemed to reach orgasm, nor to care. Watching was both exciting and disturbing at the same time—exciting because I was privy to such a private act, disturbing because I wondered whether she was fantasizing about a girlfriend while having sex with me.

We spent the afternoon shooting pool and drinking beer in a corner tavern near the apartment. Terri arranged her conversation around her movements. While describing how the Mafia burned an independent club she was working in, she would leave the narrative hanging as she popped a solid into the side pocket, then finish her sentence.

When we left the bar late in the afternoon, we were tipsy enough to be staggered by the sunlight. As we aimlessly wandered along a row of shops and bars, Terri rested her head against my shoulder and held my arm. At a street corner she said she needed to talk to a friend who was the desk clerk at a private hotel in the next block. She asked me to buy some beer and then come to meet her friend. As I set off alone, thinking about the past night, I became increasingly frustrated and disturbed. I had expected to find this affair unusually sensual and was nonplussed that it had turned out to be so sexless. I wondered if Terri's tawdry job had so infected her perception of human emotions that she had become a sexual cripple. Perhaps stripping was even an escape for her. Onstage she could allure a faceless crowd of men. But she was always able to scamper offstage before the moment of confrontation.

When I arrived from the liquor store, six-pack in hand, Terri was just turning away from the clerk's desk.

"Brian had an empty room he said we could use for a while," she said, pushing the elevator button. "He's gay, like almost every other man I know. Thank God you're not."

Though sex that morning had been better than the night before, I was surprised that Terri seemed inclined to pursue it. We had enjoyed our day together, and she was unhappy about my departure later that night. But she had also seemed more avid for billiards than sex.

The furnished room had shades but no drapes, a shower without a curtain, a sheetless bed. I started to open a beer, but Terri immediately began to undress us.

We kissed a few times in the stilted sort of way that makes sticking your tongue in someone else's mouth seem like a Three Stooges gag. Then we settled down to just stroking each other, feeling our bodies together. I rubbed my genitals against her thigh as she thrust her pelvis against mine. Soon we were not just going through the motions of having sex. Our movements were quickened by genuine passion. Terri tugged ever more insistently at my penis. I easily pushed two fingers through the wet opening of her vagina. Terri turned her head to mine and put her mouth to my ear.

"I've got a virgin ass," she whispered, "and I want you to fuck it."

She turned over, lying flat on the bed. I propped her up on her knees, licked and sucked her anus, then slid a finger in and out to relax the sphincter muscles. Then I slowly inserted my penis into her, a fraction of an inch at a time. After I had fully penetrated her, I remained still for a few moments to allow her to become more accustomed to the position. And then, gradually and gently, I began to thrust.

Terri remained utterly still. Each time I pushed forward she caught her breath. At first she sounded apprehensive. Then she began to inhale more sharply as apprehension gave way to excitement. She also rotated her ass, meeting my pressure with her own. I came hard, plunging deep into her in the final convulsion of orgasm.

Terri slid forward. I stayed on top of her, feeling my erection subside as her anus tightened and squeezed out my penis. She breathed softly, quickly, not moving. Then quietly she began to cry.

"I've never let anyone do that," she murmured as I kissed the tears on her cheek. "I guess I wanted to let you know how much I like you." Her world-weary tone of voice was gone. She had finally let the barriers down.

I did not see Terri again until nearly six months later, when my band's traveling schedule brought us through town again. After we played our first gig, Terri and I went back to the house where some musician friends were letting the band stay. We trudged past a roomful of strangers who were watching a 24-hour rock channel on TV. On the third floor we found a tiny attic bedroom with a slanted ceiling and a huge bed that nearly filled the room.

Terri slipped out of her fur jacket, sat on the edge of the bed and stripped off her leg warmers. A skin-tight black body suit was all she had worn underneath.

"I really need you tonight," she said, seductively smiling at me. From the moment I first saw her on this visit, Terri's cool manner was nowhere in evidence. She was acting like a saucy teenager who wants to be undressed and says so with a sidelong glance and ꞏ smile.

I pulled her to her feet and peeled the body suit off of her in one long motion. As I slipped out of my shirt and trousers, Terri pushed open a window next to the bed.

"It's cool out," she declared. "Let's get hot."

Taking my penis, Terri rubbed it against her breasts, by turns glancing up at me and looking down to see the head of my cock shoved against her nipple. I shifted my weight and moved my pelvis toward her mouth. She licked me a couple of times and mumbled, "I don't know if you want me to do this."

"Why?" I asked, wondering if a "reformed" lesbian has to draw the line somewhere.

"Well, I don't know. I just don't think I'm very good at it. I'm really embarrassed to tell you that."

"There's no real secret to it," I replied. "Just try it and I'll tell you what feels good." I rather enjoyed giving a lesson in the joys of sex to April Magnolia, queen of titillation. "It's most sensitive just under the head, where there's a little loose skin."

As Terri took me in her mouth, she rubbed under the glans with her tongue. "You can put more pressure on than that," I urged.

She sucked harder.

"That's good," I continued. "Now move it in and out and keep the pressure on, especially below. That's real nice."

She moved her head back and forth, hesitantly at first, and gradually with more confidence and skill.

"Bite it a little, grab it around the base with your hand," I suggested.

A few times she stopped sucking and experimentally flicked her tongue up and down the shaft of my penis. I twitched with pleasure and Terri, regarding me with curiosity, would flick me again and smile.

Then she tried to see how deep she could take my cock into her mouth. I grew increasingly excited as Terri kept trying out different ways of fellating me. I was eager to come, but every time I reached the brink of orgasm she would pause to reflect on this whole wonderful business of oral sex.

Finally I pulled her on top of me. Instantly she maneuvered my penis inside her and began to pound her pelvis into mine. Each time she slammed into me she uttered a quiet little scream. I held her ass, feeling how wet she was and slipping a finger into her anus. She pumped harder and harder, then yelped as she swayed from side to side, riding out her orgasm. Just as she finished, I grabbed her buttocks again, driving her up and down until I came, delirious with orgasm and the sense of breaking through her jaded sexuality.

For a long while afterward we lay still, smiling and feeling the cool air dry the slick sweat on our bodies.

SINGLE SWING CLUBS HARDLY SWING

By Rafael Rodriguez

A porn video was being projected on the wall of a darkened room. Five men stalked actress Vanessa Del Rio in a movie theatre. Encircled, she sank to her knees. In the flickering shadow of the movie a nude couple reclined on a mattress, casually masturbating each other. While Del Rio avidly sucked one of the men, the real-life pair increased their tempo. Briefly they engaged in 69 before the man mounted the woman and fucked her.

Couples making love to a porn film are not unusual. But on this particular Friday night in New York there was a critical difference. The couple had an audience. Five nude men sat within touching distance of their intertwined bodies. Several were masturbating, not to the film, but to the man and woman at their feet.

As the movie galloped to a climax, Del Rio accommodated all five men at once—orally, vaginally, anally and one at each hand. But none of the men in the room dared to caress the woman making love before them. Instead they merely observed—while hoping for an invitation to join in.

These men were also watched by the lovemaking couple, whose attention vacillated from TV screen to audience in a game of mutual voyeurism. The film ended with the usual "money shot"—the quintet coming over various parts of Del Rio's body. Soon afterward the couple reached a vocal, apparently mutual, orgasm and disengaged. The five men dispersed.

This bizarre scene is not unusual in single swing clubs in New York. Many men fantasize about participating in group sex, but few convert their dream to reality without the acquiescence of a willing partner. Though the number of swingers is legion and that of swing clubs ample, the standard rule of orgies—whether private or public—is that only a male and female couple is admitted. Plato's Retreat allows single males in on certain nights. But those who attend often find themselves at a stag party.

One solution to this problem is the escort service. More than 30 exist in New York and most offer a swing club package. Single men are supplied with a date at $100 an hour and up for a minimum of two hours. Thus some men must pay—including the club's entrance fee—at least $300 to attend an orgy.

But many partnerless swingers cannot afford, or refuse to spend, $300 to gain entrance to Plato's. Now they have an alternative: the single male's swing club. Advertising in such periodicals as *Screw* and *The Village Voice*, these establishments claim to attract not only males but lone females and couples. But are they really the answer to the solo swinger's dreams or are they an aberrant variety of bordello? I decided to find out.

My first stop was the Zoo in Times Square, which claimed to have "New York's largest group of regular women members eager to meet men for sex."

A representative of the club assured me by phone that it did not pay women to frequent the premises. When I expressed doubt, he insisted that the Zoo regularly attracted swinging couples with the female half obliging all of the male customers.

The Zoo was located in a cellar beneath a huge marquee reading "Adult Activity, No Escort Needed!" At the bottom of a stairway sat a man in a glass booth who took my $60 entrance fee and buzzed me through a black metal door.

Stuffed animals hung from the ceiling. I walked past a buffet table containing a few cold cuts. Nearby were about a dozen towel-clad men, mostly in their 20s, watching porn videos on a giant TV screen. They looked as if they were in a prison recreation room.

Shown to a checkroom, I deposited my clothes in a plastic bin and received a towel in exchange. Next to the buffet were two ramshackle metal shower stalls. Just beyond the video area was a small communal orgy room designed to resemble an aquarium. It was empty. On the other side was the main gathering area. Sitting at cafe tables were another dozen towel-clad men as well as three women in negligees. Opposite were several open stalls. Apparently, the sex took place here. Occupying one of them was a couple on a bench. As the woman leaned forward, listlessly giving the man a blowjob, he tried to snake his hand under her teddy.

"I said don't play with me there!" she snapped in a voice that would have deflated the erection of a satyr. The man withdrew his hand.

During my quick tour I had counted eight males for every female.

Yet the clientele seemed more apathetic than discontent. Evidently, the men were resigned to the sexual crap shoot.

The four women ranged from ugly to moderately attractive. I joined a group of men paying court to the prettiest—a dissipated blond prattling to a young man who sported an erection beneath his towel. Another fellow with a weightlifter's build paraded nude in front of her table with a blazing hard-on. She ignored him. A third tried to fondle her thigh and had his hand swatted away. I tried to determine her swinger status, but my questions received no reply.

I moved on to the boys watching video. Several were now discreetly masturbating beneath their towels. One nodded to me as I sat down. "This sucks, doesn't it?" he groused. He added that things were better last Friday when a swinging couple had showed up. "She wasn't too good-looking, but it was better than paying 60 bucks to flog your dummy," he said, nodding disgustedly toward the onanists.

Each of the women sporadically took patrons to an open stall for a perfunctory blowjob, but her rate was too slow to accommodate everyone. When the blond led a towelled youth to a stall, four other men followed and watched from the sidelines.

"I think they only have to go with boys that they like," my friend observed. "It was better at Club Xcstasy" (a club that lost its lease). "The girls got paid on a quota basis."

The Zoo seemed neither a swingers' club nor a whorehouse, but more an "anti-whorehouse" where sexual favors were dispensed by whim. On the way out I noticed that the video crowd had dispersed with their towels and were now openly masturbating.

Acquiesce, another single swinger's club, was as low key in its advertisements as the Zoo was extravagant. No address was listed —only a number to call for a reservation. The premises were described as "a discreet, posh and comfortable atmosphere." Acquiesce turned out to be a duplex apartment in one of the better commercial neighborhoods on Manhattan's East Side.

I was buzzed in from the street. A surprisingly attractive woman sat behind the front desk. The first thing I had to do was pay the $85 fee. I hoped it would be worth it. The first floor, though neither posh nor large, housed a small dance floor, bar, buffet, seating for perhaps 15 people and showers. I was led to a checkroom by a teddy-wearing black girl. My clothes went into a garment bag in exchange for a towel. Ten men were seated around the bar area. They were somewhat more refined looking and of a wider age mix than the patrons at the Zoo, but they were equally sullen, as if awaiting root canal surgery instead of an orgy. I sat next to a paunchy, middle-aged man.

"Is this your first time here?" he asked. When I nodded he pointed to a girl in a black corselet and stockings who was dancing with a young Chinaman. "Watch out for her. She likes to talk and tease but she seldom delivers." I wondered what place a "tease" had in a swing club.

Armed with a bourbon and water, I took in the surroundings. The atmosphere was more pleasant and relaxed than at the Zoo. The arithmetic was better, too—four male patrons per woman. Some of the latter looked untouchable—one turned out to be a transsexual. Several were moderately attractive. Most even managed to smile at the clientele. One gazed in my direction. Unlike the others, she was fully dressed. When I asked her why, she said this was her first night and she had not brought an outfit.

Marlene was 20, and claimed to be a part-time art student and party girl for a group of Saudi Arabian playboys. She found her way into Acquiesce after being abandoned by her oil daddies. For a half hour we talked about art and Arab orgies. Meanwhile I monitored the room. The black girl who showed me to the cloakroom had led a man with too many gold chains up the spiral staircase to the orgy floor. The corseleted teaser had followed with the Chinaman in tow. I figured Marlene and I should do likewise. "Not right now," she demurred. "Maybe later. Why don't you go if you want?" So I did, armed with another glass of bourbon.

Upstairs I found a small sauna flanked by two orgy rooms. The smaller was relegated to couples only and was empty, while the larger one featured porn videos. It was crowded with a half-dozen men and two women. The black girl was sitting on the face of her partner, while the teaser performed a business-like blowjob on the Oriental. Despite the distraction of cunnilingus, the black woman kept up an animated conversation with several other customers. This fact did not seem to disturb the tanned suitor beneath her. I joined her audience. She stared at me with mock indignation.

"Whatta you want?" she demanded.

"A blowjob!" I replied.

"Oh yeah?"

"Yeah!"

"Okay!"

And so, to my surprise, she moved forward, dragging the man below her after reassuring him that she would soon be coming all over his face. He responded to this prospect with muffled sounds of approval. She leaned over in such a way that I could not see my genitals. Soon I felt a strange sensation on my cock. Leaning sideways I saw that she had slipped a condom on me. I told her that I had not come inside a condom in at least 20 years, and that it was a record I intended to keep intact. She reluctantly removed the condom but warned me not to come in her mouth. I thought this over for a moment, then informed her I would just as soon pass. She shrugged, pulled herself up and concentrated on rubbing her crotch into the cunnilinguist's face.

Meanwhile the tease stopped blowing the Chinaman and sat up, saying: "I just remembered, I have to make a phone call." The unfortunate Oriental stared quizzically at his abandoned cock.

"See what I mean?" It was Morty, the man who had warned me about her. I asked him how often he visited Acquiesce. When he said twice a month, I ventured to ask why. "I don't always get laid," he answered, "but I like the atmosphere and even the element of chance."

Downstairs again I sought out Marlene. The boys were in a hubbub because a genuine swinging couple had entered the club. Marlene sat at the bar, still fully dressed and looking disconsolate.

Finally, Marlene, true to the name of the place, acquiesced. I followed her up the staircase feeling as if I were on a date—in a bordello. We entered the larger of the orgy rooms and found the swinging couple engaged in 69 in front of a predictable audience. Settling into a corner we were quickly attended by three men, who positioned themselves several feet away like vultures awaiting their next meal.

Marlene was only interested in the basics. She neither wished to eat me or to be eaten. After some brief kissing and fondling, she insisted that I fuck her. This I did with moderate enthusiasm, scanning the room occasionally for visual stimulation—which turned out to be the swinging couple. They were now fucking and apparently enjoying the attention.

After climaxing, and while still atop Marlene, I had a funny feeling and looked over my shoulder. My audience was masturbating. When Marlene left, they turned to watch the exhibitionistic couple. The Chinaman was now with the transsexual. Amazingly, the black girl was still being eaten by the cunnilinguist. But most of the men were without a partner. I decided to leave. On the way out I saw Marlene talking to a newly arrived young man about art.

THE FAMILY MISTRESS

By Jim Brooks

Marian was almost six feet tall and in her late 40s. She had a wild, long mane whose orange-red color came out of a bottle. She drank whisky, elbowed you when she laughed, and spoke with a twang. She was a whore, but called herself a real estate agent. She was also my father's old girlfriend.

I had never met Marian. After my father died, she kept in touch with my family only through an old-maid aunt. But one day I happened to visit my aunt while Marian was also paying a call. When we were introduced, she gave my hand an extra little tug. My spinster aunt was oblivious to the conversational subtext that Marian then began to supply through body language and innuendo. She hiked her dress up a notch, worried the frills of her plunging neckline, winked and squirmed as if in heat, and more than once remarked, "I never knew Jim was such a handsome, grown-up man." She left only after I promised to pay her a visit soon.

A few nights later Marian called and invited me over. "I told all of my boyfriends to stay away," she coyly informed me, "so an old family friend and I can be alone."

But when I knocked at the front door, a blonde woman in a tight blue dress greeted me. Introducing herself as Marian's roommate Betty, she led me into the living room. The look in her eyes and tone of voice suggested deep complicity—that we both knew why I was there. Betty was in her early 30s and identified herself as a "beauty operator." She smelled of cheap perfume and revealed even more bosom and thigh than Marian. She also flirted outrageously like Marian, telling me how lucky her friend was to have such an attractive young man for a "family friend." Giggling like a naughty little girl, she entertained me with a string of lewd jokes.

Moments later Marian entered, resplendent in an exotic dressing gown the color of her hair. Drinks were served. The women sat on either side of me and the conversation was mainly about sex. Though that was also what I had in mind, I did not realize at first that Betty and Marian were prostitutes. The decor of the house even had a bordello flavor, with a preponderance of smoked mirrors, crystal chandeliers, and large cheap prints of nudes on the walls. But the main attraction was the dining room, hidden by a silk curtain. On the pretext of needing more ice from the kitchen, Marian parted the veil and led me within.

A king-size bed sat throne-like in the middle of the room, raised up on a platform. The walls were covered with green velour and the ceiling was mirrored. The only other furniture was an ornate brass bar.

"I'm very particular about my sleep," Marian confided.

A few minutes later all three of us were stretched out on the big bed. I was nervous, never having been in a threesome before, and wondered about my ability to satisfy two professionals. But my doubts paled before the absolute certitude that I would have the orgiastic time of my life. Then the doorbell rang.

Marian rose to admit a powerfully built middle-aged man whom she introduced as Al. As a newspaper reporter I recognized our visitor as a disreputable union official. He regarded me with hostile suspicion, clearly unconvinced by Marian's story that she and I were old family friends.

"We're having a family reunion," she explained.

"And I know where you'll have it," he muttered, aiming a thumb at the dining room.

Marian and Al went off to the temple of love, leaving Betty and me alone on the couch. "Some nerve," Betty sighed. "He thinks he owns her. Doesn't want her to see other men. But," she added with a giggle, "he doesn't care who I see."

Betty brought me upstairs to her bedroom, undressed me, and licked my body from top to bottom. When I entered her she started squealing, biting and talking dirty. She came seven times in rapid succession before I ejaculated and afterwards tried unsuccessfully to arouse me again. But I did not find Betty attractive. She was cheap and dumb, and lacked Marian's *panache*. While astride Betty I imagined that I was fucking my father's old girlfriend.

In the days that followed, I called Marian several times, but she put me off. Weeks passed. I assumed that I had only been a passing fancy. Then one night she phoned and asked me to accompany her to a boat show.

We wandered for hours through an enormous arena with floatable feasts of every description. Marian showed no apparent sexual interest in me and greeted my innuendos with stony silence. She inspected this boat and that, asked pertinent questions, and collected brochures. "I'm checking them out for a friend," she explained mysteriously.

Only when we arrived before a stupendously expensive houseboat did she nudge me with her elbow. A familiar leer returned to her mouth as she contemplated its possibilities. Making our way to the captain's quarters, she sat down on the luxurious bed, testing it, and said with a knowing smile, "I'm very particular about my sleep."

That night, on the main bed in the dining room, Marian treated me to an extraordinary new sensation. As I lay on my back, she brought me to an orgasm by skillfully applying pressure on my cock with her pelvic muscles. The effect was ecstasy in slow motion, with release advancing by minute degrees.

Marian's body was voluptuous and practically unmarred by the rigors of age. She was particularly proud of her breasts, and could climax when I sucked on them. She also initiated me into anal sex, applying the Vaseline on my cock herself and urging me to be rough.

From this and other clues I understood that Marian's clients preferred primitive to missionary sex. She explained how she earned lucrative real estate commissions by acting as a broker in deals arranged by influential friends. She denied receiving money in direct payment for sex, saying that she earned her income with a higher-class brand of service.

That night our relationship as "family friends" began to bloom in earnest. She had no close relatives except for a brother whom she seldom saw. Until early morning we discussed mutual acquaintances. By the time we fell asleep it seemed impossible that I could ever fuck her again. We had become "family."

A few days later I found Al waiting for me in front of my house. Without directly threatening me, he told me to stay away from Marian. "I don't care whether you're a family friend or not," he grumbled.

I phoned Marian often in succeeding weeks, but she nervously put off seeing me. She also travelled frequently to places like Mexico, Florida and Arizona. Her sexual aloofness, the specter of Al, and our evolving relationship as "family" combined to cool my passion. Once more I concluded that I had been a momentary diversion.

Eight months went by. I never heard from Marian anymore. When she called me one night in tears, I did not recognize her voice. She phoned to tell me her brother was dead and wanted me to take her to the funeral in a little town a hundred miles away.

"You're the only family I've got now," she whimpered.

We drove down the next morning in her flashy Chrysler convertible. Marian dressed in black and sat in the passenger seat. Despite the occasion she looked sexier than ever behind her veil. The previous night I had spent long hours remembering her skills as a lover. Yet I felt frustrated by the circumstances of our getting together again. We would be spending two nights in the same motel, but a funeral hardly seemed an appropriate occasion to renew a love affair.

Despite her grief, Marian sensed my erotic obsession with her body. For two hours I monitored the crack between her knees, every gesture of her hand or flick of her tongue, the rise and fall of her breasts. But we arrived in town with me feeling more uncertain about her erotic intentions than ever.

We spent the day and night at the wake. Marian was surrounded by family and friends. By the time we returned to the hotel she was exhausted. We retired to our separate rooms.

The next morning by prearrangement I brought her breakfast in bed. She wore a lacy nightgown and made no attempt to cover herself. I sat at the edge of the bed, trying to disguise my erection. The one valuable piece of information I had picked up yesterday was that Marian and her Baptist brother had not spoken for 25 years. I also detected a faint smile of satisfaction on her face when she stood before the bier.

The day of the wake passed equally uneventfully. Again we returned to the motel exhausted by conversation and tedium. By now Marian had said her farewells.

In the morning I brought her breakfast in bed, only this time she was wearing a robe over her nightgown. All night I schemed how to take advantage of this moment—consoling arm around her bare shoulder, a gentle embrace, followed by an uncontrollable outburst of passion. According to my way of thinking, sexual release was just the tonic Marian needed to get over the loss of her brother. It was certainly the only way I knew to get rid of my 48-hour erection. But I had not counted on Marian's show of modesty. It was even more perplexing when she asked me to hook her brassiere in back. Afterwards she made me leave the room.

We did not talk on the drive back, though the tension was palpable. Marian no longer wore her black veil, but was smoking, dialing the radio, and in general acting nervous and aloof. At one point the generator light flashed red and I joked: "This car is as hot as I am." She pursed her lips, suppressing a laugh, but said nothing. A few moments later I blurted: "Why don't we stop at some roadside motel?" She shook her head.

"I'm not leaving when we get to your house," I warned her.

"Al is coming by tonight," she replied. "Remember him?"

"What do you and Al do?" I asked. "What is he like in bed?"

Marian's expression was enigmatic. "He's a degenerate," she stated simply.

When we got to Marian's house, Al was waiting in the living room. Suddenly emboldened, I decided to play a concerned member of the family and expel the outsider.

"Marian's tired and has a headache," I told him. "She has to lie down. You'd better leave. Come back tomorrow." Taking him by the arm, I ushered him to the door. There he hesitated, looking to Marian for a sign. She nodded in agreement with my plan.

As soon as he drove away, I led Marian towards the big bed, lay her down, and slowly removed her shoes. She remained silent and impassive as I undressed her piece by piece, though by now our eye contact had become fairly serious. She seemed to be saying: "You're being awfully bold, but I'm enjoying it." I was definitely sending the message: "You bitch, you're going to pay for tormenting me like that."

Gently I positioned her in the middle of the bed. Then I dimmed the lights and poured myself a drink from the bar. Undressing, I sat beside her and admired her body. She had trimmed her pubic hair. Parting the lips of her vagina, I saw that she was wet.

"Don't move," I instructed her. "Don't even lift an arm."

By degrees I caressed and kissed her feet, thighs, flank, waist, breast, and neck, before parting her legs and entering her. Moaning slightly, she put an arm on my back. I replaced it on the bed beside her. Then, as slowly as possible, I began to thrust. She writhed and twisted, shuddered quietly, convulsed a few more times, then lay still. My own orgasm flashed exquisitely up my spine. When I looked down at Marian, she seemed to be pleasantly shocked. It was probably the first time that she had remained absolutely passive in bed.

As I was leaving, Al came up the front steps. My knees felt weak, but I stopped him and said: "Don't disturb her. She's sleeping."

I never saw Marian again. Not long afterwards I moved out of town. For years she stayed in touch with my spinster aunt. Then the family lost track of her.

The Sexual Foreign Legion

✱

THE VIRGIN AND THE STOWAWAY

By Mike Durgan

I woke up feeling the hum of the ship's screws and knew that we were at sea—at sea, for God's sake! I'd done it! I swung my feet out of the bunk and sat up, rubbing my head. Jesus! I had stowed away on the boat!

I did not even know where I was going. I had been down and out in Miami. After a night of drinking I had found myself with no place to go. All my worldly possessions were locked up by a third-rate hotel that I owed two weeks rent to. So I drank up what money I had and wandered, for lack of any place else to go, to the docks. There I sat with my bloodshot eyes flinching from the brilliance of the white-on-white streamlined hull of the cruise ship *Evening Star*. The dock workers were sweating up her gangways, loading her up with good things for the trip out.

I was thinking how I would have to go to one of those dingy missions for derelicts where a Bible-slapping preacher would feed me with soup and warn me about the devil. Something crazy came over me. I stood up and stuck my hand in my pocket. My total remaining estate consisted of a quarter and two nickles. I flung the coins at the magnificent boat, nearly dislocating my shoulder. Then I did one of those lunatic stunts that can only happen when a man is so down and out that he will defy the world. I walked over to the magnificent *Evening Star* and marched up her gangway. I walked to the back of the boat and ducked down a hatchway to the cabins.

trying doors until I found one that opened. I locked it behind me, spread out on the bed, and thought, "Fuck 'em. Just let it happen."

Then I passed out.

Now I sat on the edge of the bed trying to rub the coma out of my wretched face.

I stumbled across the cabin to the tiny john and began splashing cold water on my stubbled face. And then I heard something—a key scratching at the cabin door!

I ducked into the shower, pulling the sliding door to. Over the hammering of my heart, I heard a male voice and a female voice. I saw myself being arrested as a thief or a rapist found lurking in the shower and I regretted my folly. Now came a muffled thumping like suitcases being set down and then voices again. A door closed. A lock snapped.

A sound like a shoe falling caused my heart to start trip-hammering again. Then I heard the other. I peeked carefully around the edge of the shower door. From my angle of vision I could see the bunk. The lock on a suitcase clicked open. A red print dress sailed onto the bunk, followed by a pair of pantyhose. A brassiere landed on top. I was straining to assess the cup size when it occurred to me that the woman might be about to take a shower. I wondered if this cruise ship had a brig—and would I occupy it? I envisioned the shower door opening, and almost heard the scream.

But right now she was humming. I listened. She had a young voice. Sexy. Despite my predicament, I felt my cock begin to thicken. If I were being shot by a female firing squad I would probably die with a hard-on.

Then she appeared.

She was beautiful. And stark naked. She was looking in a mirror I could see, appraising herself front and then back. So was I: redhead in her early 20s, with an astonishing movie-star figure.

She disappeared.

I was ready to leap out of the shower and sacrifice all for one more look when she put some more things on the bed next to what she took off. She rolled on a garter belt, then a stocking, and hooked it. Leaning over in this way her ass was a perfect picture. She put on the other stocking, followed by white panties and a pleated mini skirt. Still naked from the waist up, she now began to sample the effect of different blouses against the beige mini. Her breasts were full and tipped with acorn-cap nipples. Scorning a bra, she left them free beneath a flowery blouse.

She disappeared again. A minute later the door opened and closed and I heard the snap of a lock.

At least I was spared the hysterical screams and arrest. I exited from the shower with the exhilaration of a free man—though I felt haunted by a strange loss. The fragrance of perfume lingered in the cabin. I had thrown the inside lock on the door and was on my way out when something caught my eye. I picked up a thin gold ear hoop and dropped it into my pocket.

I went up on the main deck. The passengers were in Bermudas and garish prints, drinks in hand. I hoped I did not seem too conspicuous. My expensive off-white sports coat had been purchased when things were going better. I could wear it with rags and still look all right. Otherwise I wore dirty jeans, no socks, old tennis shoes, and a faded blue shirt.

I searched on three decks for the redhead and finally found her in the main lounge. She was sitting alone at the bar. Her good looks were almost intimidating. I inhaled the familiar perfume. She looked up at me. "Have you lost an earring?" I asked. Her eyes were green. She glanced at the golden hoop I held in my hand, puzzled for a second, then reached up to her ears and was surprised to find herself with an empty lobe.

"Oh! Thank you." She was pleased. "Where did you find it?"

"It was on the floor. It caught my eye." She took the hoop and seemed about to say something. "May I join you?" I persisted.

"Please do." She purred it, as if hoping I would ask. I sat down feeling a rush of unreality the way you do when something unexpectedly good is happening.

"I'm Kathleen," she breathed.

An island band, steel drums and a singer, was playing a soft merengue and she was doing a kind of chair dance to it, moving slow and sexy to the music. I asked if she wanted to dance. Seconds later I had her wrapped in my arms, her breasts crushed into me. People were watching us. I pulled her in, my nose nestled in the burnished curls of her hair. My cock stretched at the thought of returning to the cabin with her, seeing again that luscious body, exploring it, spreading her ivory thighs, sinking my hard cock deep. The prospect of it spun my head and I stepped on her toes. "Sorry."

"Yin and yang," she said, referring to my misstep. "In ecstasy we sometimes have pain."

We went back to the bar and had drinks. She told me about herself and what her sign was. I had heard all this before but she took it one step further. "I'm a Druid," she confided. "I'm one with nature. All the spirits speak and I hear them. The moon warms me at night and the sun warms me in the day. We are all one with the spirit of love—we should erase the borders and make all nations one, feed each other's hungry, love each other's children."

She went on about these things and all the while her jade eyes were wide and there was something very open about her, as if she were begging me to come into her world. She certainly understood her sexuality. She kept brushing my arm with her breasts. I tuned out most of what she was saying and lost myself in her physical beauty.

Finally I reached out and cupped her right breast in my left hand. She put her hand over mine as if to say thank you.

"You want me, don't you?" She asked it kindly as if she were offering food to the hungry. I did not answer, but only looked at her. "Don't you?"

"Very much."

"Would you like me now?"

Kathleen signed the check and we went downstairs. We had a long kiss outside her cabin door. She worked her body against me, giving me her soft lips, holding me tight. We went in and swept the clothes from the bed. I opened her blouse and devoured her breasts. I told her how beautiful she was and sat down beside her, letting my hands satisfy themselves. She lay down almost vibrating with desire, her eyes half-closed, her mouth half-opened, her chest rising, her nipples swollen. I sucked them in and out of my mouth as she squirmed; my hand caressed her stomach and thighs, then moved softly over her clit. I went down and kissed her stomach and the little mound with its sparse tuft of orangy hair. She put her hand on my head.

"Yes," she said, "like that . . ."

She was murmuring with pleasure. Her hand went to the back of my head. I tongued her slowly for a while, and then, when she began to move against me, I began to lick her faster and faster. Her juice frothed around my mouth. And then she came, pulling my head into her and holding me there hard while her body trembled. Moaning and sighing, she went limp, cooing, "Oh, oh, oh. . . ."

With my tired mouth I kissed her stomach and breasts and then her mouth, giving her back some of the juice that was awash on my face. At the same time I tried to penetrate her. My stone-hard cock, which had waited so patiently ever since my first voyeuristic sight of her in the shower, was about to receive its reward.

To my astonishment she pushed me away. "No," she said, "please." I pulled her back under me but she closed her legs. I fell back in agony.

"What is it?" I asked. She remained silent. "I'm dying for you," I gasped. Anger and frustration boiled inside me.

"Can I just do you with my hand?"

"What?" I sat bolt upright.

She looked at me in fright and lowered her head. "I'm sorry."

"Sorry?" I roared.

"Shhh. Please. Oh Mike, I am so sorry. You see, I'm a virgin."

"I don't give a damn about that. What the hell are you talking about. Virgin? Hey, this was your idea as much as mine!"

"I know. I liked you. I just thought you'd enjoy me without putting it in."

I could not believe what I was hearing.

"I am a virgin. A woman's body is a temple of holiness. It's the entry for creating life and that's sacred. A Druid woman cannot let a man enter her except for the purpose of creating life."

"So you expect me to eat you out all night and settle for a hand job?"

"Don't be crude."

"Where's all this love and sweetness you were laying on me in the lounge?"

In the end she relented. But she had to go to the bathroom first. Poking around in a suitcase, she took something out and left.

I sat back, propped up on the pillows, lit a cigarette and waited. I heard the sink faucet run for a minute. And then came a zipping —or more likely an *un*zipping—sound, like that of a medicine kit. Then the toilet flushed. A minute later the door opened and she looked out. Blinking and swallowing, she came ahead.

I took her in my arms, ready to forgive all. Feeling her against me was heaven. If ever anything was designed for pure pleasure, it was her body. But as I mounted her she once again stopped me. "Just a second," she whispered. She had some cream in one of her hands. It was cold as she rubbed it up and down my cock—but I knew it would soon make the hotness inside her just that much better. "Oh God," she said, rubbing the cream, "please be gentle."

I got on top and was about to try to penetrate her again when she said, "Let me." She guided my cock to the entry. "Easy," she pleaded.

I sank into her, knowing now what had happened. She had inserted me into her anus. The idea did not please me but my cock rejoiced inside her and it was difficult to restrain it—it had a mind of its own now and what it wanted was a whopping good fuck. But I did it slow for a few seconds. Even then she was whispering urgently: "Easy, easy." When I came, I corked-off royally, exploding into her.

Then I held her for a long time.

We docked at Nassau in the morning and said our goodbyes. I didn't know where I was going next but I knew I would always remember her: harking back to my days as a high school wrestler, I would remember her as the all-time one-hole-barred Greco-French mat experience of my life: The Virgin of the *Evening Star*.

THE CASTAWAY AND THE PROSTITUTE

By Mike Durgan

I was on the bum in the Bahamas, just following the prevailing breezes and trusting to lady luck. I had stowed away on a cruise ship and gotten off in Nassau on New Providence Island, where would I meet the girl they called The Inch.

But on my first night in Nassau I was very much alone. I had no money for a hotel and like a true castaway slept on the beach. I crashed on the still-warm sand behind the sprawling British Colonial hotel, the dowager queen of the snot-class establishment. Although the moon was out and the palm fronds rattled gently over my head, the experience proved less than idyllic.

I was hungry as hell but the only eating done that night was by the sand fleas who gnawed me unmercifully. And while the sound of the ocean was all around me, my throat was dry as the Sahara —a condition much aggravated by the sounds coming from the bar of the British Colonial, where the tourists reveled into the wee hours of the morning. Nothing, it seemed to me at the time, carries in the night like the clinking of ice and the soft titter of female laughter. I, of course, imagined these women to be pretty and sexy and my spirit was not helped by the idea that they would be bedding down with other men. Lights flashed on in the rooms upstairs and I got an occasional eyeful of a pretty girl undressing or of clutching honeymooners. But no sooner did things get interesting than the lights went out. Worst of all was the open window on the second floor from which came the sounds of a young woman in the throes of ecstasy. It continued for a long time and it ate at my lonely heart. But I had to hand it to the fellow who was with her, for he had her hitting high Cs that could have broken glass.

No Oriental torture master could have devised a more cruel night.

The next day I sold a pair of old binoculars I found to a pawn shop on Bay Street. I only got $10 for them, but it was like stumbling on gold. I could eat and have a few drinks.

And that night I met the girl they called The Inch. Not wanting more flea-bitten misery on the beach, I had wandered away from Nassau, following my nose down a narrow, unlit road until I heard music and soon came to a place called Dick's the Cat and the Fiddle.

I walked in and was surprised to be the only white man in the place. I bought a bottle of Pauli Girl beer with my last dollar and leaned back against the bar. I was in an all-night joint where the Bahamian night people go—cocktail waitresses, bartenders, dancers, musicians, and whatnot—to unwind after work. The room was about a third full, some of the patrons still in the costumes of their trade: The air was heavy with cigarette smoke. A small steel drum band was playing and a girl on the floor was dancing by herself. She was so sexy she gave me an instant zing. But she was tiny. Even in heels she was not five feet tall.

"Cute girl," I said to the fellow next to me.

"You'll be talkin' at her in about two minutes," he muttered.

"How's that?"

"Cause you a tourist and she a hooker."

She was looking straight at me now and I was looking straight back. She danced like she was born to the beat of a drum. Her ass caught every rhythm and upstairs she was moving a small but very saucy set of sidewinders. She wore a micro-mini with a little cut-off top that barely covered what it was supposed to. Her exposed navel bobbed sensuously. It was as if each part of her body was mounted on separate bearings, everything moving to the same beat but in different directions. I never saw a girl move like that and she had as cute a face as I had seen in the islands. I was so turned on I would have sawed off an arm for her.

When the number ended she approached me, the top of her head coming about half-way up my chest. "You dance like a dream," I said.

"I kin dance all night." She was smiling and looking up out of big doll's eyes.

"I'll bet you can."

And so we talked, exchanging names. Hers was Marvelanne, but everybody called her The Inch, she said, because she was so small. She undid one of my shirt buttons and wound a finger in my chest hair. "I be you girl tonight, Mike?" She said this very sweetly.

"That would be very nice. That would be the nicest thing in the world."

"You got twenty bucks, mon, so I can feed my kid?" She whispered this.

"I'm staying at the British Colonial."

"I can't go in there . . . but I know someplace we can go."

"That's not the problem. I'm sleeping on the *beach* of the British Colonial."

A small furrow creased her brow. She chewed a pretty lip. She looked at me carefully now, my unshaved face, my rumpled clothes. "Hey . . . you broke, mon?"

"I just blew my last buck."

"Shit, mon." There was real disappointment in her face. "Why you be wastin' my time?"

Her words hurt and I turned away. "Sorry," I said.

I heard her heels clicking away and pictured the hard-squeeze of her high-buttocked ass twitching above those heels. I huddled miserably over my beer. Fuck it then. I would just finish the beer and head out. I had to find someplace to sleep.

But where? I remembered passing a pair of parked dump trucks a half a mile down the road. Maybe one of them was unlocked.

I killed the beer and stood up. The Inch was sitting with another girl across the room, her crossed legs showing a fine milk chocolate thigh. She looked at me expressionlessly. I blew her a kiss and left.

Outside the night was muggy and breezeless. A mosquito sang in my ear. It was going to be another long night. I headed down the road toward the dump trucks.

"Hey, mon!" She didn't walk, she ran—a kind of kid's skip-jump run. She grabbed my arm in both her hands. "Hey, mon, you can't go sleep on no beach."

"No?"

"No, mon," she said, shaking her head. "I gone take care of you."

Well, son of a bitch, I thought.

And take care of me she did. She got a bottle of Vat 19 rum and four cold cokes and we cabbed to the Paradise Hotel, a dilapidated run down hotel on the outskirts of Nassau. The room had plastic curtains, a bare bulb hanging from the ceiling, a small oscillating fan, a squeaky floor, and an even squeakier bed—the mattress little more than a pallet. But for me that night, it was paradise.

And The Inch was incredible. We made that bed squeak like a mouse, bark like a dog, and, before we were through, we had it shrieking like a caveful of bats, the feet of the bed whamming on the floor like we were tearing the hotel down around us. Oh, what a fuck that was! The Inch, hooker that she was, had a quince as tight as a choir girl and she could manipulate it like a milking machine. I came like a fire hose and fell back exhausted.

And then I could not believe what happened. The Inch was playing with herself! I never gave a girl a better fuck and there she was, her eyes glazed, her breath catching, three fingers in and really going to town with it, her palm whapping her clit, throwing her butt up to it. I thought I had worn her out, but there she was, masturbating right before my eyes.

I sat up and poured myself a rum and coke and watched her. God, but she was pretty. But crazy. Look at her go. I wondered if she even knew I was in the room anymore. She started to whimper and then it really got weird. She began to spank her pussy! She would three-finger herself like a dervish and then pull it out and spank herself with the other hand. But really spank herself. She would slap her cunt four or five good hard ones and then the three fingers would go back in. She began to toss around on the bed, whimpering and squeezing her tits, and then she spread her legs wide and again began to slap her pussy. Only this time she did not stop. She must have spanked it 20 times, harder and harder, sobbing and gasping, and then she got off.

She lay there panting and teary-eyed. I petted her. Her skin was the color of cocoa and soft to the touch. She purred quietly beneath my hand. As I did so I noticed an odor on her breath that I had caught before but not recognized.

It was iodine. Minutes later when she sat up and I fixed her a drink, she reached into her purse for a small bottle and added a few drops of iodine.

"You drink iodine?"

"It's good," she cooed. "Make you high. Whooooie, baby, high as the sky."

I stretched out on the bed as she told me how lots of girls on the island got high this way. She sat on the bed, lotus style, sipping her "New Providence Cocktail" and examining my equipment as if she had never seen anything like that before.

"Nice one," she said. Her voice was changing, sounding more intoxicated. She tested the head of my cock with her fingers the way she might a mushroom cap at the market. It was almost full hard now and she held it at the base and waved it back and forth. "Pretty," she said.

My cock sprang to attention and she rewarded it with three slow kisses. "Oh, honey," I sighed, "suck it."

She lifted her head. "No, no. The Inch don't do that."

"What?"

"It rot you teeth you do that."

"Bullshit."

"Yes, yes. I know a girl do that all the time. She got very bad teeth. And don't none of us even talk to her."

"Her teeth are bad for some other reason. Besides, it's good for your titties."

"No."

"Yes it is."

"Nah."

"I know three girls who had little ones till they started doing that," I lied. "Two of them wear B cups now."

"Nah . . ."

"The other wears a C cup." My cock was throbbing. I put my hand on the back of her head to encourage her.

"People say bad things about girls who do that."

"I'll never tell."

"Just a liddle," she said, almost whispering. I guided her head down to it and her bee-stung lips took it in deliciously. "Oh, yes," I sighed, "that's beautiful."

She made little humming sounds and sucked like an angel. She kept a perfect rhythm, never varying, building the friction, working as if she had gone into a trance with it. The oscillating fan played over my body, cooling me, while the heat in my cock rose, as I began to go into a trance, too, as if my whole being had gone into my cock, that lovely mouth sucking so fine, and I rose up in the sky, whooooie, as if I, too, were on iodine, up there on cloud nine. When I finally got off it wrecked me, folded me up as if what I had shot into her was my bone marrow. She tilted her head back and swallowed, went south with the starch, and I felt a kind of instinctive fulfillment to have put my seed so deep inside her. When I slept it was the sleep of perfect contentment.

I spent a week with The Inch (she actually liked being called that); she was a good sport and if ever there was a happy hooker it was she. She had an almost child-like happiness. She never told me where and how she turned her tricks and I never asked her.

She was away from four in the afternoon until two in the morning. She fed me and washed my clothes and gave me drinking money every day. Every night she fucked me like there might never be a tomorrow. Especially when she was high on the iodine. Then she was insatiable. And it was then that she spanked her cunt to orgasm and gave me those trance-like sucks. I remember the last night I was with her that she snuggled up to my ear, just before we fell asleep, and whispered that she thought she could feel her titties starting to grow.

I rewarded The Inch's goodness to me by dumping her. I landed a job one day with the local newspaper, the *Nassau Tribune*, which put me into association with the island's upper-crust, a situation she could not be part of. Today I think of her often, always with regret, for she deserved better than she ever got from me.

FIRST INTERCOURSE, 1946

By Peter Duncan

In the 1940s, sex came a lot later in life for most Americans. I was 19, discharged from the USAF after World War II, before I lost my virginity—and my situation was not unusual, even for young men.

Men, I say, but most of us thought of ourselves as boys. On a pass in the Barbary Coast section of San Francisco, just before I was discharged, a gang of us were cruising along the streets lined with girlie shows and bars—bars where those of us under 21 could not be served. I had fallen behind the group when a prostitute approached me. She was a striking, very tall mulatto wearing a turban, with a huge gold earring dangling from one lobe. "Wanna have some fun?" she whispered huskily. I swung my head around to find out to what *man* she might be talking. No one. She meant *me*. I blinked and ran back to the pack and told the others what had happened. We giggled about it. I don't think any of us thought we were old enough to do *that*.

But in college, expectations were higher. You took one of the inscrutable coeds to a basketball game and went out for a Coke afterward. Then, in the sorority-house parlor, with the lights on but low, you could sit and neck on the sofas alongside all the other pairs, furtively feeling to see how far you could go until curfew.

Until I met Susan. She was a "townie," which meant that she lived at home with her parents. That gave us more flexibility about curfew and privacy.

My problem was compounded by love. Susan and I were so infatuated with one another that we assumed from the start that we would go on seeing each other through four years of college and then get married and live happily ever after. That was not to happen, but the belief affected our sexual behavior.

Until one Saturday. I showed up early because she wanted to surprise her parents by painting the kitchen, and I had promised to help. She greeted me wearing overalls and one of her father's old shirts, the sleeves rolled up. She had snitched her hair back into a pony-tail, and wisps of it were loose around her freckled cheeks. She looked adorable, and as soon as I was in the door I pulled her into my arms and kissed her deeply, my tongue plunging. By the way her hands tugged at my shoulders, I was sure her mind was not on the planned paint job.

She was tiny. Standing on tiptoes, she had to strain to reach my lips. I put my hands under her buttocks, surprised by how small and firm they were, and lifted her to me. Heading for the couch, I laid her down full-length in one motion, never removing my lips, my hard cock unabashedly pressing her thigh, and she clung to me, encouragingly. After a few moments of writhing on her leg I lifted my head and looked down at her, my face full of a silent question.

She did not smile. Her face showed eager fear. I took that for consent.

On my knees beside the couch now, I calmly unfastened the suspenders of her overalls, flipped down the bib, and one-by-one undid each button of the long white shirt. My eyes were on hers as I did this, and I saw her sweet lips tremble, but she made no protest. Her shirt was open now, revealing a slightly padded little A-cup bra (I can say say that now, though at the time I knew little about such garments). How was I to get *that* off? Carefully, I slipped one, then the other strap over her freckled shoulders. She let them drop to assist me. She wanted this, I thought. What more does she want?

I tugged at a cup and was able to slip it off her breasts, all limp and soft and pinkish white in the dappling sunlight angling in from the window behind the couch. Freckles like a golden dust came down her chest and over the top of her breast, then stopped. Her aureole was no bigger than a quarter, the little nipple like a pink raisin. Delicately I kissed it, then brushed it with my cheek as my hand worked to free the other breast. She shuddered slightly, a shudder that traveled the length of her body, but she offered no resistance. I saw little fists clenched along her denim-covered thighs.

She whispered huskily, "Let's lock the doors."

I nodded and got up to lock the front door while she, holding her overalls up by the straps, went to the back door. Then she went not to the couch but to her bedroom—a sanctum I had not seen: all lavender ruffles and pennants and pictures on the wall, her texts stacked neatly on a small desk. She closed the venetian blinds while I sat on the single bed with its ruffly-skirted spread.

With the blinds closed the room was dusky. I watched her drop her straps and reach behind her to unfasten her bra, then drop it to the floor. Her overalls slipped to her ankles. In the dim light I gaped at all that exposed skin, the little pink triangle of her panties covering the smaller dark triangle of her mound.

She stepped out of the overalls, then bent to remove her sandals while I stared at her round little ass, her soft thighs. My hands went to my own shirt buttons, but I paused. I didn't want to alarm her by seeming too forward. I felt as though I were capturing a wild bird, almost afraid to move for fear of startling her.

Susan was more self-possessed than I. Did she have experience? I wondered. No. Her hands were trembling. But this was her house, her room. And she knew she was in command. Now she lifted her arms to unfasten her pony-tail. Her underarms were bare. Shaved, I thought. Girls shaved their legs, too, I had heard. Hers looked smooth and soft. She was shaking her loose hair, which came just to her shoulders. Then she put a knee on the bed and opened her arms to invite me to her.

I panicked, thinking *Vaseline*. On the nightstand beside my parents' bed, and beside every marital bed I had ever seen, there was always a little jar of Vaseline. Little was popularly known in those days about foreplay. I assumed one had to have lubrication to get in and did not know whether one could do it otherwise. I had heard about maidenheads, and winced to think I might cause Susan pain and bleeding. I was awed by the unknowns opening before me as she opened her arms.

But I moved to embrace her, nonetheless, and bore her down to the bed. My hands now freely explored down her thighs, as I felt the nubbins of her breasts through my shirt. She was responding eagerly. Her small hands slipped under my shirt collar, over my shoulders, and she pushed me away to unbutton my shirt. I helped, unbuttoning from the bottom as she came down from the top. Now our chests were bare together, and we lay that way for several minutes, kissing, her hands lovingly exploring my bare back.

When does one go further? I wondered. I slid a hand between our bare bellies and slipped fingers under the elastic of her panties. Paused. Slipped further, the tips of my fingers grazing her pubic hair. Paused. She squirmed. Resisting? No. Encouraging. My fingers slipped further, into the hair. Further. The tip of my index finger touched dewey flesh in the midst of hair. She squirmed more violently. Onward the finger, into the warm cleft. My aching penis pressed her thigh and I began hunching as my finger dipped into her. Her clenched legs prevented my entering entirely, so I massaged. She squirmed.

I did not learn the word *clitoris* until long after I was married. Such matters were simply not popular knowledge. But Susan, of course, knew where her pleasure button was. By pressing her thighs together she kept my finger where she wanted it. This is speculation. We never talked about it, then or later. People just did not talk about such things. What a young man might learn about a woman's body was garnered from studying Varga girls in *Esquire* or bare-chested natives in *National Geographic*. And lockerroom scuttlebut. And gross jokes.

All that background seemed irrelevant to Susan. I backed away, still keeping my finger in the cleft, to gaze at her. She was smiling, her eyes closed, her hair spread softly on the pillow, the girlish length of her all bare except for those panties. My free hand grazed her chest, toyed with her nipples, traced down between her breasts and over her ribcage, her navel, the flat little belly. With her eyes still closed she shyly lifted a hand to my belt, then moved down and clenched my hard penis through my pants.

I continued fingering, but I loosened my belt with my free hand and unzipped. Her hand moved inside to the bulge in my underwear. She felt for the elastic, pulled it down, releasing the tip, and touched it gently. Then she boldly gripped the shaft. I could not believe it. I did not know a girl would actually *touch* a man down there. With her *hand*. Not since the days of playing doctor in our clubhouse, long before puberty, had a female hand touched me there. I shoved down my underwear and trousers, lifting my body to take them off. My shoes were in the way, yet I dared not stop my fingering. Awkwardly, with one hand, I untied and kicked them off. Then my pants. Socks. It seemed somehow indecent to be wearing my socks, so I slipped them off, too. All this while Susan held my cock tightly. I do not think she had any idea of how to masturbate me, so she simply clung.

And now was pulling me toward her. She wanted me *in*! Neither of us would have dreamed of oral-genital contact in those days. In the army, an older soldier told me about how he had divorced his wife for trying to "go down" on him, and I remember guessing what that meant. "I've had whores do it," he said, "but I didn't want my wife acting like a whore." Similarly, we talked about "sucking pussy" as a dirty joke. People did not actually do such things, we thought. Not decent people.

Ready or not, we were moving on. With her free hand she began shoving down her panties, lifting her hips to slide them under her. I took over that job, pulling the soft little garment down those tallowy thighs, over her dimpled knees, down her shins, over the little feet that were tense and pointing together. Painted toenails, I noticed. I flung her panties off the bed.

She parted her thighs as I moved over her, and I slipped my finger down and into the juicy channel, tentatively at first, then all the way. She gasped. She was still holding my penis, pulling it down to her. I felt the glans graze her hair, felt its tip against her moist labia, and removed my finger so that it could enter. There? No, down further. There. She guided me, but we twisted our hips trying to get it into her vagina. At last—the tip, at least. About an inch in. It was too tight. I hunched a little, going in and out that inch, and slipped out entirely. We both gasped as she gripped me and again guided me into the hole. A little farther this time. I could feel her opening. She was so slippery I couldn't imagine what people used the Vaseline for. So slippery I popped out again, and again had to be guided home. This time farther still.

Then there was the barrier I had momentarily forgotten. I was definitely bouncing against something, as though she had an internal trampoline. I could see sweat break out over her upper lip and along her temples, could feel dewy sweat on her chest. I was supposed to break that trampoline.

Could I? I pressed. My cock ached with the effort. Maybe I could just keep slipping in and out this little bit until. . . . But no, my hips sagged and something opened, something gave, and I was in another inch or so, feeling the warm ooze of fluid around my shaft. I looked at Susan's face: she was biting her lips, wincing. I stopped a moment and her hands went up to my buttocks. They felt tiny and cool. She was pulling me down, into her, into her, deeper, until finally our pubic hair crushed together.

I felt a sigh escape my lips. Victory. Yet we had only begun to fuck. Her hands still on my ass, urging me, I began pumping. She was heaving and twisting under me, her hands holding me in. Her face seemed to be twisted with agony—or passion. I could not be sure which. I was panting, sweating, pushing, thinking this was all just what I had read or heard about. But this was *Susan*, my love, my wife-to-be. I felt like I was *using* her, and something within me hated it. At the same time she had obviously encouraged me, and she seemed to be enjoying it. Was that demeaning to her? I could not worry about it now. I pumped and pumped and came, a scalding squirt, then collapsed against her, feeling my cock throb inside.

When I started to withdraw, the tip was so tender it hurt. I sank into her again and lay there hugging her. Her hands were now caressing my back and neck. Then her fingers ran through my hair as we kissed. I almost dreaded looking her in the face because of the wave of shame passing over me. Shame for what? I thought, we have done something that is, well, very *important*.

Then I thought of birth control. Women get pregnant doing this. An army training film taught us the importance of using rubbers.

Where do you get rubbers? In the army you got them from the sergeant, as I had heard. But can you buy them? At the drug store? Will they sell them to someone who is not married? Who is under 21? I could not imagine myself going in and asking the pharmacist for—what did they call them? Condoms.

I assumed that Susan was probably pregnant already. By now I had grown soft and rolled off. We lay there side by side on the single-bed looking into one another's eyes in silence. She looked worried, too. I certainly knew nothing of ovulation cycles, nor did she. Though I knew that not every screw resulted in pregnancy, I had no idea why or how it worked. So far as I was concerned, it was Russian roulette. We might find ourselves getting married within a few months and perhaps dropping out of college in order to raise and support a child.

We did not talk about it. Instead, after a few minutes of troubled silence, we got up. The bed spread bore a bloody stain. Susan ripped it off to put it into the washer, hoping it would dry before her parents returned that evening. We dressed, and painted the kitchen. When I think about the relative ease and sophistication with which young people deal with sex today, I remember with sorrow that innocent couple of 40 years ago rolling paint as though to cover their shame and worry.

PERVERSITY IN EVERY PORT

By Andrew Potter

When I was a teenager the British government gave me a choice—go to jail or join the Boys' Navy. Though a sexual innocent, I had made a reputation for myself in the East End of London as a young hellion. This was in 1965. For two years I lived with 250 boys on a four-masted sailing ship. We went barefoot, slept in hammocks, and underwent rigorous basic training. At night the biggest problem for some of us was sheer survival. Many of my mates were far tougher than I. We drank everything from aviation fuel to brass cleaner, took opium and heroin, fought and gambled, and in general behaved like animals. But I remained a virgin all this time. Homosexuality and homosexual acts were almost completely absent. Masturbating into a blanket was my only sexual relief. That—and visiting the Crown and Anchor on the London docks every fortnight when we got weekend leave.

A lot of us lads used to go to this pub, which was run by an old queer. He was an amazing person. Some nights he dressed like a woman in a formal evening gown, but the next time we visited, he might be dolled up like a lumberjack.

When the place closed down, he locked the doors. About 50 boys would be there, plus a few foreign sailors and whores. About 20 or 30 of us would stand around a table and put a pound note each into the middle of the tablecloth. The idea was for all of us to "wank off" and whoever came first collected the kitty. The owner stood on the bar, watching us and playing with himself. This was my first sexual experience, in a way. It was weird but marvelous because I thought it was better than going to school.

Later, I signed up with the Royal Navy for the minimum hitch —12 years. I was assigned to an anti-aircraft carrier and our first port of call was Malta. On shore I became friends with a drummer in the Royal Marine band who asked me one night if I wanted to earn some money. He knew an American oil executive who required his services. The marine was in his full dress uniform, complete with white helmet and gold braid. I agreed to go along with him.

The American told us that he liked to be beaten up by people in authority. Then he undressed and got under the shower with just the cold water on. He started masturbating and turning blue. Meanwhile, the drummer began hitting the fellow with his drum sticks and shouting, "Stop that wanking!"

My friend's uniform was soaking wet, and the man in the shower was getting terribly beat up. But he loved every blow. I could hardly believe what I was seeing. We were paid 50 pounds for our trouble and later did that sort of thing quite often. I became a sadist for hire, catering mainly to wealthy American and Dutch oil people who lived on the island.

During this time I also lost my virginity with an innocent young girl whom I picked up somewhere. Compared to what I had already experienced, I found the sex quite boring, really. It was not until our ship docked in Greece that I discovered what I had been missing.

Athens was the capital of degradation in the Mediterranean, attracting perverts like a magnet. To get extra drinking money a lot of us sold our blood. On one occasion we met some nurses who asked us to a party. It turned out to be an orgy, with everyone involved in something called the hump square. In this arrangement four men and women lay at right angles to one another, and on top of them would be another layer, and then another—16 people in all, a gyrating square, with each person screwing or blowing someone else.

These nurses told us some incredible tales about how they used to make love to dead men in the morgue. They had a chemical which they injected into a cadaver's penis, making it hard. When we expressed disbelief, they opened their handbags and showed us their real-life dildos—rock-hard penises and testicles which had been surgically removed from their owners. These nurses—about a dozen in all—lived together in a big house and took a lot of drugs, which they stole from the hospital.

In Athens I also met a man at a pub who invited me to come around to his flat. In his bedroom was a trapeze swing. He excused himself and reappeared 10 minutes later dressed in an Edwardian smock.

After handing me a heavy croquet mallet, he sat on the trapeze and urged me to hit him every time he swung toward me.

At first I just gave him a few gentle taps. But he really wanted me to knock him off the swing. So I began whacking him as hard as I could. After unseating him, I got paid. But there was no sex between us.

Another sordid place was Lalinea on the Spanish coast near Gibraltar. This little town was famous for its circuses, complete with jugglers and clowns. But the animal acts all involved bestiality, usually with burros. It was a very bawdy spectacle. The audience coaxed one performer on by tossing coins on stage which she picked up with the lips of her vagina. We amused ourselves by heating the coins first with a match, just to give her a little charge.

One of my mates was a fellow named Soapie. In Turkey we met a Dutchman who hired us to accompany him to his rooms. While he lay on his bed, Soapie and I stripped nude and put on crash helmets. Then we had to "chase" one another around the bed on "motorcycles," going "Vroom, vroom, vrooooom!" Our host loved it when we overtook one another. But again no sex took place except for his solitary onanism.

One of my weirdest experiences occurred in Catania on the Sicilian coast. A Russian circus was in town. A group of us went to see it and afterward became friendly with some of the performers. The fire-eater was a woman who paid us a great deal of money to treat us to her very unusual brand of fellatio. First she smeared our genital areas with thick layers of Vaseline. Then she applied a flammable gel and lit it. My mates and I stood in a row sporting these great flaming penises, while she put an asbestos shield on her gums and gave us head. When we came the air was filled with the bizarre smell of smoking, burning semen. She obviously enjoyed herself, but I personally did not find the blowjob all that hot. Rather I mostly thought about the money I was getting and worried about not catching on fire.

Nearly as strange was my encounter with a British admiral's wife in Hong Kong.

I met her in one of the local clubs and sensed right away that she was a little odd. This woman was about 45, quite attractive and with impeccable social credentials. But she kept saying to me, "I know you're the adventurous type. I'll bet you're looking for something a little different."

It turned out that she was a contortionist. She brought me to her room, and while I waited, she boiled an egg—a *soft*-boiled egg. After undressing, she bent over backward, putting her head between her legs in such a way that it was just below her anus. Next she inserted the egg—open at the top—into her cunt. Then I stuck my cock into the yolk and she would lick it off. So this went on for some time—I dipping into this warm runny egg, then lowering myself so that she could lick it off. Finally, I came. But I refused when she asked me to dispose of the rest of the egg with my mouth. I was only 19 and not yet into oral sex.

Hong Kong was also famous for its brothels. But I never went to any of them to buy a woman. Never once in my life have I ever paid for sex. It simply was not necessary, what with all the women about who wanted to pay me. Also there was a surplus of good-time girls who worked by day as clerks but due to overcrowding had no place to go at night except to a cardboard shack. So they were always available as companions to sailors who had saved up a lot of money for shore leave.

Since we were easy marks for thugs, we usually traveled in groups of four or more. Usually we hired a limousine. But we were always more interested in getting drunk than in getting laid. We went to brothels to drink, despite the exorbitant prices. One night we visited a brothel called the Rooftops. When a fight broke out among some of the customers, my mates and I escaped to the top floor to avoid trouble with the naval police. Getting caught would mean an end to our shore leave. Yet we found ourselves trapped. The cops had arrived and were charging up the stairs.

Now this floor was essentially a collection of cubicles—all occupied and divided by rice-paper screens. So we just tore through these dividers. It was like a scene out of an Oriental-style Keystone Kops movie. Above the din of the police rushing up and the gang of us screaming and laughing was the contrapuntal sound of tearing rice-paper and then an "*Aargh*!" as we stepped across the backs of the johns. We smashed through 12 walls in all and completely wrecked the place.

On a sordid note, Hong Kong also had a pub called the Chewbath where little girls aged seven or eight sat below the tables, out of sight of the customers. No sooner would you sit down for a drink than you felt your trousers being unzipped. To me, this was depravity beyond the pale—on a par with buggery. My friends and I waved the children away or gave them money just to get rid of them, but other men went there specifically for that purpose.

Perhaps I should again emphasize that we were no more than sexual animals at this time, unrestrained by morality. Yet we looked on sex as something we did only for money or a laugh. Some of our nonsexual adventures may illustrate this point. For example, one night aboard ship we saw a movie starring Jack Palance called *Ghengis Khan*. So the next time we got shore leave—this was also in Hong Kong—we had a Ghengis Khan night. If a rickshaw driver smiled at us, we punched him in the face. At a restaurant, whoever felt like going to the bathroom just stood up and pissed on the table. We had a live-rat eating competition. The winner swallowed down six live baby rats and their mother, with blood and muck running down from his mouth, and washed the lot down with cider. He became "anima of the night." In all, we were a right-wing, very racist, arrogant group—but we were very much stags, too. Homosexuality was joked about, but to screw your mate was just never done.

Also we were terrible alcoholics and supplemented our beer on shore, or aviation fuel on shipboard, with a variety of drugs. To help pay for these luxuries my mates and I made five porn films in Hong Kong. In one of them we played Hell's Angels, dressing up in leather jackets and taking part in a gang bang. With sailors like us, it was no wonder Britannia no longer ruled the waves.

Singapore was much like Hong Kong, though I saw there a sight I will never forget. One of the bars we visited featured a gorgeous Eurasian girl who sat in a glass tub and masturbated herself with a live trout. It was quite a large fish—perhaps a five-pounder—and eventually she actually maneuvered it until only its tail was sticking out of her cunt. The trout fought furiously to escape, but she allowed withdrawal only after she came. This woman was also able to put a magnum of champagne up her vagina until only the cork showed. Then she would pop it.

By far the most inventive lovers in the Far East are the whores of Thailand—attractive, doll-like women, who were sexually imaginative both on the grand scale and in small details. The most amazing brothel I ever visited was one in Bangkok where each room created a fantasy environment. For example, one room resembled a train compartment with scenery "moving" past the window. Another was a fish-and-chips restaurant, and yet another a laundry. So a customer who always wanted to ravish a waitress could fulfill his wish by having her on a tabletop. You could actually eat at this restaurant, too; and adding an edge to the experience was the fact that some "customers" were paying voyeurs.

At the age of 24, after spending 563 days in Royal Navy brigs around the world, I was discharged. For the first time in my life, I felt at sea. I took 12 jobs in as many months. And I got married to a very straight British girl. Making love to her was the strangest sexual experience of all because I was still green when it came to "normal" sex. For seven years I had sailed the seven seas, witnessing and sometimes tasting every possible perversion. I found conjugal intercourse boring—the most perverted form of sex of all—because no money was involved. Our divorce was inevitable. Now I have remarried and lead an ordinary life. Yet I cannot shake the notion that I am still the biggest pervert of all. Whereas other men grow progressively kinkier in their bedtime habits, I have followed the reverse path. Sex has become a once-a-week routine. Obviously I enjoy it. Yet, I also find myself growing increasingly unsexual. I got the sea out of my blood, and no longer act like an animal in a restaurant. But no marital invention can rival the erotic novelties of my youth. At the age of 38 I am sexually washed up.

ONE NIGHT IN BANGKOK

By Leland Street

I stood under the shower and let the steaming water pour over my body. It was my first encounter with hot water in three months. I was living and working as an English teacher in Songkhla Refugee Camp in Southern Thailand. When I felt too ripe to live with myself I had to bathe in the Gulf of Siam or douse myself with a bucketful of icy well water. But now I was getting steam cleaned.

Songkhla was a narrow strip of beach, bordered by barbed wire and crammed with 10,000 Vietnamese boat people. My job was to teach them enough English to survive their first weeks in America. So for eight hours every day, I conducted classes in a thatched hut that doubled as the Buddhist temple. It was hard work. It was good work. But mostly it was hot work. By mid-morning the temperature was well into the 90s and my wet shirt clung to me like Saran Wrap. But my students—old men, pregnant women, young children— never seemed to break a sweat.

I was checked into an air-conditioned Bangkok hotel room for a long weekend of R&R. During the war, Bangkok tended to the carnal needs of thousands of lonely GI's. More recently, droves of European tourists were drawn to Asia's Sin City by its legendary beauties and the promise of exotic sexual adventure. But just then my wildest fantasy was to park myself in front of that air-conditioner and sleep for two days. And then sleep some more. Maybe if I got ambitious, I would wander down to the pool for a cool plunge. But in the meantime, the hot water gushing against my shoulders felt just fine.

When I finally emerged from the bathroom, the icy air grabbed my chest. It felt good. There was a bucket of ice and a quart of bourbon on the bed table. That looked good too. I moved to the window and drew a two-inch wall of drapes between me and the midday glare. The room plunged into darkness—a cool dark cave. My body found the bed and I fell dead asleep.

205

Some time later I heard a persistent pounding on the door, I pulled the blanket over my head and tried to dive back into that blackness.

Rise and shine somebody called, a voice from the hallway.

It was Rick, a young doctor from the city who was also staying at the hotel that weekend. The bedside clock read 12:45.

"It's after midnight, you clown." I shouted into my pillow. "Let me sleep."

"But it's the witching hour in Pat Pong."

Of course I had heard about Pat Pong, Bangkok's red-light district. Everyone in Thailand had a Pat Pong story to tell. Beautiful contortionists who performed amazing acts, three-on-one massages, kinky sex shows. I had not been laid in months, but watching a woman peel a banana with her cunt lips was not my idea of a good time. The health factor also gave me pause. There were two V.D. clinics for every massage parlor in Bangkok.

Rick seemed to read my mind. "In case you're worried, I brought a batch of penicillin from the camp infirmary. C'mon now, Doctor's orders."

"You can tell me all about it at breakfast," I called back.

I tried to go back to sleep, but I had company now. As I stared into the darkness I saw her deep almond eyes, and if I reached far inside my mind I could almost touch her. Lé Chi was a student of mine in the camp, and just thinking of her then made the blood rush to my groin.

Once a week I taught a class in Cultural Orientation. That day's topic was The Job Interview. At the start of each interview, I explained "you have to shake hands and introduce yourself." Vietnamese are painfully bashful about any physical contact with strangers. Even eye contact is considered impolite. So I went around introducing myself—"Hello, my name is Leland Street," I said genially, extending my hand to her. She rose gracefully to her feet and warily laid her hand in mine. It was the most delicate thing I had ever touched. I squeezed it gently and she squeezed back.

"Um . . . in America, you must look the person in the eye when you shake hands." Slowly, she raised her head and our eyes met. Her eyes were somehow both shy and brazen. I was drawn inside them like Alice down the rabbit hole.

That afternoon was the weekly soccer match. Each Friday the *farangs* (as foreign volunteers were called) would play against the Catholic or Buddhist boys' team. They literally ran circles around us in the deep sand, but it was a major entertainment event. Everyone in the camp would cluster around the edges of the field and cheer wildly as we flailed around the beach.

At the end of the game I was leaning against the goal post, trying to get my breath back. I was dripping with sweat and covered with sand. "Hello, Mr. Eeland," said a soft voice behind me. I turned to find Lé Chi standing there with her hand held out. I took it and bowed my head slightly, as the Vietnamese do. "You very good," she said, smiling. Those eyes again. "No. Very bad," I replied. When I released her hand, she reached up and lightly brushed the sand off my shoulders. "Airy chest," she noted with a giggle. "Yes. Very airy." I blushed like a schoolboy.

Just then the monsoon rains let loose, as they did for an hour each afternoon. We ran for the nearest cover—an overturned refugee boat beached on the shore. By the time we ducked beneath the deck, we were both soaked. Her pajama-style outfit showed the outline of her boyish body, and her wet hair clung to her face and neck. She was shivering. When I wrapped an arm around her shoulder, she did not draw away. Instead, she clasped her delicate cool hands around mine. I wanted to do more, but this was not a college dormitory. It was a refugee camp. Lé Chi already risked scandal by visiting in private with a *farang*. So we just sat there holding hands and listened to the rain pelt against the wooden deck above. Afterward Lé Chi released my hand and skittered back to her barrack. But I could still feel the warmth where our bodies touched.

The air-conditioner roared in my head. I was too cranked up now to sleep. I wanted a drink but all the ice had melted, so I called down to room service for a fresh bucket. I drew open the drapes and looked out on the darkened courtyard. Only the pool was lit, and below the shimmering blue water I could read the words MIAMI HOTEL spelled out in black tile. I felt a long way from home.

Someone knocked on the door and I donned a robe to answer it. There, with a fresh bucket of ice cradled in her arm, was a pretty Thai woman. She stood barely five feet tall in her sandals, jeans and halter top, but every inch was in perfect proportion. Like many Oriental women, she appeared lithe and willowy despite her height. She smiled slyly at me and I cinched the robe tighter around my waist.

Leaving her shoes at the door in Buddhist fashion, she breezed past me into the room. Setting the ice bucket on the dresser, she proceeded to scan the music tapes piled there.

"Rocky roll. I like. You got Madonna?"

"Er . . . no, I don't think so."

She selected a David Bowie tape and popped it in the deck. Then she leaned against the dresser and undulated slowly in a private reverie, her long black hair bouncing against her ass in rhythm to the music.

"I only ordered ice, thanks," I finally managed to mumble.

She turned to me with a knowing smile. "Your friend Rick say you too much cold up here alone. I make warm for you." She laughed in that lilting high-pitched way of Thai women. It sounded like a beautiful birdcall.

"Thanks, but I was just going back to bed—I mean sleep."

Ignoring my feeble protest, she shut off the air-conditioner and threw open the window. The night air poured in like hot syrup, blanketing the room with its musky tropical scent. She gave me that smile again. "Better, yes? Much better for massage." She settled lightly on the edge of the bed and patted the mattress invitingly. Her eyes drew me to the bed and I sat down beside her. Everything about her was delicate—everything but her mouth, which was wide and thick lipped.

She drew a joint from her back pocket and lit it. "You nervous like monkey. This make nice for you." She took a deep drag, then leaned to me and blew a thin column of smoke from her mouth into mine. It tasted sweet and strong. I sucked hungrily at her lips, but she pulled away. Then she fed me another hit of smoke, smiling with her eyes now. Our lips touched, and her tiny tongue licked playfully against my teeth. I followed it back inside her mouth. It was warm and wet and inviting, and I wanted more.

But she eased away from me and drew back my robe. A fine film of sweat had already beaded on my shoulders. "Much muscles. I like," she cooed in my ear. Laying a delicate hand on my chest, she guided me down on my back and propped a pillow beneath my head. She stood up and wriggled out of her jeans. She was not wearing panties. Then she untied her halter top and gave me a glimpse of her bare breasts before draping the satin garment over my face. As she gently rolled me over on my stomach, the Thai-weed kicked in like a jet stream. I was off for the clouds.

She straddled my back and worked her fingers deep into my shoulders. Her hands were surprisingly strong, and soon warm waves of pleasure began to surge up and down my spine. As she worked her way down my back, my body became lighter and lighter. Only her gentle weight and small firm hands kept me anchored to the bed.

She was sitting across the back of my knees now, her hands on my buttocks. She stroked them gently with her fingers, lightly tracing the contours of my ass and upper thighs. Her caresses deepened till she was kneading my ass, spreading my cheeks with each circular motion. My whole body broke into a sweat as I clenched the pillow with my teeth and moaned aloud. Gradually, she spread my legs apart and worked my cheeks open wide. Bending down, she let her long hair dance teasingly over my crack. She lowered her head, nuzzling my ass, nipping it playfully with her teeth. Her tongue flicked upwards from my balls, slowly circling my asshole. Her lips puckered against my sphincter as her tongue darted in and across and around.

My cock telescoped outward with magnum force. She slapped my ass sharply to keep it in place, then returned to tonguing my asshole. A warm wet finger shaked its way past my sphincter. I howled softly into the pillow. She guided me over onto my back, her finger still plugged firmly in my anus.

Soon her mouth was wrapped around my throbbing balls. My cock was in a purple rage, tremendously large beside her tiny, perfect face. She raised her eyes to mine. With a mischievous wink, she pulled my shaft towards her smiling, moist lips. Her tongue peeked out and flicked against the bottom of my pulsing glans.

Then she curled her lips around my cock and plunged her head downward. Her hand massaged my balls and the molten fluid churned deep within my groin. As my cock erupted, she reared back her head to catch the steaming spurts across her face. Eyes closed and mouth agape, she laughed that laugh of hers, and I joined in with my own appreciative cries. When I was spent, she rubbed her come-smeared face across my belly and nestled her head against my chest.

I do not remember falling asleep, but I do recall my dream. I was back in Songkhla, in the Buddhist temple, but all my students had gone—all except Lé Chi. She glided up to where I stood by the blackboard and gazed at my sweating brow. Standing on tiptoes, she lightly licked the sweat from my forehead, then from my temples. She licked my neck and ear, the way a cat cleans her kitten. I kissed her, and it was salty and sweet.

Then we were on the beach, kissing still. The barbed wire was gone. Everyone was gone. And we were alone on the sand, writhing together under the blazing sun.

I awoke to find myself being ministered to by room service. She was sitting beside me, dunking a washcloth in the half-melted ice. She fed me a cube, then wiped my steaming brow with the cool wet cloth. As her girlish body hovered above me, I drank in all the beautiful naked contours that had lain hidden beneath Lé Chi's modest garments; the lithe, hairless arms, the soft amber thighs. They had always seemed beyond my grasp, but now I could reach up and touch her lovely shoulder, her tender neck.

Holding a cube between her lips, she bent down and traced icy circles around my nipples. She tweaked them between her chilly fingers till they stood up erect. My hands found her thighs and easily lifted her forward. I pulled her crotch to my mouth and hungrily explored her cunt with my tongue. Her downy hair was soft and fragrant against my nose. Soon her breath grew short and sharp, her moans building in intensity to a high-pitched wail.

"*Banh lai*!" she cried. "Do it! Now!"

I lifted her to my waiting cock. She was so small and tight I had to pull her down onto me. We groaned in unison as I entered her. My cock felt like a redwood up inside that dense tropical jungle of a cunt. I cupped her small breasts in my hands, squeezing the nipples hard between my thumbs and forefingers.

She finally broke a sweat; the hair clung to her moistened face and shoulders. She rode feverishly up and down my shaft, clenching it tightly in her cunt with each ascent. She arched her back and braced her hands against my thighs as I drove deeper and deeper inside her. I was reaching my limit when her hands found my scrotum and squeezed. I grabbed her hair and pulled her forward onto my chest, then came in violent spasms which shook through both our bodies. As my come shot up inside her, she grabbed my chest hair and brought her mouth hard against mine.

The last thing I remember before falling asleep was her long hair curtained around my head and her gentle laughter echoing in my ear.

What do Americans love almost as much as sex? Talking about it. Here, as told in their own, uninhibited words, is the state of the union between men and women today, in all its inventive, eccentric, energetic variety. The sex is unbelievable . . . and every word is true!